# SONGS FOR OTHER PEOPLE'S WEDDINGS

# SONGS FOR OTHER PEOPLE'S WEDDINGS

*a novel by*
DAVID LEVITHAN

*with songs by*
JENS LEKMAN

ABRAMS PRESS, NEW YORK

Copyright © 2025 David Levithan and Jens Lekman
Jacket © 2025 Abrams

Published in 2025 by Abrams Press, an imprint of ABRAMS. All rights reserved. No portion of this book may be reproduced, stored in a retrieval system, or transmitted in any form or by any means, mechanical, electronic, photocopying, recording, or otherwise, without written permission from the publisher.

Library of Congress Control Number: 2024948416

ISBN: 978-1-4197-7812-4
eISBN: 979-8-88707-470-2

Printed and bound in the United States
10 9 8 7 6 5 4 3 2

This book is a work of fiction. Names, characters, places, and incidents are products of the author's imagination or are used fictitiously. Any resemblance to actual events or locales or persons, living or dead, is entirely coincidental.

Abrams books are available at special discounts when purchased in quantity for premiums and promotions as well as fundraising or educational use. Special editions can also be created to specification. For details, contact specialsales@abramsbooks.com or the address below.

Abrams Press® is a registered trademark of Harry N. Abrams, Inc.

**ABRAMS** The Art of Books
195 Broadway, New York, NY 10007
abramsbooks.com

*For Mike Ross, his ancient iPod, and all it contains.* —DL

*For the 132 couples whose weddings I've played at over the years, I hope my presence turned out to be a blessing and not a curse.* —JL

This book contains original songs that are part of the story.
You can find those songs here as you read:

*Can you tell the singer from the song?*

*Can you tell the couple from the wedding?*

# THE FIRST WEDDING

Let's start at the urinal.

Two men are standing unnaturally close to one another, which would ordinarily be a significant breach of urinary etiquette, especially when the dividers are as ineffective as they are here. But in this instance, the breach is entirely pardonable, because these two men, Jun and Arthur, have just gotten married. Also, they are wearing a gigantic tuxedo that's been tailored for two people to share. The white shirts underneath are sewn together with a big bowtie on the top. The pants are appropriate for both a formal occasion and a three-legged race. The fly has been inconveniently placed.

Behind them, the wedding singer waits his turn.

In all the time Jun and Arthur spent planning for this big day, it hadn't occurred to either of them to think about peeing. In order to approach the fly at the proper angle, Arthur has found it necessary to fold himself into Jun, one arm bracing for stability, the other trying to guide the trajectory. The endeavor plays out the way most weddings do, as a messy process with unexpected challenges that test the bounds of teamwork. But in the end, there's a certain sense of relief.

Jun and Arthur are both in their early forties, and as with most gay men of their generation, their gay identities formed first as a matter of revelation and survival, next as a matter of pleasure and defiance, and finally as a matter of community and pride. When they were sixteen years old, ten years away from meeting each other, getting legally married wasn't something they could imagine. And if they had, it would have felt like a Technicolor dream sequence. Their love formed when marriage was still out of bounds, and when the bounds changed with astonishing speed, it took them a while to decide the step finally being offered was a step worth taking.

The only way they could do it was in their own fashion. Some couples have a favorite song. Jun and Arthur have a favorite state of being, and that is song. Neither of them sings particularly well or plays an instrument with any proficiency. Instead they believe in the ever-present soundtrack, the perpetual playlist. Sometimes they control the dials, manipulating their sonic surroundings to enhance or alter their moods. Other times, they leave it to chance—not just by shuffling toward randomness, but often by wandering around Gothenburg and waiting for a song to come to them, lilting from an open window or roaring out of a bar. The life they share and the songs they share are inseparable. So when they planned their wedding they knew they wanted:

1) A theme-songed wedding
2) A song-themed wedding

The second of these desires leads to the first explanation of their costume. Just as each of their guests has come dressed as a favorite song, Jun and Arthur are dressed as a tune that fits the occasion far better than a large tuxedo fits two men of different heights: the Spice Girls' mathematically simplistic yet philosophically rich ballad "2 Become 1."

As for the desire to have a theme-songed wedding . . . well, that is where J, the man waiting patiently behind them, comes in.

J is a somewhat successful Swedish singer-songwriter. If you live outside of Sweden, it's unlikely you've heard any of his songs on the radio . . . unless you are one of the bookish, folkish sort who listen to bookish, folkish stations that play bookish, folkish ditties. Then you might know exactly who J is.

The reason he's here tonight is not a longstanding friendship with Jun and Arthur. Until they emailed him out of the blue, J had never met them. This may seem like a strange thing to do, but for J, it is not that strange, because on his debut album there is a song called "If You Ever Need a Stranger (to Sing at Your Wedding)." It goes like this:

> If you ever need a stranger
> To sing at your wedding
> A last-minute choice, then I am your man
> I know every song, you name it
> By Bacharach or David
> Every stupid love song that's ever touched your heart
> Every power ballad that's ever climbed the charts
> You think it's funny
> My obsession with the holy matrimony
> But I'm just so amazed to witness true love
> And true love can be measured
> Through these simple pleasures
> They are waiting there for you to be discovered
> I would cut off my right arm to be someone's lover
> Maybe I'll meet her there tonight at the wedding buffet
> I walk up to her when she's caught the bouquet

Songs are not, by nature, self-fulfilling prophecies. It's safe to say that Bing Crosby experienced many snowless Christmases, Michael Jackson notably did not heal the world, and Florence Welch had no idea what 2020 was going to be like when she proclaimed the dog days to be over in 2010.

Over the years, many devotees of J's music have gotten in touch with him when their weddings are in the larval stage, asking if he's available to put some musical colors onto the ceremony's wings. Wedding singer gigs are usually more lucrative than busking, but J does not charge much for these efforts if (like Jun and Arthur) the couples are of modest means. Undoubtedly if you asked J as he waits for the urinal why he is here, he would answer, "Because of my song 'If You Ever Need a Stranger (to Sing at Your Wedding).' They were strangers. I am singing at their wedding."

Still, there's more to it than that. J just doesn't see it yet.

Instead he sees Arthur adjusting himself back into his underwear and Jun angling to take his own turn at the urinal.

"J!" Arthur calls out. "We're so glad you're here! We'd shake your hand, but I think it would be best if we washed off first. It's really hard to piss in this tuxedo!"

"It's wonderful to be here," J says, maneuvering around the pair to get to a stall that has freed up. "It's quite a crowd."

Jun and Arthur finish their effluent business by the time J finishes his own. They wait as he washes his hands, then wrap him in a two-armed, three-legged hug. When they step back, they take a look at what J's wearing: a deep-red beret and a wine-dark shirt covered in balloons, a number of which have already been popped.

"Oh, dear," Jun murmurs sympathetically.

In keeping with the wedding's theme, J had planned to be dressed as Nena's eighties classic "99 Luftballons," even though (a) only about sixteen luftballons fit on his shirt and (b) the song in its original German is about a group of fighter jets that open fire on balloons they've mistaken for UFOs, starting a ruinous military spiral that leads to a world where *"99 Jahre Krieg lieBen keinen Platz für Sieger"*—"99 years of wars have left no place for winners."

"What happened?" Arthur asks, assessing the red rubber carnage.

"Your nephews," J answers. (The nephews are aged ten, six, and five, and collectively dressed as Kung Fu Fighting; the balloons didn't stand a chance.)

Worried that his truthfulness has brought down the mood as only, say, the last lines of "99 Luftballons" can, J adds, "But it's okay! I can be 'Raspberry Beret' instead." ("Raspberry Beret" ends in a world where "I think I love her." Better.)

"A Prince and two queens!" Jun exclaims.

Arthur groans, but there is affection in his protest.

J smiles at the sight of them in their absurd tuxedo. It is not the kind of smile that needs any thought behind it. His heart has grown so full that his mouth must lift.

The word for what he feels is *tenderness*.

*That* is the true reason he's here.

There are a few standard questions J asks couples when trying to write their wedding song. But mostly, he improvises. He can measure immediately whether both people in the couple want him to be there, or whether only one of them is a fan and the other is merely humoring. If both are into it, the process begins.

J always starts with a simple question: "How did you meet?" (For Jun and Arthur, at a museum installation; Jun was the artist, and Arthur was doing the installing.) Then he might progress to "What did your friends first think of the two of you together?" or "What was your favorite date, from early on?" After that: free swim. "What's the stupidest fight you've ever had?" or "What's your favorite piece of his clothing?" or "What habit of hers went away after she met you?" Jun and Arthur talked a lot about the challenges of queer romance, how in their youth it felt antisocial to not be hedonistic, and how settling down now feels like a betrayal of youth, to some degree.

"So what does this wedding mean to you?" J asked.

"Well, it all comes down to Plato's *Symposium*," Arthur replied.

"Not to be confused with Plato's Retreat," Jun added, snickering.

Arthur pressed on. "Correct. *Symposium*. I'm sure you heard about it in school and thought it was boring beyond words, but it's actually amazing, in a funny and touching way. It's a bunch of Greek guys who come together, get absolutely wasted, and talk about love."

Jun picked up the thread. "Aristophanes, a comedy writer who's probably the drunkest of them all, recovers from his hiccups long enough to tell this story of how humans used to have doubled bodies. There were three different kinds: the double males who were from the Sun, the double females who were from Earth, and the androgynous who were half man and half woman and lived on the Moon."

"The double humans started to mess with the gods, and Zeus got angry and decided to split them all in half—"

"—You probably know this part from *Hedwig*—"

"Can I finish? So, yes, Zeus split them up. But he did nothing to erase their memories. *Our* memories. So each of us walks around the earth looking for our other half."

"And now I've found mine."

"And I, mine."

"So the wedding is when we're scheduled to have the surgery to be connected again."

They then explained to J their idea for the double suit.

2 Become 1.

J plays two sets at each wedding. The first is usually made of a dozen songs the couple has chosen, often a musical biography of their relationship. This set often includes "If You Ever Need a Stranger (to Sing at Your Wedding)."

The second set is exactly one song long, and it comes after the wedding toasts.

This is the song J has composed for the couple.

As J, Jun, and Arthur exit the restroom together, it is time for the first set.

It is a universally accepted fact that if asked to choose a song to kick off their wedding, 91% of all gay men will choose a song popularized by a female singer, and 78% of the time, that female singer will have died in tragic circumstances.

This is why J begins the night by playing a version of Whitney Houston's "I Wanna Dance with Somebody."

For the wedding-goer, this song is akin to a call to arms. If you happen to have come to the wedding with somebody who loves you, it behooves you to step out with them onto the dance floor. If you did not come with a plus-one of that status, or with a plus-one at all, you must either discover something fascinating about the water glass in front of you or you must scan the crowd to see what your possibilities are. It is as if the wedded couple is daring you to be resentful, and some wedding-goers rise to the challenge. (Others check their phones.)

As if to democratize the dance floor, Jun and Arthur are not dancing with one another as much as they are dancing with the entire crowd. To J, this makes sense. If Jun and Arthur are going to dance with somebody who loves them at their wedding, and they are lucky enough to have so many loving friends and family members there, then they must spread their double-wide arms and dance with as many people as can fall into their open embrace.

For the next song, a jauntier than usual rendition of "The First Time Ever I Saw Your Face," Jun and Arthur dance with their mothers—Jun's is dressed as The Rainbow Connection, Arthur's is a little more subdued Nights in White Satin. For the third song, they do not dance with their fathers—their families are supportive and progressive, but only to a point. (In fairness, Jun's father, a spirited Stayin' Alive, would have been game. Arthur's father, a more reticent Fly Me to the Moon, would rather not dance at all.)

Song by song, the revelry amplifies. As Jun and Arthur spin and swirl with an impressive level of coordination at the center, intrigues occur along the edges. Careless Whisper decides he can't stand dancing with Father Figure anymore. Smalltown Boy works up the courage to ask Sweet Dreams (Are Made of This) to dance, and now their hands are all over each other, much to the chagrin of Smalltown Boy's ex, Personal Jesus, who is going through the motions of dancing with Caribbean Queen but keeps looking over his shoulder. A few drinks in, A Little Respect is singing along, not untunefully, as they and Friday I'm in Love sandwich Dancing on My Own. (She's thrilled.) Meanwhile, Jun's aunt and uncle, Eleanor Rigby and Hey Jude, are sweetly careening through their own soundtrack, in their own dance-time, her cheek resting on his chest, his cheek resting atop her head. Both their eyes are closed.

There are some artists who are compelled by the challenge of technical brilliance, striving solely to be recognized as a virtuoso of their craft. Others are drawn to create because creation is the only way they will ever know themselves. And still others are drawn to a life of artistry in the belief that it will connect them to other people. Sometimes this connection is conceptual, as if the artist desires to plug in to humanity itself. Sometimes it narrows into a generally perceived audience, a sea of nameless faces. And every now and then, the desire for connection narrows even further, and the art is created to draw a line to one specific person. The name and the body of this person may be intimately familiar to the artist. Or sometimes the artist creates the art to conjure this person into their life.

Who is J singing for?

Of course, he is singing for Jun and Arthur and their guests.

But also:

Whenever he sings the line "Maybe I'll meet her there tonight at the wedding buffet," he always looks to the crowd.

If there's a buffet, he looks there first.

This time, he spots her immediately. She is looking at the food through heart-shaped sunglasses. But she isn't reaching for a thing . . . because she's in a straitjacket.

J smiles at this get-up.

She looks over to him on the stage.

He looks down at his guitar.

After the first set is over, J and the band step off the stage to make way for the DJ who will conjure the background sounds of the dinner hour.

Jun and Arthur come over and enfold J in a sweaty, beaming show of appreciation. They usher a few relatives (Son of a Preacher Man, Waterloo, I Want Candy, and Smells Like Teen Spirit) over to meet him. J marvels at how Jun and Arthur genuinely move as if they are sharing one body now.

As Smells Like Teen Spirit complains about her boyfriend refusing to come dressed as Lithium, J scans over her head to see if Straitjacket Heart is still by the buffet.

"Sounds like he'll need an 'All Apologies' costume next," Arthur tells Smells Like Teen Spirit.

She rolls her eyes, as Teen Spirit should.

J tries to make a show of listening while scanning the crowd.

"Looking for someone?" Jun asks.

"Yes," J admits. "The woman in the straitjacket."

"A straitjacket?" Arthur replies.

Jun shakes one of their two heads. "I haven't seen anyone in a straitjacket."

"Oh!" Uncle Waterloo utters. "I know who you mean! With the glasses?"

J nods.

Waterloo grins. "I have no idea who she is!"

"Jesus Christ," Smells Like Teen Spirit spits out. "She's *right there*."

To J's bemusement, Smells Like Teen Spirit points the way. Somehow, Straitjacket Heart has undone one of her arms so she can hold a drink. She leans away from the crowd, watching it with a cool detachment.

"Who is that?" Jun asks Arthur.

"I can't tell," Arthur says. Then he turns to J. "You should go talk to her."

"It's alright." Even though J has just been on a stage performing in front of the whole room, this conversation is far, far too public for his taste. "Why don't you tell me what song that man over there is dressed as. 'Hounds of Love'?"

Jun and Arthur both roll their eyes, Jun tilting his head to the left while Arthur tilts his to the right.

"Clark is 'Who Let the Dogs Out' . . . and you're trying to change the subject."

"Typical," Smells Like Teen Spirit mutters.

"Excuse me?" J asks.

"You know what I mean," she replies.

He does. But he doesn't understand how she'd know this about him.

Finally, I Want Candy (age five) weighs in.

"GO TALK TO HER!" he yells. And then, for good measure, he repeats it.

J, sensing that this song is all chorus and no verse, understands the only way to get to the outro is to make a move.

Even though the acoustics make it nearly impossible for Straitjacket Heart to have heard I Want Candy's cry over all the table conversations, she puts her glass down on a sill and heads to the bar.

This complicates J's route considerably, since now he must squeeze between tables to get to her. The remaining balloons on his costume squeak and whine in protest as they press against chairs and people who refuse to let J pass. A few people slap him on the back and compliment his singing, one causing a bright pop in the process. By the time he emerges from the table area, he's down to five or six luftballons.

Whether cued by the pop of the balloon or simply the keen radar most women have to tell them when an awkward suitor is approaching awkwardly, Straitjacket Heart looks right at J as he covers the final few feet to the bar. Then, when he's about five balloon's-lengths away, she turns back to the bartender for her fresh drink.

There's a part of J that wills his feet to keep walking to the end of the bar, to pretend a gin and tonic is the only intoxication he's come here for. This part warns him that the song of the awkward suitor is one he's played many times before, and it always comes to the same end.

But the greater part within J is the more hopeful part, the one that thinks love is the song that can be played a thousand different ways, and that every time you play it, a different reaction can occur.

"Hey," he says. "Where did you get that straitjacket? It looks so . . . real."

The woman looks up, her expression not at all betraying what kind of song she's hearing.

"I don't know," she replies. "I just woke up in the park like this. Barefoot. Covered in broken glass. I didn't have time to change."

"Must've been a great party last night."

She shakes her head. "No. I'm just insane."

J lights up his face. "Me, too!"

She looks at him skeptically. "In what way are you insane?"

J leans in so the bartender won't hear. "You know how most people pour their cereal into the bowl before they pour the milk? Well, I—"

"No, seriously. What's your major malfunction? What part of your internet history do you delete?"

J pulls back. "Oh."

The woman relaxes her posture and adjusts her barstool like clock hands switching from twelve to three, so she can face J directly. "Take your time." She reaches for her drink and takes a sip.

J doesn't tell her there's no reason to delete internet history if you're the only person who knows the passcode to the laptop. That isn't the answer she's looking for.

He takes too long. She says, "First thought, best thought."

"I used to have a lot of separation anxiety."

"When?"

"When I was a kid. I used to worry so much that something bad would happen to the people I loved. As far as I was concerned, the minute they walked out the door, a car would hit them, or an anvil would fall from the sky, or they would get shot by a bullet meant for someone else."

"But then you got over it?"

"I guess so. I think I became a bit scared of being close to anyone after that. I didn't like what it did to me. I didn't like how much it made me worry."

"What else?"

J smiles, briefly. "I'm a bit of a martyr. I do a lot of things for others that I don't want to do, and then I go around and mope about it. The moping is highly enjoyable to me. It's almost erotic."

He has her full attention now. She isn't faking. This interest is real.

"Keep going," she tells him.

The adrenaline of performing is still coursing through J. The fact that he can now see her eyes through her sunglasses makes this conversation feel more vivid. He knows he is in a free-associative state, but he's not trying to cage it.

"I feel for humans. Perhaps too much."

The woman takes another sip of her drink. A thoughtful sip. Then she puts her glass on the bar and says, "You know, you had me at separation anxiety. That part was cute. But universal empathy is asking for a lot of allowances."

J understands this as the challenge that it is. In reply, he picks up her drink, takes a sip, and asks, "Okay, fine—what about you? Map out your damage for me."

The woman's expression doesn't change as she folds one arm over the other, unintentionally making it look like the straitjacket is tied.

"I am very impulsive, especially when talking to men dressed in rubber," she says, but with a tone that takes the edge off of any impulsiveness. "I don't think very highly of men because our father left our family to join the circus when I was six. Which is also the reason I think every man I love will leave me. My parents hated each other so I don't believe in marriage. I'm the youngest of four siblings—no, five. Actually, make it six. My parents probably ran out of names by the time I was born. I suspect I was named after a brand of canned vegetables. The one with the yellow label—are you familiar with the brand? I'm sure you can find cans in bomb shelters around the country. When I asked my mother where the name came from, she looked like someone who'd been caught in a lifelong lie. In this case, my life. She muttered something about liking the sound of it. But that's just bullshit. It's a dirge of a name, hardly melodic. But you'd know that, being a singer."

"It seems like you've thoroughly analyzed yourself," J observes.

"Well, I couldn't afford therapy, so I had to do it my own way."

"More money for straitjackets."

The woman raises her glass. "Only the finest of straitjackets."

She takes a sip, then passes the glass to J. He doesn't even like vodka cranberry, but he takes another sip anyway.

She continues. "I appreciate you didn't try to tell me my name was melodic."

"And I appreciate your respect for men in rubber. Also, I have a confession."

"Another?"

"Yes. Another."

"Go ahead."

"I happen to like that brand of canned vegetable. Their carrots in particular."

She knocks back the rest of her drink. J likes to think of that as a signal.

"May I propose?" he asks.

"So soon?"

"I propose that we each get our own drinks and head to the balcony on the second floor to continue this conversation without so much noise around."

She smiles at him, an invitation of a smile . . . but at the same time, a man taps her on the shoulder.

"Hey! There you are!" he says.

The man is handsome in a lacrosse-player way, and the tap on the shoulder effortlessly becomes a hand resting on the same shoulder. He's covered in plastic jewelry and phone cords. An '80s-style phone receiver sits on his head. J immediately knows what he's up against.

Hotline Bling.

"Stephen's the one who freed me up so I could drink," Straitjacket Heart explains to J.

"Only left her because I promised my mother a dance!" Hotline Bling says. His hand will not leave her shoulder. J minds this more than she seems to.

Hotline Bling goes on, "You and the band were great, man. This is such a great idea for a wedding! I get to free my new friend here from her straitjacket *and* see a concert at the same time."

"You're a lucky man," J mutters.

"I know! What were you guys talking about? It looked *intense*." Straitjacket Heart swivels away from J to face the Bling.

"He was just sharing a carrot cake recipe with me. Ends up the secret is for the carrots to be canned."

"That's cool—you sing *and* you cook. Way to go, man."

All it would take is one wink from her. Not even an actual wink, but a slight tilt of the head that recognizes a wink would not work in this situation but that if she could be winking at J, she would be. J searches for that. For anything. But instead she asks Hotline Bling to get her another drink.

"Cool. Then you better eat something before they clear it all away. The crab cakes are to die for. Seriously."

To J, it has all the harshness of the end of a good therapy session. To be stopped midflow. To be told time is up. To be reminded that the only reason the other person is there is because you made an appointment. To be reminded that they don't care about you nearly as much as you care about yourself.

"I think I'll go see what's happening outside," he says.

Before his straitjacketed companion can reply, Hotline Bling holds out his hand and says, "So nice to meet you, man. Keep up the good work!"

J shakes it as forcefully as possible. Then he goes outside as quickly as he can without the spectacle of actual running.

Outside it's crowded with people smoking in the parking lot. The party is at Sockerbruket, an arrangement of buildings that look like offices aspiring half-heartedly to be castles. J angles through the parking lot to take a break by the river, and as he does, a lit cigarette grazes one of his balloons (deliberately or not) and pops it. At least two people scream. J keeps walking, wanting to be as far as he can get from the wedding without leaving it. When he gets to the water, he feels how chilly it is—he couldn't wear a jacket over his balloons.

He knows he has one song left, but he feels the urge for going. Jun and Arthur suddenly seem like strangers again. J wonders why he's doing this, why he's spending so much energy on going to strangers' weddings when there are better ways to build a career. Then he wonders why there's a cold, heavy rock in his stomach. He doesn't have to wander very far in his wondering. The answer is clear, and it's currently having drinks with Hotline Bling.

He sees a woman exit the wedding venue. She's wearing a big rose-shaped hat and far too much lipstick. She scans the crowd and then looks to the distant, antisocial shore where J has claimed citizenry. When she sees him, she scampers over.

It's only when she's closer that J recognizes her as Olivia, the friend of Jun and Arthur's who helped them plan the wedding.

When she gets to him, she says, "Kiss from a Rose," without him having to ask. He smiles. Of course.

Olivia tells him, "We're about five minutes away from the toasts, which means we're anywhere from fifteen to thirty minutes away from your wedding song, depending on how much the toast-givers have been drinking. Is that a word? Toast-givers?"

"We should just call them toasters," J suggests.

Olivia laughs—a loud, joyous burst of laughter. "*Exactly*. I guess I'm hoping the toasters aren't too toasted. We've set up two mics—how 'bout you stay at one plug and I'll stay at the other, and if they start to ramble on or tell stupid jokes about stupid things Jun and Arthur did that have nothing to do with them being a couple, we pull."

"Sounds good," J says. But what he's really thinking is, *I guess I have to go back inside.*

"You're the best," Olivia replies. Then she takes a look at him and says, "Your poor balloons. Did you bring any extra? We have about two minutes, and I could help you put them on."

"I'm afraid not."

"Drat. Well, then . . . no rest for the wicked. Let's go make some magic."

J takes a deep breath and exhales. There's no saying no to women like Olivia.

The wedding is drawing him back in.

"Do you have any role models for your relationship?" J had asked Jun and Arthur as part of their interview.

"Well, my parents," Jun said. "They bicker all the time and love each other like bodies love oxygen."

"I wonder if that makes my parents carbon monoxide," Arthur said.

"They're not that bad!"

"They're *fine*," Arthur told J. "But their roles are a little too rigid for them to be role models."

"What about outside of your family? Who else?"

Arthur looked instantly giddy upon landing on his answer. "Do you know the story about Genesis P-Orridge and Lady Jaye?"

J shook his head. (He did, in fact, know the story, but he wanted to hear how Jun and Arthur would tell it.)

"Genesis was in Throbbing Gristle," Jun went on. "Which does *not* mean we want you to play any Throbbing Gristle songs at the wedding."

"In fact, please don't," Arthur agreed.

"Anyway," Jun said, "Genesis and Lady Jaye were married but they weren't satisfied with that. They'd shared a kiss once that made them leave their bodies and become one and they wanted to feel like that again. So they started dressing alike—"

"As identically as possible," Arthur continued. "But that wasn't enough, either. So then they started to surgically alter themselves to be a single nongendered being, and invented their own identity: *pandrogyne*. Genesis got breasts. Lady Jaye got her eyes done to match Genesis's. Beauty spots were tattooed on Genesis's chin to echo Lady Jaye's. And so on. They wanted to become a *we*, so that became their pronoun. Even after Lady Jaye died, Genesis kept referring to themself as we."

"But doesn't love require distance, separateness?" J asked.

"Of course," Jun said. "But the way I see it, we've spent almost half our lives with separateness. We wasted so much time figuring things out, partly because the world made it so hard for us to figure things out. You don't know what that's like, to believe the world actively wants you to remain separate and alone. Maybe in a few generations, queer kids won't know what that feels like, either. But for us—it took too much time and too much navigation to come together comfortably."

"I don't think we want to share the same body," Arthur said, "but we do want to share the same heart. We've lived long enough with separate hearts. Let's be together the rest of the way. Let's live together, and then when we die, let our ashes be mixed in the same urn and buried together."

"Making up for lost time," J offered.

"Yes," Jun told him with a sad smile. "There has been so much lost time. So doesn't it make sense that we want to spend the rest of our lives found?"

The toasts are not as awful as wedding toasts can be; neither J nor Olivia needs to pull their respective plugs. Because Arthur's father is the most uncomfortable with what's going on, he gets the most tears when he gives in despite himself, calling Jun the piece that had been missing in their family, the piece that made the whole jigsaw suddenly make sense.

As the assembled crowd raises its glasses for the father's toast, J looks over to the bar, where Straitjacket Heart is still perched, Hotline Bling beside her. He despairs slightly that she has not freed herself of him, but at least takes some solace in the fact that every time Hotline Bling's tried to talk to her in the past five minutes, she's shushed him so she could listen to the speeches.

Once Arthur's father is done, it's J's turn at the microphone. Even though it is a single song, he feels much more vulnerable with this set, much more naked in the spotlight. In a concert setting, if he messes up, the only thing he's ruined is his own reputation. But these performances always mean more. He has been asked to conjure a blessing, fill the room with this couple's shared heartbeat. It is not at all in his nature to be confident that he can pull off such a feat.

He looks to Straitjacket Heart. From the stage, he can't really read her expression. But he does see her nod, just once, so he can take the momentum from that nod and ride it into his opening chords.

There is no net here. No lyric sheet. Nobody wants a blessing that's read from a piece of paper. No, it has to seem like the truth is sung straight from the soul.

The song he's written for Jun and Arthur is called "55%."

It goes like this:

> **Think of life as a battery**
> **Ticking backwards slow**
> **Instead of being 37**
> **We've got 55% to go**
>
> **Think of all the time**
> **We've practiced and rehearsed**
> **For an ending that never started**
> **For the other to strike first**

We gotta hurry up and love
We might not have much time left
Give or take—45 years
Of not being dead
I have so many questions
While we're still alive
I'll never know you completely
And it tears me up inside

We met in the wrestling ring
We were young and we brawled
I got to gently unmask you
And tell you what I saw

Not a savage beast
With a heart made of metal
When you waved the white flag
That's when you won the battle

We gotta hurry up and love
We might not have much time left
Give or take—45 years
Of not being dead
I have so many questions
While we're still alive
I'll never know you completely
And it tears me up inside

As he sings, Jun and Arthur joyfully dance along, surrounded by so many people dressed as so many other songs. When J is done, he sees that Jun and Arthur are teary as they beam and bow to him. This is the first time they've heard the song, and it moves them to see themselves within it, to know it is yet another marvel that would not have existed if they'd never met.

The wedding guests cheer and applaud. Hotline Bling whoops. Next to him, the straitjacketed woman looks like she is holding her own reaction inside, to examine it better before she shares it.

J now wishes he had a lyric sheet, because he has nothing to give Jun and Arthur in this moment except a bow back, an acknowledgment that what they've created has led to the song's creation. After he steps to the side, the DJ announces that now there will be karaoke for anyone who wants to sing the song that inspired their costume.

"That was amazing!" Olivia cries, wrapping J in a spontaneous hug and popping another balloon in the process. "Did you see how happy Jun and Arthur looked? That was such a highlight. You're incredible."

A guy dressed as a juicebox has jumped onstage, swigging from a bottle of gin. The DJ cues up "Gin and Juice."

"This is not going to be a highlight," Olivia groans. "Here, come with me. I have a surefire coping mechanism for amateur karaoke."

J looks over to Straitjacket Heart, but she hasn't extricated herself from Hotline Bling. If anything, Bling seems to have dialed it up, and it doesn't take a doctor to see how it makes J ache.

"I happen to be very into coping mechanisms," J tells Olivia. But still, he's surprised when she pulls him into a catering office and offers him a rough powder.

"Don't worry—it's just Molly," Olivia says. "There's a guy out there in a Cannibal Corpse t-shirt who says he's dressed as their song 'I Cum Blood,' and he plans to sing it. You're going to need this."

J has never tried MDMA before, but he's been around people who were on it, and they seemed to be pretty happy. Also, Hotline Bling and Cannibal Corpse are too much for any bookish, folkish sensibility to handle at the same time, so J opens up his mouth to new possibilities. He is startled to discover that swallowing MDMA feels like inhaling crystallized hairspray.

"Now we dance!" Olivia says, in a way that makes it sound like this is part of the official MDMA protocol.

Luckily, Gin and Juice has been replaced by Dancing on My Own, who ironically fills the dance floor as she carries the tune to heights that karaoke rarely reaches. J starts to feel a lightness, but he isn't sure whether it's because of the song, the fact he no longer has to perform, or the drugs he's just snorted. Olivia is very handsy in her dancing, but in a friendly-more-than-flirty way.

The next person to take the stage is dressed in an aqua/periwinkle/navy/sky combo. With orchestral seriousness, he launches into "I Guess That's Why They Call It the Blues."

Those who'd been rockin' to Robyn start to slide from the dance floor. J assumes he and Olivia will, too, but instead she wraps her arms around him, careful not to crush the lone balloon between them as she leans her head in. Her hand starts to strum the small of his back. He strums hers in return, because it feels like the friendly thing to do.

J gets lost for a moment and later will not be able to remember if his eyes were open or closed as he swayed with Olivia. There was just the sensation of the music, and hands on backs, and then a poke higher on his back, not like a strum at all, and then another poke, this time popping the second-to-last luftballon, which had been dangling off his elbow.

He turns, and there's V. Who he knows he should be thinking of as "Straitjacket Heart." But she's really his girlfriend V, playing a part. Because they thought it would be fun. And he's having fun. Really, he is. But V doesn't look like she's having as much fun.

"I need to talk to you," she says.

"Okay, sure," J replies. He tilts his head forward. "This is Olivia. She's a friend of Jun and Arthur's. We were just—"

"It's urgent," V interrupts.

J doesn't want to be rude. He wants to be friendly.

"Okay," he says, his hands now off Olivia's back, but still on her waist. "But Olivia and I were just—"

V reaches between them and playfully pops the last luftballon. Olivia startles. V reaches into J's shirt, wraps her finger around one of the buttons, and pulls him in the direction of the door.

"I think it's time to go home," she says with a smile. "Slip out of our costumes." Then she lets go and heads outside.

"You should follow her," Olivia tells J. "It's okay. I should probably make sure people know they can take home the flowers."

"Thank you," J says. Then he goes outside to find V standing alone in her straitjacket. He momentarily thinks it's smart to lead with, "What happened—did Hotline Bling hang up on you?"

"Says the man who was about to deflower Every Rose Has Its Thorn!"

"Kiss from a Rose."

"Well, wouldn't you rather seal the deal with me?"

J likes the sound of this.

"Well," he says, "we're never going to survive unless we get a little crazy. Is that what you're saying?"

V cozies up to him and whispers in his ear. "I'm not just crazy . . . I'm Crazy in Love."

"Oh!" he says, voice full of childish revelation. "The straitjacket and the heart-shaped glasses. Now I get it! Are we stopping the game now? Let's keep going! Tell me all about your four, five, or six brothers and sisters. I have to say, I love all of them!"

"I don't want to talk about them, not after they died in that tragic canning accident."

J doesn't know why this statement is making him feel so euphoric. He understands this definitely means the role-playing is over. But . . . someone inside is singing "Dancing Queen," which makes him wonder . . .

"What does the beat of a tambourine really feel like?"

"Excuse me?"

"Sorry. Be my Dancing Queen."

Because that's what she is. Even in her straitjacket. The thought bubble forms over his head in its puffy, puffy cloud: *She is my dancing queen.*

"I have a better idea," V says.

Six minutes later, they are making out furiously in the back of a cab. It is understandable, even admirable, to feel bad for the cab driver in this situation—but let's focus on the back seat, where it's getting hot in more ways than one.

"This feels so good," J moans. "Your skin, it's so . . . soft. Soft and . . . welcoming."

"Yours too," V says, although what she's caressing is really a collapsed balloon, not his skin.

"So welcoming," J coos. "Your skin is like . . . ABBA."

V kisses him hard, grabbing the back of his neck with the one arm she has available. After a little back and forth in this respect, she pulls away.

"Your mouth is dry," she observes. "And you're sweating a lot."

"I'd stop the world and sweat for you."

"No, like even more than normal. Are you okay?"

"I'm great. Really, really great." J nods, agreeing with himself. Then he sings, "Having the time of my liiiiiii-ife."

"Right here," V tells the cab driver.

"I've got it!" J says, reaching for his wallet. Then he pays the driver all the cash he has.

Once in J's apartment, he and V tumble into the bedroom. J thinks: *The game isn't over! This is still the game! And it's a fun game!*

V stops kissing him and says, "Hang on—you're really warm. Like, super warm."

"The clothes—the clothes are the problem!" J says, pulling at his shirt without recognizing it would be wiser to remove the tie first. Then he looks at V. "Or shall I free you from your constraints?"

"Did you take something at the wedding?"

"Haha, yes. It tasted like hairspray."

V seems amused. Although to J, the bed also seems amused. And the window. And his shoes.

"I really love my shoes," he says. "And I suspect they love me back."

"Was it ecstasy? MDMA? Did you even know what you were doing? You don't take drugs. You've never taken drugs."

"I know. But I wanted to do something you would do. I wanted to impress you. I'm really sorry you're not on it, too. I think Olivia would have given you some. But you were talking to Drake. And then you were pulling me away. And the next thing I know we're in a taxi and my heart is racing and I want to touch you so badly and . . . whoa."

V undoes her straitjacket and lets it drop to the floor. She takes her glasses off and levels J with a look.

"Oh, honey," she says. "How does it feel?"

"So far, sooooooo good. Why haven't I done this before?"

"I'm so happy for you."

"I want us to become one, V. Let's become one."

V laughs. "I'm not sure your balloon's going to inflate tonight. That's a common side effect of MDMA."

"Shit. Olivia didn't tell me that."

"Probably would've ruined the mood."

"I'm sorry."

"It's okay." V sits down next to him on the bed. "Did you have a good time?"

"Yeah, I did. Jun and Arthur have it, you know. They got there."

"It was very sweet to see. And your song was nice."

J would normally wince at the adjective *nice*. But he decides to let it wrap him as a compliment right now.

Then he remembers Hotline Bling and says, "I did get jealous, though."

"Yeah, me too. Obviously."

"I liked this little experiment. I guess even though it was painful to see you flirting with someone else it also made me want you more."

V leans back on the bed. J follows suit.

"We were strangers again!" V says to the ceiling.

J turns on his side to face her. "We don't have to do this too often, though, right?"

V reaches over and takes off his beret. Then she softly runs her fingers behind his ear.

"No," she says, "but I'm glad we tried."

J reaches around to the small of V's back and lingers there, forgetting where he got this motion from.

"I love you," he says. Then he repeats it as a pronouncement. "I love you *so much*."

"Yes, I know," V says, gently stroking his arm, then moving her hand away. "That's a side effect, too."

"I want us to be together," J says sleepily. "But I also want us to be separate. Is that wrong?"

"No. That's not wrong at all. After two years, that's the hard part, isn't it? Figuring out how to do that?"

"I love you."

"I bet you love the world right now."

"Yes. Them too. But mostly you."

Later, Jun and Arthur will laugh uproariously as they stumble their way out of their tuxedo and into each other's arms. Smalltown Boy will go home with Sweet Dreams (Are Made of This) and will stay far longer into the next day than either of them is expecting. Back in their hotel room, Smells Like Teen Spirit's boyfriend, the one who refused to be Lithium, will get back into her good graces when, after turning the lights out, he whispers to her, "It's less dangerous." Olivia will be the last person in the dancehall, smiling because even though it's empty, the music will still be playing in her ears, the sound of joy made human. And throughout the night, J will lie awake and whisper his love to V, but never so loud that it wakes her. You might say that, at this moment, he is crazy in love.

Or, in other words: Ninety-nine years of wars suddenly seem to have opened up a single spot for a winner.

It is either daybreak or J's snoring that pulls V from her dreaming. This is a novel occurrence; J is many things, but a snorer is not one of them. Usually.

V gets up quietly and heads to the bathroom. It had been her idea to role-play, after J had told her about the wedding's costume conceit. Why not take it a little further? He would dress in his apartment and she would dress in hers—their alter egos would have the thrill of meeting for the first time, and maybe, just maybe, that thrill would carry over.

On the toilet long after she's done using it, V ponders whether the night was a success. It was fun to see J's response to her other suitor. It was even more fun to talk so directly with J at the bar, even if every single thing she said about herself was a lie, while he characteristically opted to tell the truth. She wonders if this is a warning sign: She used disguise to explore the person she wasn't, while he used it to bring up the person he was.

What tempted her the most was the opportunity of it all. She knew she wasn't going to go home with anyone but J, but at the same time, she liked having options—especially options who brought her drinks and found her attractive. Weddings often depressed her, to a degree that she's never really shared with J. Some people see a balloon and see color, lightness. Others only see the coming of the pop. Weddings make V confront the fact that she feels the pop is inevitable.

For this reason, V isn't too surprised by J's costume choice. He wouldn't have seen the pops coming. She is jealous of this. More jealous, in fact, than she was when she saw J dancing with the woman who gave him the drugs. Because while V craves opportunity, she and opportunity have a very complicated relationship, probably even more complicated than her relationship with J. She hasn't often gotten the things that she's wanted, although she's frequently been the thing that someone else has wanted and gotten. The wonderful thing about being with J is that his desires are not demanding; he wants good company, good sex, and a sincere sounding board. She enjoys being all those things. But she's not so sure they add up to her in the same way they add up to J.

She flushes the toilet a second time, just in case he's awake now and wondering why she's been in the bathroom for so long. But when she returns to the bedroom, she finds him snoring away. It's not a buzzsaw snore or a choking snore, but more like his body has chosen to put a little more emphasis on breathing.

Her phone buzzes; no doubt a work text coming in from some American, even though it's six in the morning on a Sunday. She doesn't check it.

Instead she waits for the screen to unlight itself, then takes the phone from its charger and pulls up the microphone. She holds it by J's snoring face for a minute, to record the sounds he is making. At the very least, it will come in handy the next time he accuses her of waking him with her own snores.

She puts the phone back down, not even bothering to plug it back in. She didn't meet J at a wedding, but if she had to pinpoint the moment she fell in love with him, it would be a wedding over a year ago. Ordinarily she wouldn't have been at a wedding where he was playing, but in this case she was the reason he was there in the first place, because it was an old family friend who had a serious wedding budget and an appreciation of her newish boyfriend's music. The theme was Swing Time, and J had been given a big band to back him with horns and strings. He gamely tackled a number of jazzier standards, but it wasn't until he slowed everything down for a rendition of "Blue Moon" that V's heart truly took note. He wasn't afraid to share the longing of the song, and instead of throwing everything off, it brought everything together. V looked around at all the couples leaning into one another, swaying under a moon that was only present in the song, and when she looked up at J, he was holding his hand out to her. She had felt so lonely out in the crowd, but once she stepped onto the bandstand and into his arms, she felt profoundly unlonely—if only because he had seen her loneliness and had joined it to his own to create the antidote. He continued to sing as they danced, and nobody in the wedding hall thought it was unusual, not even V.

*So what now?* V thinks. The enormity of such a short question nearly paralyzes her, as such questions often do. That was another benefit of being Straitjacket Heart: to have her story only exist in the present tense. In the bed, J turns, moans, and subsides into sleep, the snoring now gone.

V slips back in and sees that J—consciously or not—has arranged his body in a position that makes it very easy for her to pull close. Whether it's an invitation or serendipity, V takes her place. She puts off any other thoughts of opportunity, of what's next. She surrenders to being one half of this comfortable drowsing. For now, it's enough.

# THE SECOND WEDDING

"I have a favor to ask you," J's childhood friend Tom had said, nearly two months ago now. Then he clarified: "Actually, it's a favor for Mom."

The phrase *childhood friend* applies here in two connected ways: J and Tom grew up together, and as a result have a friendship forged in pillow forts and bicycle grease, video games and vague adolescent ruminations. When J got his first guitar, Tom pleaded with his mother for a drum set. J still plays the guitar; Tom gave up the drums in a matter of months, and he was realistic enough about his own lack of interest that when J formed his first band and needed a drum set, Tom was happy to "lend" his, never to be returned.

So, childhood friends. Friends since childhood.

Also, when they get together now, they tend to act like children. This is one of the advantages of having friends for so long—you get to extend your childhood whenever you're with them. Unless you've given in to age, which neither J nor Tom has.

The downside is that sometimes their mothers ask for favors.

"Does she want tickets to my next show?" J asked. Lisbet loved getting free tickets to J's shows. Even when the shows were free, she liked him to arrange for tickets to be waiting for her, so she could have that moment of being "on the list."

"I'm afraid it's something more than tickets to a show," Tom replied.

Tom has, by and large, grown up into a likable unhappiness, loosely defined by an aggregation of minor disappointments that he's always managed to fit under comedy's mask. It is possible J and Tom have never had a completely serious conversation, and J felt a slight terror that they might fall into one now if he's not careful.

"She's not marrying George again, is she?" he asked, mostly joking.

Tom all but gulped. "I'm afraid so."

J laughed. "For a *fourth* time?"

"I'm touched. Most of my other friends have lost count," Tom said. "She swears that this time they're going to do it right."

"It's an obsession, Tom. An addiction!"

"It's just that they get so lonely without each other. They forget how much they hate it when they're together."

J looked heavenward for a moment, then back to Tom. "It's a pretty obvious pattern."

"But it's like a crop circle—you can only see it from the outside. When you're in it, it's just . . ."

"Crops?"

"Exactly!"

"And are you defending this pattern?" J asked. "Do I have to get your head checked, too?"

"No! I'm aware it's ridiculous."

"But?"

Tom sighed. "But . . . I think maybe my mom is at her happiest when she's marrying George. From the moment she starts planning to the end of the honeymoon—that's the best time for her. And, honestly, I think the same's true for George."

"I've always liked George."

"Right? Me too. They always find a way to mess it up—but before the mess comes, it's pretty great."

"It's always a good party." The only one J missed was the last, which had happened on a cruise ship. J loved Tom and his mom, but not to a weeklong-cruise degree.

"So here's the thing: Remember that time you were supposed to come with us to the lake house, but then you had to play a wedding in Düsseldorf? Well, obviously I had to tell Mom why you weren't coming, and I guess she made a mental note of that thing you do with the wedding songs, because maybe twenty seconds after she told me she and George were giving it another go, she asked if I'd get you to be their wedding singer. She says it will make the wedding really special. And honestly? I think she's nervous that some of her friends won't want to come, even though she hasn't asked for gifts since wedding number two. You're the lure."

"Does your mother even like my music?" J asked. In his mind, this question was only 40% serious. But in truth, it was probably nearing 70%. Tom's mother had once, in his presence, described his music as "like an oddball Simon and Garfunkel"—but she had clearly put her emphasis on the Garfunkel.

"She loves your music!" Tom replied. 100% sincere, maybe 64% accurate.

"When is the wedding?"

"She says she'll plan around your schedule. But, you know, not *too* long."

"And what does George say about this?"

Tom shrugged. "Not a word. They're in that stage right now, where he understands that the road to contentment is paved with his silent acquiescence."

"I'd say he's a wise man . . . but I'm not sure if marrying the same woman four times counts as wisdom."

"Maybe hitting sixty-five will change the pattern."

"Your mother's turning sixty-five?"

"You are *not* allowed to put that in the song."

"I haven't said yes yet."

"But you're going to, right?"

"If I don't, she'll make me watch some Bette Davis movie with her."

"That only happened once!" (She had caught them staying up late, sneaking a comedy famous for its female nudity on cable, and had told them if they were going to be up past midnight watching a movie, it was going to be the movie of *her* choice. Neither of them can remember its name, only that it was black and white, starred Bette Davis, and was not at all what their eleven-year-old selves could bear to watch.)

"No, it's fine," J said. "I can't say no to your mother. Which is, I believe, something I learned from you."

"Fair enough. I'm considering that a yes. Thank you." Tom kicked J's foot lightly in gratitude.

"I'd say 'any time,' but honestly I will not play the fifth or sixth wedding. Please make that clear."

"Holding out for the seventh—noted."

"Will it be a big ceremony?"

"More like a party. And I'd guess it'll be big. Mom doesn't really do things on a small scale. Don't worry—you'll get a plus-one. You can bring V."

Tom's tone was 91 percent playful as he said this. But J still couldn't help but think, *There it is. I knew it.*

Tom's simple statement—*You can bring V*—could be interpreted in two ways:

1) V is your girlfriend, and of course she will be your plus-one. How nice it will be to have her there.

2) May I remind you that I, Tom, was on a second date with V the first time you met her? And while I appreciate that nothing happened between the two of you until months later, well after V decided there wouldn't be a third date with me, and while I have come to peace with the fact that V's

decision to not go on a third date with me was in no way related to the fact that she wanted to go on a first date with you, and while I naturally feel like farthest point of the triangle whenever the three of us get together, since I don't currently have a girlfriend myself to balance such situations out—despite all this, I hope I have proven to be nothing but welcoming to the fact that the two of you have proven to be a better couple than she and I ever would have been, and expressing my desire to have her at my mother's fourth wedding is merely another gratuitous confirmation that I am totally okay with the fact that had I not brought my date to that party, the two of you might never have met.

"I'm sure she'd love that," J replied, addressing (1) instead of (2), just as most men would.

"Wonderful! I'll tell Mom." (*How much,* J wondered, *does Mom know?*) "Do you have your calendar on your phone?"

Soon a few dates were sorted, and Tom's mother was called on speakerphone. J appreciated how unapologetic she was about the fact that she and George were getting married for a fourth time, as well as the fact that at no point did she promise that this would be the last time, that this would in some way be different. No, it sounded like they just wanted another spin on the dance floor . . . and if they wanted him to play some songs as they followed their steps, who was he to say no?

Now, nearly two months later, the wedding is upon them, the weekend following Jun and Arthur's wedding.

V isn't sure she can attend.

"If Thor has to fly out for this meeting in New York, I have to go with him," she tells J. "You know this."

Thor (not his birth name) is V's boss. V can sense that J would love to say, *Thor's a big boy—he can take care of himself.* But the problem is that while Thor is still a boy, he's not a particularly big one. Rarely can he take care of himself. He's only nineteen, and it's an open debate whether he's a genius or just really lucky.

When J and V first reconnected after her inconsequential dalliance with Tom, the conversation seemed to hit an invisible fence when J asked her what she did for a living.

"I can't tell you," she said. "It's a secret project."

She didn't say this to tease, but as a contractual obligation. J could tell she was embarrassed to find such words coming out of her mouth. So he let it slide, and over the course of their next few dates, he pretended she worked for an organization called Secret Project.

This had unintended consequences.

Before working for Thor, V had been working at a publishing house, and when it shut down, she looked for employment with a certain desperation, since her time in publishing had not led to a deep reserve of savings. When she was approached about Thor's endeavor by a friend of one of her former professors, she wasn't too interested. Then they told her the starting salary, and she became very interested. Long story short: As a kid, Thor had started programming an online world-building system for himself and his friends, where you'd design an elaborate space for your friends, invite them over to experience it (like a party), and then when the party was over, the space would go away and you'd start all over again. And that had been the jumping-off point for something much larger, involving a whole lot of new technologies that V barely understood.

V was brought on to do PR, thinking it wouldn't go anywhere. Much to everyone's frustration, while Thor was good at world-building, he sucked at words, and for far too long, the site was only known as Untitled Thor Project. Then one day, V made a joke in a meeting about how the guy she was dating called it Secret Project . . . and that was the missing piece, the phrase that got everyone excited. In what could only be called a frenzy, Thor got more funding than most charities ever saw, and big American companies started sniffing around, thinking they smelled The Next Big Thing. At this juncture, the sniffers had turned into suitors, and it was decided that V's ability to judge character was crucial, since Thor would have probably sold the company for jellybeans if they'd been the right color.

J still likes to think of V's employment as something between a lark and a dark comedy. Most times, V agrees with this assessment—the stakes shouldn't be high when dealing with imaginary worlds. But she will also admit (often to herself, occasionally to J) that she's become invested in Secret Project's fate. Both literally (if it becomes the next *Minecraft*, she will have more money than she ever imagined having) and figuratively.

After telling J that Thor might need her in New York, she prepares herself for the joke, the jibe, the groan. She is unprepared for J to lean in the doorway of his bedroom and say, "I know he needs you . . . but I would love for you to be there. I have no other plus-one in my life."

"Come on," she says, keeping her voice light. "It's her fourth wedding. I missed the first three. I can't imagine my absence will be noticed."

"I'll notice it," J responds. There's a vulnerability in his voice that's not characteristic; he doesn't usually get pre-show jitters. "It's going to be weird for me. Besides Tom and his family, odds are good that other people will be there who've known me since I was a tadpole. I want it to go well . . . and having you there always helps."

"Don't worry," she says. "I doubt the trip will end up happening. The money guys want to make the Americans come to us. And if we're going to New York, it'll probably take more than a week to organize. Thor is neck-deep in the Beta, and I don't think the design team wants to lose him, even for forty-eight hours."

"I don't get it," J says.

"Which part?"

"Why do they call the demo stage 'Beta'? Shouldn't 'Beta' be second? Who *are* these people?"

They've swapped back to their old positions—now J is joking, and V is feeling like the serious one.

"Also," he adds, "how many chances do you get to see the same people married for a fourth time?"

V knows she should take some satisfaction in being so needed. But instead of filling her up, it drains her a little, and she isn't even sure why.

After J had agreed to sing at her wedding, Lisbet took him to lunch. Tom came along because J wouldn't let him get out of it.

Lunch with Lisbet wasn't a particularly risky endeavor, as long as you didn't plan to say very much, and as long as you weren't the server. ("I don't think this glass is clean" was a particular favorite of hers. Back when J was a teenager, he'd once seen her return three water glasses in a row, due to smudges his own eyes couldn't locate.)

For a half hour, she told them about the details of the wedding—especially how exhausting it was to put up with the planner's shortcomings. George's name wasn't mentioned once, not even when the subject veered into J's field.

"About the song," Lisbet said, after at least ten seconds of staring at a lettuce leaf with intense displeasure. "There will be an original song, correct? Tommy told me you write a song for all your weddings. It's a *darling* conceit."

J had been hoping he'd get out of writing a song for George and Lisbet. At their third wedding, the highlight had been a sterling rendition of Shania Twain's "You're Still the One"—somehow seeing a middle-aged, third-time's-the-charm couple dance to it made it uncommonly moving. J had assumed he would just have to whip up some similar hits from bygone eras. Now, Tom was looking apologetic even before J turned his way.

"Of course there will be a song," J replied.

Lisbet used her fork and knife to cross out her salad, then pushed the plate away as if it had been inching closer to attack her.

"Look," she said, "this is very important to me: I want you to be *truthful*. I know that often your songs attempt to be funny, and I know there's an audience for that. But not at my wedding. I am aware—painfully aware, one might say—that there are people who are laughing at me for going through with this yet again. As far as I'm concerned, there's already been enough laughter on the subject. I do not intend to sit there at my wedding and give an opportunity for further jocularity. Can you see where I'm coming from?"

J couldn't help but smile. *Can you see where I'm coming from?* was Lisbet's inadvertent catchphrase. Memorably, in the middle of a silly fight over staying out late for a Weezer concert, Lisbet had asked this question and Tom had foolishly replied, "The kitchen, Mom! You're coming from *the kitchen*!" There had been hell to pay for that.

It was a lesser hell to be paid for the smile now—but the smile was noticed. To J's horror, it was met not with anger or rebuke, but with a flash of sadness.

*Oh, no*, J thought. *She thinks I'm laughing at her, too.*

Quickly, he collected himself and tried his best to look sincere.

"I promise I'll stick to the truth," he said. "It's a truth worth celebrating."

"Exactly," Tom said. "That's exactly right."

Lisbet leaned back, satisfied.

The truth.

The truth is that the wedding is three days away and J hasn't written a word yet.

The truth is also that J has never gotten back with an ex for any lasting period of time. Not for lack of trying.

Getting back together three times is unimaginable.

He wants to talk it over with V, which is both scary and thrilling. In the past, his creativity was a castle where he'd wander from room to room, pacing the chambers and ransacking the drawers to find the perfect phrase or the right instrumentation. The castle was his and his alone—all others were requested to stay on the other side of the drawbridge, allowed in only when it was time to perform in the ballroom. At first, the drawbridge applied to V . . . but she must have found an underground passage, maybe a service elevator from the dungeon. Whatever the case, he started to bump into her when he wandered the halls. Every now and then he'd ask her if she'd seen where he'd placed his chorus, and she'd tell him to check the closet off the vestry. Then she'd keep walking, leaving him alone again.

Now J is in his apartment, trying to get to the castle. V is working late, and he's starting to wonder if he needs to talk to her to find his way.

While he waits, he tries to find the phrase that will gain him entry.

> **The fourth time's the charm when it comes to love. . . .**

No, not that.

> **Can't live with you,**
> **Can't live without you**

Please.

> **Fuel my folly**
> **And hold me tight**
> **Grow old with me**
> **Because what other choice do you have?**

Tom's mom would kill him.

V comes home at ten, which is three hours later than planned, and (to her) at least an hour earlier than expected. The office is in

Thor's house, and he often forgets that his employees have a longer commute than he does.

"Why would you marry the same person four times?" J asks as soon as she comes through the door. If she is surprised by this, it doesn't show.

"Addiction? Boredom?" she answers, hanging up her coat and kicking off her shoes. "Love? Loneliness? Whatever the condition, it has to be mutual."

"It's like a wound you don't want to heal."

V shakes her head. "It's a game you keep pausing but still want to get to the next level."

"No. It's a flavor you forget, so you have to keep ordering it again."

"An old shirt you keep deciding to wear."

"A crime scene you keep returning to."

V, who has walked into the bedroom, pops her head back into the living room.

"That one. That works."

The drawbridge lowers a little. J squeezes in, and V leaves him alone in the castle as she reheats some chicken and watches the news, because (perversely) it helps her relax.

It's only when J emerges from the castle ninety-seven minutes and six lines later that he asks how her day went.

"New York is off," she says. "For now. Thor's become a little . . . obsessed. He wants our person to ask for a Times Square billboard as one of the terms."

"Has he been to New York before?"

"On a school trip. I think they took lots of drugs and wandered around the city. Whenever it comes up, he says, 'It's so inspiring. Such an inspiring city. An inspiration for the world, because of all its *inspiring* qualities.'"

"Just don't leave me if Secret Project suddenly becomes a big American company based in New York," J requests.

She comes over to him and kisses his forehead.

"Don't worry. I don't find New York nearly as inspiring."

"Good. And I hope this means you'll be joining me at the wedding."

V smiles. "A crime scene I keep returning to, it appears."

Later that evening, J works on his song while sitting on the toilet (clothed) with his guitar, while V gives notes (naked) from the tub.

Early on, her naked presence would have been too distracting, and she probably would have insisted on his presence being naked as well. Now it feels normal for them to be like this. As J experiments with chord progressions, V closes her eyes and treats the music like steam. Were she in a different mood, J's volume might feel intrusive. But she's in this mood, ready to welcome his presence as part of her recovery from the workday.

Her friends had teased her at first, for dating a musician. *You just want him to write songs about you.* Or, *Aren't you worried he's going to write songs about you?* Or, *Guys like that never stay in the same place for too long.* Plus the usual concerns about his financial and mental stability.

V understood what she was getting into . . . but she'd had no idea what it would feel like. J's stresses are so different from her own, and his ability to create something out of nothing isn't a talent she feels she shares. It is astonishing to her how he can pick phrases out of the air and string them together into something other people want to listen to. She feels that creative part of him will never really be accessible to her—she can help him shape the final product, but she has no idea where the raw material comes from.

His work is as much a secret project to her as hers is to his. Only, he doesn't realize it.

As it happens, V loves baths and doesn't mind being serenaded. She thinks J's obsession with weddings is a little strange, but she'd never tell him this. Based on her own parents' wedlock, V is a glass-half-full person—and that half is full of poison. What Tom's mom and stepfather are doing is insane to her.

Does J want to get married? Sometimes V thinks yes, and sometimes V thinks he'd rather have it be something other people do.

V admits to herself that she loves J more when she thinks the latter is true. But she isn't sure why. It's one of the many questions she'd rather not ask herself. Some people take baths so they can let their thoughts run wild. V takes them for a silence of the mind.

"What do you think?" J asks.

Early on, V would have told him it was wonderful, or requested he play it again to cover for her own lapse of attention.

Now, she says, "I'm sorry. I drifted off. How did it sound to you?"

"It needs work," he says. "Can I play it again?"

That's the thing with these wedding songs, V knows: He doesn't just want them to be good for him. He wants them to be good for the couple, too. She likes him better for it, but also feels she can help him less. They're strangers to her. She has no idea what they'll like.

This time, she keeps her ears above water.

When he's done, she tells him what she thinks. Whatever that's worth.

The first thing J notices about the wedding is that it's about half the size he expected.

He's come early to make sure the sound system at the banquet hall works. Now he's standing beside the table with the place cards, chatting with Tom, who looks as nervous as he had in high school when the hot girl from the swim team asked him out to a concert two hours away, assuming he had an idea of how to get there when he didn't.

Tom notices J doing a mental count and says, "A lot of people didn't want to come. One 'friend' of Mom's wrote back *I'm tired of this, Lisbet* on her response card. George's daughter lives in South Africa now and wasn't going to bring her family all that way, which I kind of understand. But George's son lives in London—he could've come. He said he was busy. I told Mom if she'd really wanted them to come, they should have combined it with George's birthday. The kids couldn't have said no to that. It's a big birthday. They can be real pains, but I don't think—"

Tom looks over J's shoulder and stops abruptly. Two seconds later, a hand lands on that shoulder, and a rough voice says, "Well, if it isn't our wedding singer!"

"George!" J says, turning. Then he, too, stops abruptly. It is indeed George, but it's a gaunt, old version of George. His hair is gray and his complexion is almost the same color. Everything he's wearing looks a little too big, but it has a worn quality that makes it clear it's his usual size. His hand remains on J's shoulder, either for camaraderie or support—J can't tell which. He stays steady, just in case it's the latter.

"I'm looking forward to your song, kid!" George says, and it's like hearing a pop song coming out of a haunted house, because even if his body language is beleaguered, there's a brightness to his voice that J clings to.

"It took you two long enough to ask me," J replies, keeping his own voice bright.

George lets out a laugh that's half cough and takes his hand off J's shoulder—but only so he can punch him in the arm.

"Such a kidder. You were always such a kidder."

"Takes one to know one."

"Well, you got me there."

They make small talk for a few minutes, until the planner comes over to say the guests will soon be arriving, so they should move into the room where the ceremony will be taking place.

George allows himself to be ushered off. Tom instinctively holds back with J.

"I know," Tom says before J can ask anything. "I know what you're thinking. And here's the thing—we're not talking about it, okay? George doesn't want to talk about it. Mom doesn't. We're doing this like nothing's wrong. He hasn't been well, but it's all under control for now, okay? I'm sorry I didn't tell you. She told me I couldn't."

J finds himself asking, "Do his kids know?"

Tom shakes his head. "When I say they're not talking about it, I mean it. They're *really* not talking about it. They've got each other. They don't want anyone else. Mom didn't even tell me at first. I had to force it out of her. Eventually she let me take him to chemo, so she could get a break . . . but I couldn't tell anyone. I had to say we were going shopping."

J doesn't know what to say. He feels ridiculous because now it's Tom squeezing his arm when he should be the one giving the support.

Someone comes over and tells Tom his mother needs him for a second. J goes out to where the guests are starting to gather and finds V, looking splendid in a floral suit. One look at him and she can tell something's wrong.

"What is it?" she asks.

The other guests are too close, chatting away. J is afraid of being overheard.

"I'll tell you later," he says.

She's curious, but she is willing to carry her curiosity for a while, which J appreciates.

Instead she whispers, "Do you realize that we're the youngest people here?"

J looks around. She's not wrong.

She goes on, "Do you think at a certain point you just stop meeting new people? So you decide to marry one of the old ones?"

When V asks a question like this, J always tries to find their own relationship within the riddle, to figure out whether there's a right answer or not.

"We're far from old," J assures her.

"I know. That's why we're the youngest people here. But in a way, it's nice, isn't it? To have this many people stay by you. If I got married tomorrow, I doubt I'd have this many people show up. Not from my side. I wonder what that means."

Before J can even begin to think of the right response here, a woman interrupts, asking if J remembers sitting next to her at wedding number two. (He does not.) V recedes, and he only gets her back when the announcement is made that the doors are now open to the room where the ceremony is taking place.

"Will you sit with me?" he asks.

"Are you in front?"

"Yes."

"In that case, I'll stick behind. Is that okay?"

"Of course," J says. Because he understands not wanting to sit at the front when you barely know the couple getting married.

Still, he would feel better with her beside him.

It is only after the ceremony has started that J realizes how inappropriate most of the lyrics in his song are, if George is that ill. He tries to rewrite it in his head, but his head doesn't work that way.

Tom walks his mother down the aisle. George stands at the front of the room, beaming even brighter.

He looks at her like it's the first time, like it's all brand-new.

J is sitting in the front row because they've asked him to sing "I'll Be Seeing You" as part of the ceremony. It isn't until he takes his position and faces the audience that he sees V toward the back. She smiles at him, and then he looks and sees that many other people in the audience are smiling at him, too. To look at them, nothing is wrong. They are here to celebrate.

J starts a cappella, then fills the music in.

> **I'll be seeing you**
> **in all the old familiar places . . .**

He looks over to Lisbet and George. George's eyes are closed, and he is smiling as he listens. Lisbet is mouthing along the words.

Even though, technically, the two of them aren't married yet, they are holding hands like they've been married a long time. When J finishes, there's applause. This is not usually the case during a wedding. But since it's the fourth time around, people figure, why not?

V understands what J didn't tell her earlier. She also presumes she now understands why Lisbet and George are doing what they're doing. They don't want to die alone. Fair enough. V can think of far worse reasons to get married. But she's not sure it's a reason she ever wants to consider.

J cannot look over at Tom, who has tears in his eyes. J has never seen Tom cry, or even come close.

J has to turn away. He does not want to cry in front of all these people.

The vows are simple.

"You will be my reason," George says to Lisbet.

"You will be my reason," Lisbet says to George.

They use the same rings, because even when they weren't together, they kept them.

*What is my reason?* V wonders. But as she and J walk into the reception, she says, "That was sweet."

J wonders if she noticed anything wrong, anything off. She has no frame of reference—this is her first time seeing George.

He doesn't say anything. Not for the first time, and not for the last, he wonders whether love, for all its complications, is really very simple. Even though there may be dozens or hundreds of reasons to say no, you say yes to it, and that is that.

He's already picked up the place cards, so he leads V over to Table 2. When they get there, he sees that V has been seated between him and Tom. He wants to alter this arrangement, but he knows Tom must have planned it this way and will notice if it veers.

"Well, this isn't awkward," he murmurs.

"What?" V asks as she seats herself.

"Nothing," he says. The woman to his left arrives, a flight attendant who's known Lisbet "longer than you've been alive." The table fills, then falls into conversation, many of the guests tallying how many of George and Lisbet's weddings they've been to. Tom is the last to arrive, his nervousness badly masked by his attempts at good spirits.

"It's lovely to see you again, V," he says once he's sat down and his napkin is in his lap.

"Oh?" V replies. "Have we met?"

With a sense of dread, J can see that Tom doesn't realize she's joking.

"Why yes," Tom sputters. "We—"

V offers a forgive-me smile. "I know. I just couldn't resist."

Tom isn't laughing. Instead he looks like he's just been startled by a camera's flash.

"Oh, I see," he murmurs.

"I don't understand," the woman to J's left says. "Do you know each other or not?"

It is noticeable to all three of them that neither J, V, nor Tom jumps in with "It's a funny story . . ." J waits to see how Tom or V will answer. V waits to see how Tom will answer.

Tom finally says, "Yes, we've met. But it was some time ago."

"And how long have the two of you been together?" the woman asks J and V.

V answers, "For some time."

J has never felt guilty about how he and V met, only awkward. It was clear even on that night that the chemistry wasn't there between her and Tom, and nothing that J has learned since has led him to believe that she and Tom would have made a good pair. When he and V had reconnected, he'd even checked with Tom to make sure it was okay, and Tom had said no blessing was required. It's true that J had avoided them going out as a trio in the intervening two years . . . but he hadn't hesitated to invite Tom to group activities where V would also be. Tom never said yes. Not, he assured J, because of V's presence.

J now feels maybe he should have forced the issue a little earlier, so the reunion, as it was, wouldn't occur at a table set for ten.

Both Tom and V are looking at him now, each expecting something from him that he can't discern. All he can do is turn to the woman on his left and ask her which airports are her favorites. Ten minutes later, he is in the middle of hearing about a carnal free-for-all in a Hyatt by LAX when the wedding planner comes over and tells him the speeches are about to start; he is on directly after.

George and Lisbet take their place at the microphone, George in his ill-fitting tuxedo, Lisbet in a dress the color of a carnation and the cut of a rose. George has to say "Hello everyone" three times before the guests quiet down. He turns aside to cough away from the mic, then comes back on.

"Hello! I just wanted to say—" (another cough) "—how grateful I am that you've joined us today. I realize that our approach to marriage—" (two coughs, then an abashed smile) "—isn't particularly conventional. We must seem like two of the most fickle people in the world. But I'll tell you, I wouldn't have it any other way. A lot of people have asked, why now? Why again? Well, I'm gonna tell you: The older you get, the more you understand what you like, and the more you understand that you should be spending your time on what you like, not all the other crap. You know what I mean?" (Pause for breath; J sees many of the older guests nodding—one even calls out "Yes, we do!") "This lady beside me—she and I have had good times, and we've had hard times. But there's a difference between hard times and bad times, and lately I've been realizing how hard times can bring out some of the best times, when it comes to what love is worth. So here we are. I won't promise you this is the last time, because life has demonstrated that it doesn't give a damn what I think. But if I can't control what life does to me or any of us, I can certainly choose who I want to spend it with. Sometimes she gives me grief, and a lot of the time I deserve it. But when she knows I can't take it—well, there's no one who's ever been more on my side. The love of my life, four times and counting. Here's to having cause to celebrate."

He raises a toast, and the room rings out with the clink of glasses, like wind chimes announcing the breeze of a new morning.

Lisbet then steps to the microphone and says, "I don't know I have anything to add to that. We know who our true friends are—and they're here in the room with us. And George's children, of course, who are scattered all over the globe and couldn't be present. I know they're sending their love, and I'm also so glad to have Tom here with us. Anyone who's been to all of our weddings will be receiving a bread maker—I'm not kidding about this!—and Tom's will be the most deluxe bread maker we can find." There's some laughter. Tom blushes and looks down at his plate.

"Now," Lisbet continues, "we have quite a treat for you. One of Tom's longtime friends is an *internationally acclaimed* performer, filling concert halls and stadiums. Even though I'm sure he could be playing to a much, much larger crowd than this, he is here to debut a song he's written just for George and me. We haven't heard it yet, so we're as excited as you to hear it. You've already given him one ovation today, but please put your hands together again for . . . our wedding singer!"

It is with a profound unease that J gets up from his seat. Not because he's been introduced on false pretenses (he's never played a stadium), but because he knows the song he's written is wrong for this moment. It does not match the bragging glee with which Lisbet has welcomed him forward. It does not match the deep breath George is taking, and the trouble he seems to have standing for so long. It does not acknowledge that hard times can bring on the best times, a phrase that J can't get out of his head.

It is never a good idea for singers to try to explain away a song before they sing it. J looks to V for some help, but she's clapping along with everyone else, even though she knows what's in the song—how can she seem so supportive, so ready for him to open his mouth?

J picks up his guitar and gives himself a thirty-second-long grace period of tuning before he says anything. Then he steps to the mic and begins.

"It's so wonderful to be here, to celebrate with Lisbet and George. I've known Tom since I was a boy, and when I met him, George was already on the scene. I wanted to write a song that . . . celebrated the magnet that keeps drawing them back together. Because most couples . . . at a certain point they don't even question what they have, and whether they want to have it. But Lisbet and George—they are always questioning it. And the answer is always the love that leads to us being here today."

He looks at George, who gives him a thumbs-up. Lisbet is impatient, wanting him to start singing.

J takes a deep breath. After the exhale, he says, "Okay. This is called 'Still in Love with You.'"

> **I tried not thinking of you**
> **cause the thought was a truck**

    parked uphill, handbrake almost loose
    keys still in the lock
    I know that it's been years since we were through
    But I'm still in love with you

    I tried not thinking of you
    Cause you were an empty casket
    A silhouette outlined with chalk
    covered by a blanket
    a crime scene I keep returning to
    I'm still in love with you

    And when you try to not think of something
    You can only think of that thing
    The one thing people tell me I shouldn't do
    But I don't care what they say
    I no longer want to be saved
    there's not a cure in this world I wouldn't refuse
    If I go down at least I want to go down with you

    I know that it's been years since we were through
    But I'm still in love with you
    I can't stop thinking of you

He repeats the last chorus once, twice. George looks like he is struggling to breathe. Lisbet looks as if she doesn't know whether to be angry or pleased. Tom is glaring at him—*What are you doing?* V is glancing around at other people's reactions. He's still playing, so they haven't hit that moment yet, where people will either applaud or not. In his heart, J knows he can't stop. No one is laughing—at least he's honored that request—but no one is smiling, either.

So J keeps playing. He makes it look like the song hasn't ended. He changes his chords around. He reaches for something, anything, that can give him an exit from this moment.

And then, God help him, recalling the song that brought George and Lisbet so much joy two weddings ago, he starts singing Shania Twain's "You're Still the One."

He actually starts on the second verse, because he doesn't remember there's a first verse.

> **Looks like we made it**
> **Look how far we've come, my baby**

Since his recollection of the lyrics is fuzzy at best, it comes out as:

> **Looks like we made it**
> **Look how far we've got now, baby**

Somehow he gets to the safer ground of the golden chorus, and he's giving it his all. The bewilderment he sensed in the air is gone. He dares a glance at George and Lisbet, and sees George hold out a hand to her, and Lisbet, both smiling and crying, taking it, and now they are having an unplanned first dance.

J looks over to his table. Tom is crying, too. V has her phone out—she must be looking up the lyrics, because as he gets to the end of the chorus, she mouths, "Ain't nothin' better," and yes—there it is, the rest of the song. She guides him through.

J looks back at George and Lisbet. He sees how tightly Lisbet holds George, and once again has no idea if it's out of affection or support, or if there's any difference between the two. Both of them have their eyes closed. Both of them sway into the second chorus, the third chorus. J wants to make the song go on and on, so they can dance like this for days, for years.

The song inevitably ends. The guests erupt in applause. George and Lisbet linger in their dance for a few beats after the song is over. Then they open their eyes at the same time, smile at each other. George kisses Lisbet. Lisbet kisses back. The guests cheer.

J's work here is done. The wedding band has been gathering behind him. Now he steps aside as the bandleader comes on, calling in a carnival-barker tone, "We'd like to invite you all onto the dance floor for a celebration of George and Lisbet's fourth wedding!"

J puts his guitar back in its case and heads to his table. Tom stands, walks over, and gives him a hug.

"Nice save," Tom whispers. Then, when he pulls back, he says, a little louder, "I hope you don't mind, but I'm going to ask V to join me on the dance floor. I feel I should be there now, you know. And since I don't have a date of my own . . ."

"Of course," J says. "Go ahead."

The two of them turn back to the table.

"J has been kind enough to allow me to ask you to dance," Tom says to V.

"Oh, has he?" V replies. She puts her napkin on the table and pushes back her chair. "Let's go, then."

J is too wiped out to do anything besides sit. He is relieved to find that someone else has asked the flight attendant to dance, and that the other couples at the table have also joined the newlywed-agains on the dance floor. The band is, strangely, playing "Save the Last Dance for Me" as their first dance. Though when he thinks about it, J wonders if this isn't fitting, after all.

At the end of the song, J sees George whisper something to Lisbet, and she lets him move away from the dance floor. J assumes Tom will glide into the breach, but Tom doesn't seem to want to dance with anyone other than V. Another adult, Tom's uncle Gustav, steps in instead.

J is so focused on this wordless dance negotiation that he doesn't notice George's approach until George is nearly upon him. He moves to stand, but George says, "No, no—better to sit." Then he lowers himself into V's seat.

Immediately, J approaches an apology for his song. "I know that probably wasn't what you were—" he begins.

George cuts him off. "It was perfect."

"That's very nice of you to say, but—"

"No buts. I don't know how you did it, but you got it exactly right. What it's like. And I don't mean that Shania Twain crap. I mean *your* song. That's what it feels like to me. I can't speak for Lisbet—I'd never be fool enough to speak for Lisbet, not at this point. I'm guessing those probably aren't the words she would've used. But I honestly couldn't have said it better myself. Which I guess is why you're a songwriter and I'm an accountant."

This is too many words for George to get out without a breath. When he's done, the coughing comes back. J, feeling helpless, reaches for his water glass. George doesn't look thrilled to take it, but he does. When he's done with it, it shakes in his hand as he puts it back on the table.

"Are you alright?" J asks.

In response, George looks him in the eye and says, "I've never been better, kid. It's a great day." Slowly, he rises from the chair. "Now, you better go save your girlfriend from my son. He's been waiting for that dance for way too long."

As George shuffles off to greet another table, J looks and sees that Tom is holding V in a way that would signal to a casual observer that she is, in fact, his date to this wedding. The fact that the song is "Always on My Mind" doesn't help matters.

J makes his way to the dance floor. Nobody stops him to compliment him on his lyrics—but no one throws dinner rolls at him or asks about empty casket imagery, either.

Tom seems surprised when J cuts in.

"Go dance with your mother," J tells him. "I'm sure she wants you to."

"I'm sure she'd love a dance with you, too," Tom replies. Then, hearing himself, he lowers his arms and takes a step back. "Eventually. If you have the time."

J isn't sure he's ready for Lisbet's review of his performance; he's going to rest on George's laurels for as long as he can.

The band strikes up "I'm Still Standing." J offers his hand to V. For a second, it appears she won't take it.

"You do recognize I'm a sentient being?" she says. "The last time I checked, I wasn't an inflatable doll to be passed from friend to friend."

Their hands clasp. She puts her other hand around his waist.

"I am aware of this, yes," he replies.

"I just had to be sure."

"And why is that?"

"Because, if you didn't realize, he asked you if I could dance with him before asking me. And then, during the first song, he felt the need to tell me how much he's missed me."

J's spine straightens. "Missed you?"

"Missed me. And do you know what I said to that?"

"No. What?"

"Nothing. I said nothing. Because I really don't want to be a friendwrecker."

"A friendwrecker? Is that a thing?"

"It is now. You know what I mean."

"Well, I'm sorry. I had no idea."

"No, you wouldn't, would you?"

J twirls V around. They are quiet for a minute, and then he says, "Thanks for the save, by the way."

"I knew you were in trouble when you skipped the start of the song."

"I didn't skip the start of the song!"

"According to lyrics.com, you did."

"I will gladly turn in my wedding singer license, if you want to press charges."

"Oh, please," V says. "You love this kind of thing."

"What kind of thing?"

"People in love."

"And you don't?"

"It makes me uneasy, all these expectations gathered in one room. But at least this time nobody gave a speech pestering the couple about when they're going to start having kids. That's progress."

J kisses V. "Look at you, so down on love."

"Just down on weddings. Not the same thing."

"I'm glad you're with me," J says.

And V tells him, truthfully, "That's the reason I'm here."

Two songs later ("I Will Survive"), Tom tries to cut in.

V laughs and J tells him, with aggressive jokiness, to back off. Tom avoids them for the rest of the night. Even when J is sitting alone (V has to take a call from Thor, who has forgotten the name of a financial advisor), Tom keeps his distance. The flight attendant slips into the conversational space and wants to know if being a global superstar means J has platinum status on more than one airline.

When V returns to the table, J asks her how the call went.

"I have to keep reminding myself that when I was nineteen, I could barely remember how to figure out a tip, not to mention budget my spending. And Thor's trying to run a company. It's not his fault he's not an adult yet."

"So you get to be the adult?"

"Isn't that strange?" V says. "My nineteen-year-old self would be disgusted."

"And what would she say to me asking you to dance again?"

"Honestly? She'd have no concept of being here. She'd be in her dorm furtively masturbating to one of the Backstreet Boys while pretending to be masturbating to Rilke. So to hell with her. Let's dance."

Lisbet doesn't breathe a word to J about his song, positive or negative. She just says to him in parting what she's saying to all the other guests—that it was lovely to have him there.

But George—George goes out of his way to pull J aside at the end of the night.

"If you get lucky," George says, "every once in a while, you find someone who loves you so much that you're not troubled by the meaninglessness of it all. By that measure, right now, I am a lucky man. A very, very lucky man."

They hug each other goodbye. It lasts longer than it usually would.

"Good luck," J finds himself saying.

And George has the grace to reply, "You too."

# THE THIRD WEDDING

Two weeks later, V is on a plane to New York.

Nothing happens, and nothing happens, and then everything happens—that's how it feels to V. How do you react when the possibility that's been dangling in front of you is suddenly in your hands? All she could do was say goodbye to her apartment, say goodbye to her friends, say goodbye to J, without being able to say with any certainty when she'd return.

It should feel terrifying.

It does not, in fact, feel terrifying.

Her gut is telling her they are going to ace this test; Thor and the tech team have cast a spell over the financiers, and V is going to do her best to make sure nothing wobbles.

In the meantime, she wants to enjoy this flight. She and Thor were given business class seats—which, they discovered, could be folded down into beds. Even though Thor is a programming savant, he still reacted with glee upon seeing the amenity fortress the airline provided. V was right there with him, snapping photos to send her friends before she had to turn her phone off. (This was before she understood she had free wi-fi.)

"We're traveling in style!" Thor proclaimed from across the aisle.

V couldn't discern a single ounce of nervousness within him. This was also part of his gift.

Thor fell asleep before they'd left Swedish airspace, but V has stayed awake well past the last European land mass. Once upon a time, she might have imagined that such a journey would make her feel the pull of home even stronger—Gothenburg was where she'd anchored her life, so it made sense for the tug to come from what was being left behind. But instead, V has the strange sensation that she's tethered to the future, and that her anchor has been shifted to New York before she's even gotten there.

She has no idea what any of this means. All she knows is how it feels.

There's an echo here: That moment, age sixteen, when she took the things that mattered to her from her room and left her parents' house. Their mess, their noise, had infected her, and she knew she had to get out before it turned her into the people they had become—drunk and angry, drunk and sad, drunk and bitter. Only with distance could she understand that not everyone was so hateful, and that finding an unhateful home was worth all the hardship of making a new life from scratch. Her best friend Glenda's family had taken her in, and then a year later she'd had her own place . . . with three roommates. A year after that, she moved in with the first of a string of non-starter boyfriends. It wasn't until she was in her midtwenties that she finally understood what it meant to live alone. Later, when she met J, she loved that he understood the value of this. While they'd talked about living together, they agreed that having separate spaces worked well.

When she'd left her parents' house, she had mostly felt resentful. It was only later that she felt grateful. Now, there isn't resentment. But there is gratitude, even though she knows it comes at a cost.

She and J had dinner last night, and she could tell he was putting on a brave face. There was some irony in this; he traveled all the time on tour, and she had grown very used to him leaving on a jet plane. Of course, the next line of that song is "don't know when I'll be back again"—something that was never the case with J, but was true now for V.

"You go to New York all the time," V reminded J. "You have friends there. It's not like I'm moving to Perth."

"*She's moving to Perth*," J had spontaneously crooned over the dinner table. "*So far from the land of her birth. / I think she's taking all my mirth . . . / but I'm proud of her, for what it's worth.*"

"I appreciate that," V had said. And she still appreciates it now, as she pushes back her absurdly expensive plane seat and looks out at the pulsing lights at the edge of the plane's wing. But it's only a minor chord in her mind's current symphony.

She always knew she'd make this next step in leaving home. She just never imagined she'd leave like this. First class, with a nineteen-year-old genius as her flying companion. There's a part of her that wishes she'd had the bravery to leave at eighteen, to forgo the first non-starter boyfriend, put her prized possessions in a backpack, lose that backpack at a train station, and then discover there were prizes to be found all around the world. She knows she has wired herself to be responsible—that is, after all, why she's indispensable to Thor and Secret Project. But any person wired for responsibility looks every now and then at the fuse box with longing.

She knows how strange it will be for J. She's been acting like his anchor, his Penelope. Which she knows is overstating it . . . but, again, it's how it feels. Or how it's felt. Up in the air, he feels a long way away. She is not waiting for him for anything. He may have to wait for her.

The flight attendant comes by and asks V if everything is okay.

"How could it not be?" she replies.

The flight attendant smiles. But, really, how could she understand?

For V, this is the great adventure. She's not doing it for survival. She's not doing it because there's anything she needs to escape. This is the big journey she always secretly (even to herself) had her bags packed for.

She wants to be open to whatever comes next. She wants to see where her anchor now lies.

Nearly two months later, V is living in New York and J is trying very hard not to be heartbroken. They are still together, he reminds himself. But he finds himself needing the reminders more and more.

She has been gone for seven weeks and five days, with no return date on the horizon. Things are going well for Secret Project. People are buzzing that "a new way to do socially constructive, invitation-exclusive media" (V's phrase) could lure people to their computers and phones for extended amounts of time and ego. Thor has been heralded (mostly by V, but increasingly in the press) as an oracle of things to come. Interviewers don't mention that he can still take up to half an hour to decide where to have dinner.

J and V talk every day. Well, most days. V's days seem to pass more quickly than J's, and there is also the six-hour time difference, which cruelly ensures that their conversations are more informational than carnal. When J is feeling sexy, V is inevitably caught in an afternoon meeting or navigating the aforementioned dinner plans. When V is feeling sexy, on the rare night where she feels sexy after a fifteen-hour workday, J is sound asleep. He tried waking up at six in the morning to chat with her, but some parts of him were more amenable to an early wake-up than others.

When V had left ("I promise, it'll probably be two weeks at the most"), she'd sold it as the perfect opportunity for him to finish writing the songs for his next album—as if her presence impeded his creativity rather than inspiring it. This theory of hers has proven to be a spectacular failure. Not only is it hard for J to write new songs that aren't mopey-in-a-bad-way, but her absence is now tainting the older songs that were fueled by his thoughts of her. Even an anodyne phrase like "I wake up to the sun poking through a hole in the shades" becomes a summoning of morning acts that can't be repeated when your lover is an ocean away.

The only songs J can write are the wedding songs, because those allow the illusion of belonging to another couple's lives. Two weeks after Lisbet and George's wedding, he played for a more customary fee at a stranger's wedding. Anton was a punkish guitarist, and he'd fallen madly for a cellist who was not from the same scene. Instead of playing clubs, Sara played with the National Orchestra of Sweden. She also had a superbly perverse sense of humor, so she didn't mind at all that J's wedding song contained the punch line:

> I'm not known to be
> a Classical fellow
> But even Beethoven
> could hear
> You had me at cello.

What nobody had told J was that Sara was also minor Swedish royalty, and as a result, a prominent columnist from a prominent newspaper was present. The columnist absolutely *adored* J's song, and once Sara told her the backstory, she decided to write about what J was doing. This article, in the higher-selling Sunday edition of the paper, brought him a surge of wedding invitations—some of them quite enticing, financially. At first, J let them sit in his inbox, reading aloud the funnier requests ("a wedding entirely on horseback!") to V. It was only after she had decamped ("I'm sure I'll be back before you even notice") and his desire to write his own songs had dissipated that he looked at the invitations in earnest.

J is old enough to know you should never do something *just* for the money. But he figures (correctly, for the most part) that if you have nothing else to do with your time except wonder how an extreme bout of long distance will affect your relationship, you might as well go for the distraction that will make you some serious bank.

J relies on his wedding gigs to supply a significant share of his income; what started out as a lark spun off from a song became something a little more reliable than a lark. This is the reality of the music industry right now; if he wants to actually live off of music, he has to be a part of the gig economy. As streaming transformed how people listened to songs, music became like tap water, something people took for granted, that they expected to be there for a monthly subscription fee. And in this process, music itself was transformed into something that could only be profitable if it was sold via another commodity. There is no stability in being paid $0.003 every time your song is played. The choice for J was between having an energy drink logo tattooed on his forehead or finding a way to make his music exclusive somehow. Transform it from tap water into . . . well. Maybe not a bottle of Acqua di Cristallo, but at least a bottle of Evian.

So when times have been tight, J has found himself playing for some entrepreneur who talked to him endlessly about the music they'd heard at Burning Man. He's played for a very sweet couple who had at least one arms dealer in the audience. He's played for a "struggling artist" whose father was listed in *Forbes* as the eighty-first richest person in the world. At that wedding, every guest got their own Tiffany bracelet to commemorate the day. As an afterthought, J was given the bracelet of a man who hadn't shown up. He didn't feel bad selling it for a nice profit.

When J scrolls through the post-column invitations, he finds one invitation in particular that dangles a sum equal to about half a year's salary as a barista. He almost spills his coffee over his laptop when he sees this.

J emails this couple first.

As he waits for a response, he does a little googling and discovers that the groom-to-be works "in finance" (which is to say, he does something involving lots of theoretical money that J will never even try to understand). The bride-to-be owns a boutique named after herself. Its logo is her name in cursive leopard-print. She has far more Instagram followers than a boutique owner would ordinarily have, especially in Sweden. It's from this that J deduces she is of that strange breed known as *influencer*—people known for being known who leverage their known-ness exquisitely.

These should be warning signs, but the dollars signs block them out.

J hears back from the bride-to-be's assistant within an hour, even though the particular hour is midnight. He wonders if the assistant is in another time zone or if she is always on standby.

A video interview is set up for the following Tuesday, at precisely 6:15 p.m.

J has no idea whether he is going to be the interviewer or the interviewee.

Since he is up after midnight, J calls V.

"Oh, hello," she answers.

"You sound surprised it's me," J observes. "Didn't you see my name before you answered?"

"I just figured it was late there. I'm surprised you're awake."

J can hear voices in the background.

"Are you still at work?" he asks.

"It's only eight here. Of course I'm still at work."

Male voices. There are male voices in the background.

"Is Thor there with you?"

V sighs. "No. He's out with Meta."

"Meta?"

"I told you about Meta. The NYU student?"

J sincerely can't remember any NYU student being mentioned. But he doesn't always remember everything V says when the conversations happen after midnight.

"I'm not sure you've told me about Meta," he confesses.

"Well, Thor's in love. With an NYU student. Named Meta. In her defense, her name predates Mark Zuckerberg's appropriation of the word."

"So she's old-school meta, then. How'd they meet? A warehouse rave?"

"They met in the park. Thor was walking his dog, and Meta is, apparently, a sucker for mutts, so they started talking and now they're out at Momofuku while I'm still at the office."

J knows it's not the point of the story, but he gets stuck on one of its secondary facts.

"Thor has a dog?" he asks.

V sighs again. "Yes. He adopted a dog from a shelter last week. He's still trying out names, to see which one she likes best. We have a betting pool. I chose Cherry. I'm not even sure why. She just seems like a Cherry."

"Is she a small dog or a big dog?"

"She's a medium-size dog, but she's still growing. Why does that matter?"

J tries to control his breathing. "V," he says, "nobody—not even someone as cloud-headed as Thor—adopts a dog if he thinks he's going to be moving back home in a few weeks. He's not planning on coming back."

This time V doesn't sigh. But J can sense her shaking her head.

"Is this why you called? To have this conversation?"

"No! I didn't know anything about the dog when I called. I was going to tell you about this couple that wants me to sing at their wedding. But now you've mentioned Thor's dog and there's no going back."

"Have you been drinking?"

In his most sober tone, J says, "No, I have not been drinking. Do I sound like I've been drinking?"

"No. You sound tired. Go to sleep and we'll talk tomorrow."

"You haven't argued my point."

"What?"

"You haven't said, 'No, just because Thor's adopted a dog, it doesn't mean we're going to be staying here.'"

"Do you seriously need me to say that? To prove to you that Thor's impulsive behavior is never an indication of anything? The fact that Thor adopted a dog means that, at one singular moment, Thor wanted a dog. It's not a part of a grand plan. Thor doesn't have a grand plan. That's why he has the rest of us, to turn his impulses into a grand plan."

"And the grand plan still involves you returning here in a few weeks?"

The sigh returns. Were V a tire, she'd be out of air by now.

"I don't know when I'm returning," she says. "It might be a few weeks or it might be a little longer than a few weeks. But I know for sure we're not moving here so Thor can keep his dog. Okay?"

J says it's okay.

But it doesn't feel okay.

Neither J nor V is a fan of any particular sport. J will turn on the World Cup, maybe. V thinks the Williams sisters are incredible, but she never got much thrill from watching them play full sets. Highlight reels were enough.

Still, even if neither of the two people involved in this conversation is sport-inclined, a sporting truism occurs to each of them at this point. It's actually one of the most basic truisms in all of sports: You don't get much of a game if both sides are on the defense. Pride might be saved, but the match won't be won.

It stands to follow, then, that if you're both going to be defensive, you might as well save the energy and leave the field.

"You know what," J says, "you're right. It *is* late. I *am* tired."

A soothing tone returns to V's voice. "I know. And I'm super stressed and, frankly, sick of working late every night."

"I miss you."

"I miss you, too."

"Good luck with the rest of your night."

"Sleep well."

J knows he is not going to sleep well. He knows he shouldn't have been the first one to say "I miss you" because the "I miss you, too" is never, ever as satisfying to receive. All V needed to say was "I can't wait to come back to you, whether or not Thor has a dog."

J loves that V will always avoid being an outright liar. But that makes it harder when there's a truth he wants her to confirm and she steps away from it rather than addressing it.

J feels alone in his apartment and stuck in his aloneness. Because the only person he wants to call is the person he's just hung up with.

At 6:14 p.m. the next evening, J clicks the video chat link.

At 6:15 p.m., another box appears without its camera on.

"Please hold for Celestia Vaughn," a voice—presumably the assistant's?—intones.

J waits. And waits.

At 6:28 p.m. the shades of another virtual window are drawn and he's face-to-face with a woman who can only be Celestia Vaughn. She is no doubt younger than J, but already has the semi-android look of someone who is using surgical means to tame all the personality from her face. While J is at his kitchen table, lit by the usual lighting fixtures, Celestia is ring-lit, in a study where the book spines have been arranged into striped patterns. Books with small titles have been deliberately chosen, since longer titles would interfere with the effect.

None of this is particularly unexpected. What is unexpected is when Celestia opens her mouth and takes the tone of an early teenager who's had a little too much fruit punch at the slumber party.

"Oh my god, it's so amazing to see you!" she launches with. "I'm honored, really. I've been listening to your albums nonstop since I read that article, and the fact that you'd be willing to even consider our wedding—I can't tell you what that means to me. Truly. I was telling Roger, 'You have to listen to this guy. He knows things about love that you and I really need to learn.' The fact that you write songs for couples—what a kind way to share your talents. A gift. Like, totally a gift."

J doesn't know what to say to any of this except "Thank you."

"Now, before we get into it, I also have to apologize to you for the sum we quoted in our initial email. That was before I heard your music. Roger would hate me for saying this, but we're definitely willing to go higher."

Again, J finds himself thanking her. The weird part being: He can tell she's not bullshitting. She actually listened the songs, and they meant something to her. That means as much as the money, although the money of course is more helpful when he's out in the wider world.

"So tell me, how does it work?"

He gives her the rundown about the conversations they'll have so he can shape the song, then the two sets he'll perform—one with favorites of theirs, one with the wedding song. They can incorporate the sets into their wedding wherever they see fit.

Celestia starts to flutter her hand in front of her face. Her eyes are tearing up.

"That's just so . . . special," she says. Then she looks to her side, sees someone, and gestures for them to come closer.

"It's the wedding guy," she explains to the person off camera. "You really liked that cab song of his, remember?" Then she turns to J. "Roger's just gotten home. Roger, say hi."

A guy in a suit comes into the frame. He puts a hand on Celestia's shoulder and kisses her head. Then he looks at the camera, smiles, and says, "Just do whatever she tells you. That's what I do." Celestia swats at him playfully, he squeezes her shoulder, waves to J, and walks out.

"He's a joker," Celestia says. Then her eyes widen in revelation. "Write that down! That can be part of your song. How he jokes all the time. But only out of love."

She looks at J so expectantly that he grabs a notebook and writes it down.

*Joker.*

Before J can ask anything else about their relationship, the presumably-assistant's voice returns.

"Celestia, I'm so sorry. But your six-thirty is waiting."

Celestia seems crestfallen to hear this.

"But we just got started! Why did you only schedule us for five minutes?" Then she looks to J. "I'm *so* sorry. But this is a start, right?"

Yes, he agrees. This is a start.

Ten minutes later, the definitely-assistant emails him with a revised offer that makes this the most lucrative gig J has ever had.

He accepts.

He texts this news to V, and then feels foolish for how often he checks to see if she's read it.

It's still unread as he falls asleep.

The next morning, there's a response from her. But all it says is $$$$$ ☺

He wants her to point out that the sum is more than enough for him to fly over for a visit.

He doesn't need her to be happy for him, but it would be nice for her to be happy for that.

J considers the day in front of him; he doesn't have a single plan. In certain moods, he would find this liberating. But in his current mood, he finds it depressing. He realizes he should be taking this time without V to see some of the people she doesn't particularly like. There's a roster of friends he sees maybe twice a year, one-on-one. Why not use this as an opportunity to get some of these engagements over with now?

He texts Ginger, a woman who he didn't date long enough to consider an ex and doesn't see often enough to consider a close friend. She is an actress of great range and little depth, and one of the great attractions of dining with her is how little she demands, other than being listened to.

When the lunch is over, J walks to his car and writes a *good morning* text to V.

She replies, *I've been up for hours.*

J does the math in his head. It's 8:44 there. And, really, the good morning was meant to reflect the time between the two of them, not empirical time.

He decides not to engage in this distinction, and instead texts, *I just had lunch.*

He waits for her to ask who with.

She doesn't reply.

J realizes there's no point in turning his head. If he wants to work on songs, he has to face what's right in front of him.

> Between your time zone
> and my time zone
> how do we find
> our comfort zone?

That feels elementary.

> No hugs, no kisses, no sex
> You don't even answer my texts
> I'll take heartbreak for 500, Alex

True, but where does it go next?

> Love is the fifth natural force
> Making rings on the ocean with its oars
> Reshaping the planet to its core
> Oh I just want things to be like before
> Well, if anything's worth melting the glaciers for
> it's you

Better, songwise. But depressing to think about.

He checks his email and there's one from Celestia's assistant.

*Celestia is compiling her list, v. excited. Will have it to you next week. In the meantime, please sign the attached contract and NDA so we can proceed.*

J isn't sure what the assistant means by a list, but figures he'll find out soon enough. In the meantime, the contract and NDA are an astonishing thirty-four pages long. J understands the bottom line is that he can't speak of anything that happens at the wedding; fair enough. He also sees that Celestia wants to maintain control of the song after the wedding; she won't own it outright, but J will need her permission to record or perform it outside the wedding. J decides for this price, he can agree to that.

It is only one song, after all.

If J's week is somewhat formless, V's appears to grow more and more intense. The investors have been wooed, and now offers are starting to be made. When he meets his financial suitors, Thor is savvy and strategic and enigmatic. Outside these meetings, he is a complete mess, suddenly paralyzed by the notion that he could make the wrong choice and doom the whole endeavor to failure. Rather than talk it out with V, he runs off to be with his new love, Meta, and their new dog, Macdougal (Mac for short). It has been left to V and the chief financial advisor, an American named Grant, to play the potential investors off each other to get the best offers possible.

J has pieced this narrative together from shards of quick conversations. Since V is always at work, he is always catching her at work. Time and time again, he offers to stay up for her, to be ready when she is done, even if it's three or four in the morning, his time. But in response he always gets the same refrain.

> Don't stay up.
> I'm so tired.
> Don't stay up.
> I'll talk to you tomorrow.

At one point he gently suggests that maybe she needs to take a break, take a few hours for herself.

"You just don't understand," she tells him.

"What don't I understand?" he asks.

"This. *Work*."

As soon as she says it, she apologizes, says it came out wrong. She tells him she is only getting three or four hours of sleep each night, and even her dreams are work-related nightmares.

"Is it worth it?" he has to ask.

"When they give us tens of millions of dollars to do this site the right way, it will be worth it," she tells him.

Then she says she has to go. Another call is coming in.

He finds himself at strange hours (day or night) doing a deep dive into Celestia's social media. Nothing that she's talking about—skincare regimens, the right amount of cleavage, self-enhancement—are of particular interest to him. But he is fascinated by the balance that Celestia strikes between sincerity and the sell. He believes that she believes in what she's doing, and that belief is something he can't help but admire . . . even if it scares him a little. Because the intimacy is an illusion of intimacy—she's not confiding or conversing, she's *broadcasting*. But judging from the comments section, many of her followers believe it's a two-sided interaction. That's why they keep coming back.

As promised, celestia's list of "song elements" (J is impressed with her phrasing) arrives via email.

*You see, V?* J thinks. *Work.*

The only thing that can be said about the list is that it is most definitely a list, with twenty-eight numbered items. What the items have to do with Celestia, her husband, and their marriage is much less clear, even for someone who's recently spent a good deal of time on Celestia's social media. A few are clearly either nicknames they have for each other or the names of their pets. Many others are designer brand names. J is familiar with a few from magazines, and others he just assumes are brand names because they are capitalized and seem to go along with names like Gucci and Balenciaga.

In fact, the only nouns that aren't proper nouns are *toaster*, *bedtime*, and *ambition*.

At the end of the list, there's a note with a phone number:

*If you have any questions, just call!*

J calls.

"Celestia Enterprises, Mikhail speaking," a lilting voice answers.

J explains who he is and why he is calling. Mikhail explains he is on Celestia's communications team, and that he should be able to answer any questions J has.

"Is it okay if I just go down the list?"

"Please."

"So . . . Salty and Pepper?"

"Those are Celestia's poodles."

"Safe to assume that one's a white dog and one's a black dog?"

"Oh—Celestia does *not* use that word."

J thinks for a second about what he's just said, then has to ask, "Which word?"

"The d-word. One of Celestia's hallmarks is her *specificity*. Salty and Pepper are always to be referred to as poodles. Not . . . you know."

"I *do* know. Thank you. Next one—the Queen. Is that a reference to Sweden's queen? England's queen?"

"That's a reference to Celestia herself."

"I see."

"It's what Roger calls her. Though, between us, I think she came up with it, so I wouldn't give him credit if you can avoid doing so."

"How about *bedtime*?"

"They have a running joke about their bedtimes, since they're often so wildly different. Celestia's day often starts much earlier than Roger's, for reasons I can't disclose. So she's trying to go to bed earlier."

J figures he understands why ambition is on the list, so he asks about *toaster*.

Mikhail is silent on the line. Finally J has to ask, "Are you there?"

"Sorry. I was just texting Belgravia on my other phone. She's on Celestia's appearance team. If anyone knows, she will."

"Well, I can just ask Celestia when I do my interview for the song," J says.

Mikhail actually laughs. "Oh, I'm afraid that's not going to be possible. I think it's a miracle you got this list. Celestia's calendar is insane for the next two weeks—even for her. Getting married creates so much demand."

J is disappointed by this, but not *that* disappointed.

"So," he says, "about all the brand names . . . are these favorites of hers? Are there any stories that tie them to their courtship?"

"Their courtship! I love everything about you! It's easy to see why Celestia is so excited about your song. Can I trust you?"

J answers yes, and tries to keep a question mark off the end.

"And you've returned your NDA?"

J can answer a firmer yes to that.

Mikhail's voice lowers to a whisper. "Well, this is so exciting . . . but really you can't tell anyone." (J has a feeling Mikhail has said this to many people before.) "Celestia's event was already going to be the wedding of the year. But what her public doesn't know is that for the past three months, she's been recording the new season of—" (here, Mikhail mentions a reality TV franchise that revolves around the girlfriends of rich men) "—and the wedding is really going to be the season's centerpiece. A lot of extraordinary, visionary brands are on board, and those are the brands reflected on Celestia's list."

J has encountered people who've wanted their favorite things in their wedding songs before, but this is starting to sound uncomfortably like product placement.

"So I can't sub in another brand if it rhymes better?" he asks.

"Ha! Just be sure to get us the song by next Tuesday; Celestia's approval process usually takes a week, but with the wedding, we'll want ten days. She needs to approve all lyrics, as I'm sure you understand. And then we'll see you for the run-through on the twelfth."

J doesn't remember a run-through being mentioned in the contract, but perhaps it was buried in there between the translation rights and the streaming royalties. Considering his fee, a run-through certainly makes sense.

"I'll be there," J says, in a tone that is perhaps not quite a match for the wedding of the year.

"Oh! And please be sure to send me your measurements, as precisely as possible. Celestia is a very visual person, you know! Let me know if you need anything else," Mikhail says. "I'll get back to you about the toaster!"

J gets back to Mikhail about the measurements, but Mikhail does not get back to him about the toaster. And J has five days to write the most expensive song of his career.

He tries to convince himself that these are brands Celestia likes, that he is not selling out by taking on the burden of her wedding's corporate sponsorship. The principle doesn't entirely sit right, but neither does the principle of being paid only $0.003 when someone listens to your song.

Since he's been given a list, the best way to go seems to be a list song. The greatest of all list songs being Cole Porter's "You're the Top" (which also featured a brand name or two). J figures if he's going to crib, he might as well crib from the best.

He also thinks it will help to be really, really stoned.

So he takes the necessary measures and starts drafting a song from the list. At first, it's mostly gibberish, with long breaks for him to contemplate his phone and why V isn't calling. But slowly a song starts to take shape . . .

> Oodles of poodles
> Look up from their noodles
> When they see you passing by
>
> Whether Pepper or Salty
> Their perception's not faulty
> To see love tinting the sky
>
> It's New York fashion
> To speak of your passion
> There can be no wondering why . . .
>
> You're a Balenciaga ball gown
> You're a Hermès tie
> You're a Prada feather
> Gucci leather
> Nike sneakers
> Bose's speakers

> You're the best...
>     money can buy.

"You're kidding, right?" V chimes in, in his head.

J looks up. She's not here. But she also . . . is.

"This is just a draft," J protests. "I haven't even made it to the second verse."

"You're insulting them."

"I am not!"

"The best money can buy? You don't think that's an insult?"

"Not to them!"

V snort-laughs and sits on the bed. Well, his hallucination of her sits on the bed. It's not like the bed sags under her weight.

"New York isn't on her list," V points out. Then, sarcastically, she adds, "I wonder how it got there?"

"You don't have to be this way."

"What way is that?"

J doesn't want to be having this conversation. Not with an imaginary V. Then again, if she's imaginary, maybe he can get some imaginary answers.

"Why don't you love me anymore?" he asks. "Or at least not enough to want to be here right now."

V looks like he just asked her where she bought her dress. "You don't want the answer to that question."

"I do!"

"No, you just want reassurance that I love you."

"Yes, of course. But I'd still like the answer."

"I've told you multiple times that I'm coming back. I've taken great pains to make it clear to you that we aren't breaking up. Why are you so afraid?"

"You've been gone so long."

V tilts her head to the side. Levels him with a glance.

"You go on tour for months at a time. We've never broken up over that. We've always managed to reunite. Don't you think you're being a little hypocritical?"

"I just don't understand . . ."

"What? Tell me."

"Yes, I'm afraid. I don't even know why. It's just . . . there. And the thing that makes me most afraid is that you don't seem afraid at all."

V makes a gesture like she's putting out a cigarette on the blanket. Then she stands.

"You want me to be afraid," she says. "That's fucked up. Now, go back to your stupid sellout song. Although, really, I like it better when you improvise."

"I like that better, too. But that's not what they're paying me for."

"In that case, I have only one thing left to say to you. Do you even know what that is?"

J stands up and reaches for her. "What?" he asks. "Tell me."

She leans over and whispers into his ear.

"*Toaster.*"

And with that, she disappears.

The next morning, he wakes up groggy, but still texts V, *You up yet?*

It isn't until the afternoon that she replies, *Things are intensifying here. Will try to find a moment later.*

J finishes a draft of Celestia's song. He can feel other songs starting to form underneath.

None of them are happy songs.

He sends in the draft of his lyrics and receives Celestia's "notes" two days later. She isn't at all put off by the "best money can buy" refrain. She just wants to add a few more brand names.

"There are still a few sponsorship opportunities," Mikhail confides. "So there may be other additions or substitutions. Stay flexible."

"I'll try," J grumbles.

What's absurd to J—what's truly absurd—is that his acceptance of the product placement in the song isn't just about the money he's being paid and his need to make a living off his art.

No, there's something even more desperate underneath.

He's reminded of another wedding he did—for not one but *two* influencers. They weren't rich like Celestia and Roger, and they certainly had time to sit down and talk to J about their song, which they wanted to be about how they met (skiing) and not at all about their individual platforms.

The influencers were in their twenties, as influencers often are, and most of their guests fit that demographic as well. There was only one child at the wedding, a girl who was about five or six years old and dressed like a princess. After J played, the girl came up to him and asked, "Are you famous?" It was a question J would usually sidestep or laugh off, but coming from a young kid, he made an effort to give himself a little glory, so she could reflect in it.

"I've been a little famous," he said.

With a deep assurance, she replied, "I am going to be famous, *very soon*. Princess is my brand." She showed J the Instagram account that her mother had set up for her. In each image, the girl was dramatically clothed as a different princess—some fictional, some historical. When J was a child, this would have been called "dress-up" and would have occurred in a haphazard way after school. But nothing about this was haphazard. To J, it was all hazard.

Princess Girl's mother appeared and said, "Darling, have you shown the man how many likes you got on your latest video?

Everyone loves you when you're Diana!" The girl showed J the video, pointing out how many followers she had, how many likes she got, and how many famous people were following her. Later that night she had a fit when she didn't get enough attention, sitting on the floor, crying, "Am I not pretty enough to be a princess?" It was very unsettling.

But just as unsettling—now as then—was how J secretly wondered whether the girl had the right strategy. In this day and age, was it foolish to still be touring and releasing albums? It used to be that a big break would come when a famous DJ put your song into heavy rotation on an influential station, or maybe a song of yours would appear in a movie or a TV show. But now your best chance is for your song to be playing in a fifteen-second burst as a very passionate teenage girl you've never met complains about her heartbreak to her seven million followers. (Your song will get even more attention if she's sobbing.)

So that's the desperate hope under J's acquiescence to Celestia's whims: What if this ridiculous wedding is the thing that makes people take notice of him and his work? What if some of her almost arbitrary fame rubs off on him for a night?

J and V facetime. He is in bed, and she is pouring herself a glass of wine at her small kitchen table.

"I'm not even sure if there is such a thing as selling out these days," V says after he explains how he's feeling. "When everyone's become a brand, isn't that essentially the triumph of capitalism? It almost feels inevitable at this point."

"What's my brand?" J asks.

She laughs. "Are you serious? Swedish troubadour. Shepherd of the lonesome and the clever."

"Fair."

"And do you know what my brand is?"

There's no challenge in her question, not really. But J finds himself utterly stumped.

The easy out would be to say, "I don't want to think of you as a brand." But instead he starts with "You're . . ." and then lets it trail off.

"That's my brand, then? Invisibility?"

"I'm sorry. I wasn't ready for the question."

"That's alright. You may be more accurate than you know. I'm really good at being other people's voices. But I have to work on my own."

"I like your voice."

"I know you do."

*But it's not enough.* She doesn't say it, but J hears it in her voice.

The rest of the conversation is strained. She asks him about his days, but it doesn't feel like she's a part of them. He asks her what's going on at work and he doesn't really understand what she's talking about. Thor's growing relationship with Meta is the only thing he can really wrap his head around, because when something really big is happening, wouldn't you want someone to share the excitement with?

He does not ask V this question.

Two days before Celestia's wedding, at 6 p.m. New York time and 11 p.m. Gothenburg time, J gets a text from V: *WE HAVE A DEAL!*

He calls her immediately and is pleasantly surprised when she picks up on the second ring.

"Congratulations!" he cheers.

"Thank you. We're all celebrating here." He can hear Motown blasting in the background, and giddy laughter.

"It's a good deal?"

"It's a *great* deal. Not just because it's a lot of money, but because these investors really believe in what we're doing and, frankly, have more expertise than any of us do in terms of how to get it done."

"That's amazing," J says. "And it means you can come home now?"

There is a pause, and at first J doesn't understand why. He's asked a fairly straightforward question.

"Really?" V says. "You're bringing that up *now*?"

J is still lost. "I just assumed that since the deal is done, I'd get you back."

"I am telling you we've pulled off this incredible feat, and all you care about is when you'll 'get me back.' You you you you *you*. Do you ask me how we pulled off this deal? Do you even ask me who the deal is with? Do you ask me what the next steps are or what my role is going to be? No no no. You you you."

J knows he's taken a misstep, but V's thrown up a wall before he can step back to where he was. So he digs in. "It's selfishness to want you back here?" he asks. "The last time I checked, it wasn't only my ego that was missing you. My heart was in there, too."

"What you don't seem to understand is that I miss home as well. More than I thought I would. That's one of the reasons we stay in the office so much, because when we're here together, we can pretend we're still back home, with each other. This wasn't my plan at all. But you know what? I know it isn't that much of an achievement, it isn't that special, to be one of four or five people involved at the ground level of a start-up company. Those come and go. But it *is* an achievement, and it's a big fucking opportunity, to be one of four or five people involved at the ground level of a start-up company that strangers are willing to invest tens of millions, potentially hundreds of millions, to support. This is the wild ride, and I'm on it. So, no, I'm not coming home. I'm staying where I have to be. And when everything settles down, I will figure out where I want to be."

J can't believe that after pining for so long to have her talk to him, this is what he's hearing. "I don't factor into this decision at all?" he asks, his voice taking on a plaintive tone that he rarely uses with V, or anyone else.

This time there isn't any hesitation before the response. "Of course you're a factor. But you can't be the decisive factor. Even though I'm sensing you want to be."

Now it sounds like the people behind her are laughing at him, celebrating her liberation.

"So we're through?" J asks. "Is that what you're saying?"

"That was never my intention," she says, her anger subsiding into something that sounds more like sadness. "It still isn't my intention. But if we're going to stay together, you're the one who's going to have to adapt for once. And right now, I'm not sure you're capable of that."

"Thanks for that vote of confidence."

"Look, I'm going to go. You're ruining what was, up until this point, one of the best days of my life."

"Well," J can't help saying, "that was never my intention."

"I'm going."

"I'll talk to you later."

"We'll see, J. We'll see."

Then she hangs up.

J puts the phone down before it can do any more damage.

He can't figure out if his relationship just fell from the sky, or whether it's been at the bottom of the ocean for weeks now, and nobody bothered to tell him.

Some people would drink in response. Get stoned again. Put a fist through a wall. Sob.

J paces. Back and forth through the apartment, back and forth. Tiger in a cage, pendulum with a loose leash. It gets him nowhere.

He thinks about calling back and then tells himself calling back will only make it worse.

He paces some more, his footsteps beating out a tune for *What-is-happ-en-ing? What-is-happ-en-ing?*

He decides he needs to distract himself. Might as well rehearse Celestia's song a few times before the wedding. He picks up his guitar, starts to sing—and doesn't make it past *poodles*.

So that's not going to work.

*What do I feel?* he asks himself.

Then: *What do I want to feel?*

Then: *How can this be saved?*

He still has the guitar in his hands.

He stops pacing. He sits down.

He stays up another seven hours.

Then he sleeps for seventeen hours.

He misses the wedding rehearsal. Which means that when he wakes up there are seven messages from Mikhail and none from V.

He looks first to social media, imagining he'll find lots of ecstatic posts from V, dancing in celebration with her colleagues. But there's no word there, either. Possibly because she's still hungover. More likely because Secret Project has to remain a Secret Project.

Then J listens to Mikhail's seventh message—he sees no point in listening to the first six—and texts him back, assuring him that he'll be on time—early, even!—for the wedding the next afternoon.

After some coffee, he checks his phone and finds a six-hour-long voice memo, confirming that last night he crawled into the dark cavern of his most morbid creativity, and decided to record whatever came out.

There is a lot of wallowing in the key of gibberish. There is some profanity. There are many questions. At one point, there is a lapse into a bastardized version of Celestia's wedding song.

At this point, panicked, J checks his call log, and he is relieved to find there is no record of any contact with V for the last twenty-four hours.

Amidst the doggerel and the bluntly articulated misery, there are a few phrases that stick, especially one he implores over and over: *We're working on a script.*

Meaning: This isn't over.

Meaning: By being honest with each other, we're finding our way.

Meaning: Even if our way is rocky right now, that'll only get us to the smoother terrain.

After the six-hour-long voice memo, there is a much shorter one, only twenty minutes long. The phrases are gathering now. It's shapeless, rambling, with a few da-da-da-da's for lines he hadn't yet written. It's about that first big fight in a relationship, how unsteady it makes you on the balance beam, wondering if all it takes is one big wobble to make you fall off completely. It's strange that J can't really think of a major fight that he and V have had before—they've bickered and been temporarily nasty to each other, but never on the level that calls the whole relationship into question.

J picks up his guitar again and starts to shape his thoughts.

An hour later, he has written a song in his notes app. And the song has convinced him that this doesn't have to be the end. No, a fight can also be an opportunity to work things out.

That is what he and V are going to do.

Since it's still early evening in New York, he records the song as another voice memo and sends it to her. It sits on her phone, unopened for minutes, unopened for hours. He works on the song some more. Sends her a new version. It's almost sunrise again, and he knows he needs to get some sleep and set an alarm this time.

He can't be a mess for this wedding.

They're not paying him this much to be a mess.

He wakes up at seven in the morning because the wedding is in Torekov, a small coastal town a three-hour train ride away. There are more texts from Mikhail, and a call asking him to confirm he knows the time and place of where he needs to be and that he'll be there. Mikhail also says to be sure to leave time to change into the sponsor's suit. J had forgotten he wouldn't be wearing his own clothes and wonders if he gets to keep the suit after. Probably not.

There is still no word from V.

And J . . .

Well, J is starting to wonder if there's ever going to be a word from V again.

He knows this isn't rational. At the bare minimum, she'll have to be in touch for her things. But also—there had been some tenderness, even in that final (not *final* final!) phone call, hadn't there?

> **We're working on the scene.**
> **We're working on the script.**

How could she not answer? Or is a lack of answer her answer?

J plays the song, over and over, as if a new verse will emerge from her point of view. He barely rehearses Celestia's wedding song.

So many things of V's are scattered throughout the apartment. J imagines they've turned against him, too, hold him responsible for their abandonment. The hairbrush in the bathroom wonders what will become of her. The unread books on her side of the bed assume this is the point where she gives up on them completely. A blouse in the closet pledges to wait, however long it takes.

A love hangover is far worse than the drunken kind, because with a love hangover, you know it isn't going away in a matter of hours. J's head is beginning to pound. He wants to call someone for some sympathy, but he also doesn't want to make the situation any more real than it already is. Because if he doesn't tell anyone, and he and V manage to overcome this, then it will be like it never happened. No one will ever know. As far as the world is concerned, J and V are still a great couple. Nobody knows otherwise. Except maybe the people in V's office, and anyone else she's told.

His head pounds some more. He has to control himself. He has to get to the wedding. He reminds himself it's a big deal, and a big paycheck. Then he laughs at himself: Look at him, grateful for thousands when V is playing with tens, maybe hundreds, of millions.

He quickly runs through the last verse of the wedding song.

> You're a Tiffany diamond
> You're a scarf from Dubai
> You're a Burberry trenchy
> Bright socks from Givenchy
> Moët champagne
> A Porter refrain
> You're the best . . .
>     money can't buy!

It's far from a flawless performance, and he takes his lyrics notebook with him, not trusting himself to remember the way the brand names fall in Celestia's song, and fearing she'll have set a trap door for him if he gets her sponsors wrong.

He intends to memorize it on the train ride to Båstad, but he ends up napping instead. When he catches the bus to Torekov, he is discombobulated. The setting doesn't help—there's no particular reason for there to be public transportation in this town, which has a population of under a thousand, except that it happens to be a town where the rich and famous like to cavort. As J walks from the station, he stares at the large seaside houses and vaguely recalls that one of them is owned by the actor Hugh Grant. V probably told him this once. How else would he know?

While the wedding is being held in a church, the reception is in a vast tent complex by the beach. When J arrives, he spots some photographers hanging out in front. At first, security stops him, but after he brandishes his guitar and explains who he is, they let him pass.

When he enters the ballroom tent, he nearly thinks he's entered a greenhouse instead. The large room is a topiary explosion of trees, plants, and vines that must have taken days to arrange.

"Welcome to Eden," a woman in a green and lavender cocktail dress greets. "Can I help you?"

J says his name and asks if Mikhail is around.

"Oh yes! You're the missing singer!" the woman says.

"No longer missing!" J clarifies.

The woman talks into a headset he hadn't even realized she was wearing, and within a minute, a man in an impeccable tuxedo arrives. From their exchanges, J had assumed Mikhail was in his twenties, but this man looks like he could be George Clooney's slightly older brother. He thanks J for being on time.

"What do you think?" Mikhail asks, gesturing to the garden Celestia has assembled.

"It's paradise," J says.

It's also humid as hell. As they pass by the tables, J sees all the glasses are sweating.

There are two stages at the head of the ballroom tent, facing each other. The first is set up for what could easily be a full orchestra. The other looks like the judges' table from a singing competition show. Since there are only two seats, J assumes this is Celestia and Roger's perch. A set of six stairs leads down from the platform to the dance floor.

Mikhail explains the run-of-show. An internationally renowned soprano is performing at the church ceremony but will be gone before the reception. While the guests mingle in the first-six-days-of-creation cocktail area, Celestia will be in her suite changing into her Eve-themed gown (Dior) and taking photos for a popular weekly magazine. Then at 7:07 p.m. sharp—because seven is

Celestia's luckiest number—she and Roger will make their entrance; J will be offstage and the band will play the couple's first dance, a new "pop-forward" arrangement of "It Had to Be You." A Very Famous Action Star (who invests with Roger and was available, like J, for a fee) will then make the first toast. When he is done, he will introduce J, explaining that the song is one of Celestia's gifts to her new husband, because she is such a believer in both love and the arts, etc. J will then sing his song. He may take a bow if he wishes; the Very Famous Action Star will then return to the stage and introduce two dancers from the Royal Swedish Ballet, performing a piece that Celestia commissioned on Roger's behalf, in her name. It rewrites the story of Adam and Eve, so the two of them get to stay in the garden and become king and queen of all creation.

As J is listening to this, all he wants to do is call V and tell her about it so they can laugh together at the evening's absurdity. He wants to sneak her into the wedding so she can see it. So they can talk about it for years and years . . .

He has to focus. Mikhail is asking if he has any questions.

"This whole thing is being livestreamed?" he asks Mikhail.

Mikhail looks back at him sternly, as if expecting J to object. "This was spelled out in your contract—"

"No, no—I'm fine with it. I'd just love the link to send to my girlfriend, so she can watch."

Mikhail smiles. "Of course." He tells J it will be available on all of Celestia's platforms.

J feels like a liar as he types out the message to V, that *my girlfriend* echoing in his ears.

*You need to see this*, J texts. *I should go on around 7:30.*

A smaller tent has been turned into a backstage area, and that's where Mikhail escorts J. Inside there are band members in green suits and lavender suits, as well as ballet dancers in green costumes and lavender costumes.

"Celestia's two favorite colors," Mikhail explains. Then he goes to a rolling wardrobe and pulls out a suit composed of green and lavender swirls. J almost expects it to come with a top hat, for in this suit he will certainly look like Willy Wonka crashing the Garden of Eden.

"Go see if it fits," Mikhail says. "We have two backups if it doesn't."

In the changing area, J tries to imagine how much all of this has cost . . . and honestly can't. V would have a guess. He goes to call her to ask, before stopping himself. She still hasn't answered the text about the link. Or any of his texts.

As the guests arrive and the pleasant babble of overlapping conversations resounds from another room, J talks a little with some of the players from the big band and checks his phone constantly. At 6:52, Mikhail comes back in and says, "Places, everyone!" J picks up his notebook and is about to follow the band when Mikhail looks at him strangely and says, "Not you. You come with me."

J figures he's being taken to wait somewhere with the Very Famous Action Star who will be introducing him. Instead, Mikhail takes him to a small meeting room, where he comes face-to-face with . . . an enormous cake. It's at least five feet tall, and mercifully neither green nor lavender. No, this is the most angelic wedding cake imaginable, a pure froth of white frosting and decoration.

"It's a lovely cake," J says, not entirely sure why it's being shown to him.

Three hotel workers wheel in a ladder, and a caterer gingerly steps up the ladder to remove the top of the cake, which is really just a smaller cake placed atop the larger cake.

"Are you ready?" Mikhail asks J.

And J has to ask, "Ready for what?"

Mikhail laughs. Then he sees J is serious.

"No one told you about this in your first conversations? Celestia's vision?"

J shakes his head.

"You will be making your entrance from within that cake. At first, everyone will think her gift to Roger is the cake itself. But then . . . it's you! We'll have a piano already onstage."

Slowly, J says, "I wasn't . . . aware of this."

*What-is-happ-en-ing? What-is-happ-en-ing?*

"That's why you were chosen! Celestia saw how thin you were and knew you'd fit *perfectly* inside the cake."

"Okay then," J says. He's never been inside a cake before.

It will be another thing to tell V.

If she'll listen.

He's walked around the cake and finds there's a very narrow path up the layers for him to walk. Using the ladder to balance himself, he gets to the top and lowers himself to stand inside. He must hold his arms above his head in order to avoid touching any icing. The cake has been constructed around a white plastic container, and when J stands on the bottom, his head is still visible.

Mikhail looks at his watch. "We don't have much time," he says. "When you hear the cue, just pop out and say something charming. I promise, it will be a memorable entrance!" Then he pauses, remembering one more thing. "You did get my message about changing the song, didn't you?"

J has no choice but to ask, "What message?"

Mikhail sighs. "This is why rehearsal is so important! As I told you in my voicemail, Celestia had a change of heart about the song. She decided that especially with the other brand placements already in place, it didn't feel right to have them in her wedding song. I'll be honest with you—she and Roger had a big fight about it, because Roger was seeing it mostly as a financial arrangement, making the customers happy, et cetera, et cetera. But Celestia put her foot down. She wants you to sing something else. From the heart. 'He knows what love is really like,' she said to me. 'Have him sing about what love is really like.' We'll just pretend you wrote it for them. Understood?"

"Understood," J says calmly. He has no idea what do to. Except take the next step . . . into the cake.

Slowly, J lowers himself into a crouching position. It is extraordinarily tight.

"You okay?" a voice (the caterer?) asks.

"I'm great," J says. Because maybe this is his punishment, for wanting money, for wanting fame.

"Alright. Here we go."

The top cake is put back in place, and J can hear what sounds like whipped cream being released from a can, to cover the seam.

J waits, expecting they will roll him in at any moment. He doesn't wear a watch and his phone is in his back pocket—he's afraid if he tries to reach for it, he will hit the side of the container and cause part of the cake to collapse. He can't imagine how much a cake like this costs. It must have required an engineer as well as a pastry expert.

He tries to figure out what to sing. It's not like Celestia and Roger have given him much insight into their love or their lives. The only song in his heart right now is "HELP!" To comfort himself, he looks for the air holes in the plastic. Which is when he realizes there aren't any air holes in the plastic. They've forgotten the air holes.

J is not by nature claustrophobic, but he does like to be able to breathe. And he's starting to feel like he can't. He takes deep breaths to calm himself down, then panics that his deep breaths are only making things worse. So he takes small breaths. At long intervals, at first. But then more frequently because it really does feel like the walls are getting tighter, and time is either moving slowly or not moving at all, and he twists to get his phone to text Mikhail, and there's a jolt and he gasps and—

. . .

. . .

. . .

. . .

... the world comes back frame by frame, like a film projector that's rolling slowly. J can't see much, just darkness and white plastic, but he hears indistinct voices yelling, and then suddenly there's light—J looks up and this must be a dream because this Very Famous Action Star is staring down at him, asking him if he's okay, and that's when J realizes he passed out—passed out inside of a wedding cake—and this Very Famous Action Star is reaching down for him, and the first time J tries to stand, his legs do not agree with the plan, and he is so embarrassed to wobble in front of the Very Famous Action Star, but the Very Famous Action Star doesn't make him feel ashamed, he actually says, "This whole thing is such bullshit!" as he leans over more so J can grab his hand and let himself be pulled up. His head clears the top of the cake, and he's not sure he's got the steps, so the Very Famous Action Star keeps hold of his hand, and because the little stairway on the back of the cake is facing the Big Band, that's who J sees as he emerges. They all have their instruments down, and they're looking at him with such concern, and life really can't get much worse, can it? Not just because they pity him, but because they're pitying him for the wrong reason. They have no idea he's lost V. He's made a fool of himself and lost V. He's made a fool of himself by losing V.

"How do you want to play this?" the Very Famous Action Star whispers. They're both smeared with white frosting and whipped cream. "I've already introduced you."

"I'm good," J replies, some ridiculous instinct kicking in. Now he can hear a further murmur throughout the ballroom, and he understands that he's just stopped the wedding cold. When he turns around, he can see Celestia and Roger staring at him with something between worry and irritation. He also sees that numerous guests have their phones out and are recording his every move.

He goes first to the nearest microphone and repeats what he said to the Very Famous Action Star, "I'm good." Then he adds, "It was a little tight in there!"

There's laughter and applause. Yes, applause. Just for the fact that he's made it out of the cake and his legs are still supporting him. He still feels wobbly, though, so instead he walks over to a nearby piano and takes a place there. And what hits him hardest, what makes him shakiest, isn't the utter humiliation of being a frosted Willy Wonka, nor the awkward silence that he's launching into. No, what guts him is the fact that V is not here, in person or in spirit, and the lack of her presence is the loudest kind of absence. She is no longer in the wings, and so the wings begin to fold.

He tries to keep it together. He is generous in his introduction, talking as if he knows the wedded couple beyond their fondness for toasters. "It is extraordinary that you have built this kind of paradise together," he says. "Not just for yourselves, but for everyone here. That is magnificent of you, and I am so honored to be able to add my humble song into the gift of your day." The last part barely makes sense, but it sounds good, and now J can see Roger smiling like a pleased Medici. Celestia, however, is giving him a different kind of look—both vulnerable and curious. He recalls what Mikhail told him, how she thinks he has some insight into how this whole love thing is supposed to work. And that, he realizes, it what she's looking for: some insight. She fought with Roger over getting rid of the old song, because for all its grandiose trappings, she still wants her wedding to be about love, so her marriage can be about love.

There's really only one song that wants to be sung. If Celestia wants to him to sing something true about love, this is what he's got. It's only thing right now her money can buy—a possible path on the balance beam. Clumsily, he takes his phone out of his back pocket and pulls up the lyrics on his notes app.

"My girlfriend always tells me she prefers it when I improvise," he says the crowd. Then he stops himself. Corrects himself. "No, that's wrong. She's not my girlfriend. She's the woman I love. And she always tells me she prefers it when I improvise. So here's a very new song about love. A song from my heart." Then he looks straight at Celestia. "It's about how messy it can get, but how you can push through that, so it all works out."

She smiles then, a little less vulnerable, a little more curious, and he begins the song.

> When we've had a fight
> When we sit there in the stillness after the storm
> Quiet like two butterflies dipped in chloroform
> I think: Hold on
> Just hold on
> Remember it's not always like this
> We're still working working working on our script
>
> Working on a script
> Working on a script
>
> We're working on the scene
> Where a simple gesture like a laughter
> gives away you're really not an actor
> And maybe it's true
> that I can trust you
> Honey, forget all your lines
> I like it better when you improvise
>
> Working on a script
> Working on a script
>
> This is
> the mapping
> of what's happening
> when the credits have rolled
> This is what happens
> when two atoms

>    bump into each other
> 
>    and explode
> 
>    This is
> 
>    a movie
> 
>    you'll never see
> 
>    The greatest story ever told
> 
>    This is
> 
>    an ending
> 
>    to endings
> 
>    That's you and me when we get old

For the first few seconds, it feels like a good idea to offer this song. But he hasn't counted on how real it would feel to sing it, how real V's absence would sit at the center of it. He's no longer in control of the song or its outcome. He's not in control of anything anymore. He is singing these lines as if they are the most honest words he's ever penned, and he is bereft because he's not sure that's good enough. He has slowed them down and is offering them as a hymn, trying to turn his heartbreak into something loving. He is starting to tear up, and the guests are starting to tear up, too. They think he's overwhelmed by the couple before him, and they have no idea that he is sad because the only person he wants to be watching is not watching, that the only person he wants to be here is no longer here for him. He is crying because while he wants it to be her fault, he suspects it's his own, that he leaned on the wrong lever and sent the train careening off the tracks.

As he gets to the final verse, there is a reverent silence that's rare even for a concert.

>    This is
> 
>    the mapping
> 
>    of what's happening
> 
>    when the credits have rolled

> This is what happens
> when two atoms
> bump into each other
> and explode
> This is
> a movie
> you'll never see
> The greatest story ever told
> This is
> an ending
> to endings
>> That's you and me when we get old

His voice quavers on the last line, and that's how he gets them, that's how he reaches into their hearts and pulls out their sympathy. When he finishes, there's an abundance of applause. J looks out at the large ballroom and thinks that this is the world that V is entering into, this is the place success will take her. She will measure in millions. He will measure in thousands. She will applaud when he sings, but she won't really know what he means.

He knows she has the livestream information. He knows other people still have their phones up, recording as if he's famous, or maybe just because he passed out in a cake.

"I dedicate that to the woman I love. And to making it through." Then, remembering why he's here, he turns to Celestia and Roger and says, "I wish you a lifetime of belief and love, and a script you both write together, long into getting old." Celestia mouths the words *thank you* while Roger looks at his watch. There is more applause, and Roger looks up from his watch and smiles as the Very Important Action Star comes onstage to make his next introduction.

"Well done," the Very Important Action Star says, and as J walks off, he wonders if perhaps they'll become friends. No one will be waiting for him backstage, or at home, or in his voicemail. As he walks off the stage, the ballet dancers take their places.

J does not stay to see them give Adam and Eve their happy ending.

## THE FOURTH WEDDING

J decides that maybe it's time to take a break from weddings.

He's not in the mood for love. He and V have been in contact, but their conversations haven't been those between lovers. J is not expecting reconciliation, but even negotiation or argument would be comforting at this point. Instead, it feels like they are trading Wikipedia entries summarizing their past few days, a bloodless rendition of a world gone right (for her) and wrong (for him).

J is too embarrassed to tell his friends what's happened, in no small part because it isn't entirely clear what *has* happened. V has not said, "It's over." Even though she ignored the song he sent and his darkest-hour questions, she now answers his texts with something approaching promptness, as long as he doesn't type anything that could be construed as emotional. He suspects that if he asks her *Are you still my girlfriend?* she will respond *Why are you asking me that?* Or *The fact that you're asking the question should give you an answer.* Or *Is that what you called it?* Anything besides a yes or a no.

He tries to tell himself that there's nothing to worry about, that this is the way they are. After all, he would often leave for weeks or even months of touring, and there wouldn't be pressure to be in constant touch. Or even significant touch. They had always been chill about such things.

He's starting to wonder, though: What if that was, in fact, a problem? What if being so comfortable with being at a remove meant there'd been something missing all along?

They liked reaching out for each other when they were close by. But why hadn't they ever done it when they were far apart? No long phone calls. No postcards or letters. Just a passionate going-away kiss and then a passionate welcome-back kiss, with everything blank in between.

He goes back to blaming the distance. Of course he blames the distance. V's only response to Celestia's wedding was to say, *Maybe in the future, you need to insist they build you a bigger cake.* If they were in bed next to each other, he knows the conversation would continue from there—*What do you feel my ideal cake size is?* And maybe then *It depends on whether you're wearing heels, doesn't it?*

But that's not how their texting works. They might as well be using a transatlantic telegraph.

Meanwhile videos of him being yanked through the tiers have gone viral, and at first he wondered if his career was over, punch-lined to the curb. Not just his wedding career, but his entire career.

Instead it's made him more popular. It hasn't increased streams of his music, but his inbox is now flooded with wedding requests. Most of them involve him popping out of things.

It is very easy to say no to these, and to think he's taken the wedding gigs too far.

What had his original wedding song said?

> True love can be measured
> Through these simple pleasures
> They are waiting there for you to be discovered

Well, that was then and this is now.

These couples want a canary, not a Cassandra. J worries that if he attends one more wedding, he will become the person who raises an objection. Not to the specific couple (maybe), but to the principle. And maybe not even the principle of being married. No, to the con job that goes back to Adam and Eve, Noah's Ark—one by one, people giving themselves up to two by two.

What hurts is that he's pretty sure by now he didn't do anything wrong with V. He just didn't do anything right enough.

J knows the sense of power he feels deleting all the requests that come in is pathetic. This, and only this, is something he can control.

No, he will not pop out of a giant éclair.

No, he does not do toddler birthday parties.

No, he does not want to tell a Swedish gossip blogger the "real" story behind the "wedding of the century." (He suspects this is really Mikhail trying to see if he'll abide by his NDA.)

No, he does not want to sing a wedding cake shop's jingle for a radio ad. He didn't even know that radio ads were still a thing.

He is done with weddings. Done done done.

That is, until Andreas calls.

Andreas is a relatively young guy who loves relatively old things. He and J met when J was looking for a vintage car to use in a music video. "Oh," everyone told him, "you need to talk to Andreas. He's the nicest guy in the world."

Even though Andreas did not himself own a Rolls-Royce, he knew someone who did, and because Andreas indeed turned out to be quite possibly the nicest guy in the world, the owner was willing to let J drive his precious heirloom along the seaside while playing an acoustic guitar and singing about love gone wrong. Since then, J has returned to Andreas a few times for very obscure items, mostly as props and sometimes as gifts. In every exchange, Andreas has been the embodiment of kindness and graciousness—the sort of man who would not just give you the shirt off his back, but would then take out a needle and thread to make sure it fit perfectly. Even when they didn't have any business to attend, J would get a call from Andreas every few months, asking him to drop by his store. There, Andreas would have an object that he thought would delight J—an old flashbulb from a 1940s camera, or a rare 45 of Al Bowlly and Ray Noble and His Orchestra singing "Hang Out the Stars in Indiana." The fact that Andreas would never, ever accept payment for these items both endeared him to J and left J a little mystified. Surely no one could be this chipper, this generous all the time. They aren't friends, really. But they're not business associates, either. They're just two guys who every now and then have their orbits connect.

When J sees Andreas is calling, he assumes it's because another item has fallen into his possession that he feels compelled to pass J's way.

"I have wonderful news," Andreas begins. But instead of saying, *I found the perfect velvet Elvis for you*, or *Do you think you could use a lime-green couch in your next video?* he follows with, "I'm getting married!"

"Congratulations!" J replies, even though his heart is still stuck on something akin to *You have no idea what you're in for*.

"I had to tell you because Kerstin, my wife-to-be, loves your records. The first time I went over to her house, there was one sitting by her phonograph, and when I told her that I knew you, she couldn't believe it. It felt like serendipity."

"I'm glad I could help," J says, somewhat awkwardly. "When is the big day?"

"The day after tomorrow! We decided yesterday. It's going to be a very small, very quick ceremony."

J waits for the request to come, the *real* reason for the call. But as Andreas goes on with some of the details of the wedding (hillside, the bride's sister as officiant), J realizes Andreas has no idea that he sings at weddings, and that this call isn't meant to be a request in disguise. Andreas just wanted him to know he played a small part in getting them together.

Which is why J finds himself offering to sing at the wedding. Andreas replies with genuine surprise and deep emotion. J explains the whole thing about the wedding song, and at first Andreas says no, no, that is way too much at such short notice. But J insists, happy to be able to do a good deed for someone who lives by good deeds. Andreas in turn insists on paying, and J gives him something between the friend fee and the stranger fee. After arrangements are made, and Andreas has said thank you more than J thought was humanly possible, J hangs up.

Instantly, he is returned to the emptiness of his apartment.

They meet the next day in a coffee shop not far from J's apartment. Andreas first, with Kerstin to follow.

When Andreas arrives, he is genuinely anguished to find that J has already bought himself a coffee and a pastry.

"It should be on me!" he insists. Then, once he has gotten his own sustenance, he sits down and more than makes up for it with a silver cigarette case he hands J as a thank-you gift.

"I'm not doing this to encourage you to smoke," Andreas says. "Just to possess beautiful things."

"You really don't have to give me anything. You've already given so much," J says.

Andreas waves this off. "I won't hear of it!"

J knows it's pointless to prolong the argument, and that he only has twenty minutes with Andreas before Kerstin arrives for her turn.

"So," he says, picking up his pen and hovering it over his notebook, "a simple ceremony on a hillside?"

"Yes, that's all we want."

"But I would have thought . . . you know."

"What?"

"Considering all the access you have to props, you could have constructed something elaborate. If anyone in my life can find a horse-drawn carriage at the last minute, it's you."

"Yes, but that's *work*. Do you think of singing at your own wedding?"

The truest answer is: J thought he'd be together with V for a long time. But he didn't think they'd ever want to get married. Or, really, that *she'd* ever want to get married.

"Honestly," J says, "no."

"With all the weddings you do? You've never thought about your own wedding?"

"I mean, details, sure. We'd say, 'Oh, we'd never do *that*.' Or, 'Those canapés were a nice surprise. Maybe we'll make them our next dinner party.'"

"Interesting."

"Why is that interesting?"

"I guess if I walk in a room and it's a lovely room except for one really ugly lamp, I'll imagine the lamp I'd put there, and by doing that I'm starting to imagine living in that room, making it mine. Not for long. But for a little bit, I role-play every room I walk into. I figured you'd do that with weddings."

J wonders if this is actually a problem, that he's never looked at an altar and imagined standing there with V. It's hard to imagine her in a wedding dress; she has nothing but contempt for lace.

"Maybe I'd keep it simple, like you," J says, more to keep the conversation moving than out of any deep belief in what he's asserting. He doesn't know what he'll do if Andreas asks him about V. "There's something very appealing about that."

Andreas takes a sip of coffee, then smiles and says, "We'll see, won't we? Now, what do you need to know for your song? Really, there's no need to write a new one. We'd be perfectly happy with a song from one of your albums."

"Absolutely not," J says. "I want to give this to you." Then he starts his questioning predictably, pen in hand. "Tell me how you met."

Andreas smiles with even more intensity; remarkably, he's not tired of this question. "I admired a scarf she was wearing," he says. "I thought it was a vintage Yves Saint Laurent—it looked like the wings of a butterfly. As you know, I don't ordinarily have an eye toward clothing, but this caught my attention. I didn't even register how beautiful the woman wearing the scarf was until I caught her looking at me. I told her I admired her scarf, and she told me it had been her grandmother's. Before I knew it, we were going for a drink. It's a very old-fashioned way to meet someone! But I suppose that's to be expected for someone like me."

"And now . . . how does she make you feel?"

"Good. Happy. Very happy."

J shakes his head. "I need a little more than that. Something more personal."

"I mean, what can I say that hasn't been said a thousand times before?"

"Try." J takes out his phone and puts on the timer. "I want you to talk about it for three minutes. Just say whatever comes into your head. Are you ready?"

He knows Andreas won't say no.

"Sure. Has it started? Okay. Um . . . she makes me laugh? But she's not one of those people who makes you laugh because she's shooting someone else down. Or herself. No, it's just the way she sees the world is a little bit off from mine or anyone else's, and when she shares what she sees with me, it's really funny because it's absolutely true, in a way I never saw before. And maybe she makes me that way, too. Like, when I focus on her, it clears away the noise. There's so much noise all the time, and a lot of the time, it drowns me out. I'm not the kind of guy who yells, who says *hey, look at me!* No, if you want to get to me, you have to really clear the path.

And that's what she does. It's not like anyone else I've been with, the way that path is clear. When we're alone, we're not competing with the outside world and we're not competing with each other. That brings out the best in me, I guess. Or at least the part of me I like the most. I'm making her sound like she's this Zen person—you'll meet her, she's not. But—let me put it this way. Everything's in the right place with her. It's unique and it's unusual and maybe it's not perfectly balanced, but nothing's a mess. When you're with someone like that, and when the two of you have complementary notions . . . I guess I can put it in musical terms, can't I? We have harmony. But I also get to hear her melody, and she gets to hear mine, and it's the most honest, clearest melody I've ever made. For her ears only. Is that time?"

"Yes, you were a little over. But I wanted to hear where you'd go. And I promise you, it wasn't something that's been said a thousand times before. The feeling underneath, sure. But not those particular words in that particular order."

J admires how pure Andreas's feelings seem. He also thinks Andreas is a fool—hasn't he ever been hurt by love before? Maybe this is his first serious relationship, and therefore his first serious potential heartbreak. J doesn't want to be the guy to warn him. But he also hopes someone does warn him.

"Is something the matter?" Andreas asks.

"No, just had an idea for the song," J covers. He is awful enough a person to blatantly lie, but not so awful as to submerge Andreas in his own treacherous depths on the eve of his wedding.

"That's so exciting," Andreas says. "You're so kind to do this."

J looks down at his notebook. While Andreas was speaking, he jotted down a few words, but he's not sure yet if there's anything he can particularly use.

He thinks of the other questions he could ask.

*What makes you so sure?*

*How can you possibly know?*

*What will you do if it doesn't work out?*
*Why risk so much pain?*

Yes, he wants these answers. But he also knows they won't do him much good unless it's V answering.

In his silver cigarette case, J sees his distorted self and thinks it's a pretty accurate reflection.

"What would you miss the most about her if she were gone?" he asks. Immediately, he wants to take it back, but it's too late.

"Myself," Andreas replies. "I imagine I'd miss myself. The person I've become without the noise."

"You know this already? How long has it been?"

"Eight months. And, yes, I know this already. Isn't that remarkable?"

*Eight months,* J thinks. *You can spend years in a relationship chasing after where you were at eight months.*

He remembers what it was like with V around that time. Navigating between their two apartments. If V mentioned a favorite movie that J hadn't seen, they'd watch it that night. If J was going out of town, he'd leave her with a favorite book of his, to "keep her company." Sometimes he'd take a second copy with him, and they'd talk about it when he got back. (Not the same as reading it to each other over the phone, but he puts that out of mind.)

"And here she is!" Andreas announces.

J has been staring at his notebook, and now he looks up just as Kerstin appears from behind him. She looks a little older than Andreas, but J isn't sure if that's because of her age or her demeanor. Her red hair is cropped short, and she has a light purple birthmark under her left ear. She's wearing a bright blue blazer that matches the bright blue frames of her glasses.

Andreas stands to greet her, and the two of them kiss as if she's just gotten home. J stands too, but that only makes his observation of their affection more awkward for him. If this were a cartoon, they would be the source of a rainbow and he would have a cloud over his head. Or maybe the floor would open up beneath him and he'd hang in the air for a moment, wondering what to do.

This is a pattern that J does not like to admit to himself: When he is dating somebody, he doesn't really feel competitive with any of the lovers around him. He takes their happiness at face value, because he knows the value of his own happiness. He doesn't need what they have, as long as he has his own version.

But when he's single, he suddenly feels like he's putting all his weight on a phantom limb. He doesn't envy the couples around him as much as he feels the world is teeming with inadequacy. His own. Theirs. It feels like everyone is playing a parlor game called Don't Be Lonely! and while others have forgotten it's a game, he understands that a winning hand only lasts until the next cards are dealt.

Andreas is now introducing J to Kerstin, and Kerstin to J. She tells him what an honor it is to meet him, how she loves his music so much, how it never occurred to her when she was at one of his concerts that someday he would be playing a song at her wedding. She repeats the story of Andreas seeing J's record the first time he came to her place. Instead of calling it serendipity, she calls it fate.

"Thank you," J says. "The honor is truly mine. The man you are marrying is the nicest man in the world."

Andreas immediately protests ("I killed a fly just the other day!"), but Kerstin agrees.

"I'm very, very lucky," she says.

Andreas looks at his watch and says he needs to be going—he's called in a favor at a bespoke tailor, and it would be rude to keep the woman waiting.

Kerstin kisses him goodbye, then takes his seat. J asks her if she wants anything to eat or drink. She says she's happy just to talk, and to finish the coffee Andreas has left.

J explains again how everything will work.

"Really, it's unbelievable of you to do this," Kerstin says at the end of the explanation.

"If the roles were reversed, and I needed a silver tea service or a Bentley or a robe once worn by Greta Garbo herself, I know Andreas would do the same."

Kerstin smiles. "You're absolutely right. But not everyone reciprocates his kindness. Most of his family takes from him without giving much back. And some of the people he's dealt with in his business—well, it means so much to him to see the best in people, but they don't always deserve that." Kerstin pauses, as if she's just overheard herself talking at another table. "Listen to me! What an awful way to start. Please don't put any of that in your song."

J is now concerned. "He's okay, isn't he?"

"Oh, yes. Through his eyes, everyone is his friend. And I'm very careful what I share with him about what I see through my eyes, because he has so much faith in everyone, and I don't want him to lose that. And, please, don't get me wrong—there are many, many people like you, who understand his kindness and are kind in return. Because we believe that is how the world should work."

"To be loved, and love in return," J says.

Kerstin leans back in her chair. "Not exactly."

"Not exactly?"

"Just because you love someone . . . it doesn't mean they have to love you back. Whereas with kindness, you should be able to be able to be kind to anyone who is kind to you."

Her words repeat themselves in V's voice. *Just because you love someone . . . it doesn't mean they have to love you back.* Has V actually said this to him? Or is it just that he can imagine her saying it to him, in response to him saying he loves her?

"I'm so sorry," Kerstin says. "I've come off to you as cynical about love. Let me put it this way—if kindness is easier to reciprocate, then that means love is more meaningful to receive. Because love must include kindness, but kindness does not have to include love."

"I can't disagree with that."

"You are with someone?"

And there it is, asked by someone who has no idea how her innocent question brings out something akin to guilt.

If he says *I am*, he's a liar . . . isn't he?

If he says *I'm not*, he's given up . . . right?

"Oh," Kerstin says. "I see. I'm sorry."

"No, no—it's not as bad as that. There's no need to be sorry."

"I wasn't apologizing for your relationship. I was apologizing for asking the question."

"It's fine," J says. "My girlfriend and I are in different places. Geographically. Perhaps emotionally. But that doesn't mean we won't be in the same place again."

"When did you last see her?"

"Eight weeks ago."

"And when did you last talk to her?"

"Does texting count?"

"No. I mean the sound of her voice responding to the sound of your voice."

"Ten days."

"That must be very hard."

It honestly wouldn't have been a problem before, when he was out of town and feeling more secure about their relationship. But now, hearing this observation, J feels as if he's been walking around bleeding, and finally someone has noticed and asked him if he needs a bandage. And at the same time, he's embarrassed to have been caught walking around bleeding, unable to bandage himself.

"It *is* hard," he manages to say. Then he recovers and adds, "But that is not what we're here to talk about! I want to get a better sense of you. For the song."

"May I ask . . . how is the sex?"

J is startled by such a forthright question, but also feels it's very V-like for Kerstin to inquire. Which might be why he answers, "If that's your way of asking if that is the cause of our problems, I think you'd have to ask her."

"That's a good answer. Good that you're not presumptuous."

The truth, of course, is that to the best of his knowledge, J and V have both gone without sex for the past eight weeks. It's been a strange inversion of the way things usually are for him, because to him monogamy has meant that sex was something that happened at home, not on tour (unless V was along for the ride). He's pleasured himself in the interim, and he's sure she's pleasured herself—but rarely in tandem, which is how they used to get through some of the longer spells apart. J knows this is a huge factor in the aloneness he is feeling—not missing sex, per se (though he does miss that), but more having her body and his body expressing closeness. Any kind of closeness.

He is not going to tell all this to Kerstin. So instead he goes back to his usual questions and asks, "What are some of the things you and Andreas enjoy doing?"

"Well, the sex is very satisfying. He's got the enthusiasm of a seventeen-year-old and the knowledge of a forty-year-old. It's a good combination."

Since Kerstin seems intent on steering the conversation here, J asks, "And is that why you're together?"

"Hardly. We're together because he enjoys my company and I enjoy his. I've dated many men before. Many, many men. And I don't think I could have said that about any of the rest of them. They were too busy broadcasting their needs to tune in to mine. Ends up that's what I was looking for all along. You can write that down, if you'd like."

J has forgotten all about his notebook. Hastily, he scribbles down some of what she's said. Then he flips back a couple of pages.

"Andreas says that being with you clears away the noise. Do you feel that way, too?"

Kerstin reaches for J's hand, the one without a pen. It's not a romantic gesture. She just wants him to hear what she has to say.

"No, I don't feel that way. The noise is still there. It doesn't go away. But I can always hear him through it, and I know he can hear me. It's like when you're in a dentist's office. They're cleaning or drilling or whatever, but through that, you can hear they're playing a song you love. Some Fleetwood Mac, maybe. So you latch on to that, you try to push your mind as far into the song as you can, because that brings you some joy, or at the very least distraction, and you can sing along in your head while whatever is being done to you is done to you. In this scenario, Andreas is the song."

J jots that down, then says, "So tell me about how you two met."

"Really?" she asks, as if the question is beneath both of them.

Kerstin's stubbornness is just like V's.

"Really," he tells her.

"I was at an auction. Mind you, I am not like Andreas—I've been to maybe three auctions in my entire life. In this case, I was doing a favor for one of my mother's best friends. She had just been through a horrible divorce, and her ex-husband, out of a mix of spite and greed, was auctioning off his share of their art collection. There was one piece—a very small sketch by Hammershøi—that she wanted, but she didn't want him to know she was doing the bidding. I'd never met the man, so I was deemed a safe proxy. As I was leaving my mother's house, she ambushed me and insisted I wear this fancy scarf that had belonged to my grandmother. I don't know if my mother has ever been to an auction in her life, but she said quite confidently that it was important to look wealthy, so other bidders would assume you'd go higher if you had to. So I wore the scarf, and I won the sketch. After, this man came up to me admiring what I was wearing. And I'll admit—at first I thought it was a lame pickup line, like, 'Nice scarf, lady . . . I'd love to see it tied to my bedpost.' But then I realized I was wrong. This guy was genuinely admiring the scarf. I assumed this meant he was gay, but then he seemed to be admiring me as well, and I thought, *Oh, well, this is more interesting.* I asked him if he wanted to get a drink, and one thing led to another. I never returned the scarf to my mother, but I haven't worn it again. I tend to lose things. And usually, because I know I do this, I don't get too attached. But this time, I knew almost immediately that I didn't want to lose that scarf, that it had become far too important to be risked."

J and V met at a party. Should he have kept the glass she was sipping from? Crawled through all the chatter to discover what song was playing in the far background?

He can't even remember what either of them was wearing.

Somewhere in his closet, there's probably a pair of jeans with a story to tell, but he'll never know to ask.

"You felt right away that it was something serious?" he asks Kerstin.

"Let me put it this way: Have you ever stumbled onto a restaurant, a little neighborhood place that makes astonishingly good food? And you wonder, *How is it possible that this place doesn't have a line down the block? How does this not have a Michelin star? Why isn't everyone talking about how great this place is?* And at first, you want to bring everyone you know there, to be the person who put it on the map. Then you realize, no, that will only ruin it. You want to keep it to yourself. Maybe take one or two close friends and swear them secrecy. It's your find. That's how I felt about Andreas. I couldn't believe no one else had found him. I couldn't believe that I hadn't needed to do anything special to bring him into my life. All I needed to do was show up at the auction that day and recognize him for who he is."

J writes this down, *recognize him for who he is.*

"Does she recognize you for who you are?" Kerstin asks.

J isn't surprised it turns back his way. He almost welcomes it, to finally be talking with someone about what's going on.

"I think she does," he answers. "But that might be the problem."

Kerstin's phone goes off; the theme to *Jaws* is the ringtone.

"It's my sister, Elin," Kerstin says, waiting out the ring. "I'm supposed to meet her soon. She'll be there tomorrow to perform the ceremony."

"How many people will be there?"

"You. Me. Andreas. Elin."

"When he said it was going to be small, I didn't realize it would be *that* small."

"This isn't about anyone else. It's about the two of us. His voice, my voice. His ears, my ears. No one else needs to watch over us. Elin makes it legal, but at least blurs the line between government obligation and family tradition. And you bring the spirit of something random, singing our own voices back to us in your song."

"No pressure," J jokes. But it's only a joke because he's saying it out loud. He *is* feeling pressure.

"I love your songs and my husband-to-be treasures you as a friend. That is the perfect combination."

"But I think I've proven to you already that I'm hardly an expert when it comes to love."

Kerstin's phone rings *Jaws* again. This time, she picks it up, says she'll be there in ten minutes, and hangs up. Then she turns back to J.

"I would never trust anyone who claimed to be an expert in love," she says. "Surely you understand that? Love has more unknowns than knowns, more questions than answers. Why delude yourself into thinking otherwise? It's the second largest thing we experience, after life itself. There's no way you're going to get all of it right. You just have to hope you get enough of it right, with other people who also get enough of it right."

It's only when she stands that J realizes she never even took off her coat.

"Andreas has told you where to be?" she asks. "Ramberget at one? Right by Keillers Park. Andreas will send you the coordinates. It's a nice spot."

"I'm sure it will be."

J stands to say goodbye. They hug with the awkwardness of two people who've crossed the line from strangers but haven't yet made it to the territory of friends.

"I hope I gave you enough to work with," Kerstin says.

J looks at his notebook on the table, and the few lines scribbled within it.

"It's enough," he promises.

He runs some errands, but as he does, the song is forming. A number of his thoughts are melding, preparing the words to be there when he reaches for them. There are too many words, and not all of them make sense. But they are being assembled. Dancers at the ready, waiting for the choreographer to show up.

The problem is, when he finally sits down to summon the song, a lot of the dancers end up looking like V. He puts them off by focusing on the chords, the melody. He puts them off by picturing Andreas and Kerstin on a hillside, Kerstin in her scarf. He puts them off by vowing not to call V, not tonight.

Then, nearing midnight New York time, he calls her.

He's surprised when she picks up, and surprised further when her "hello" seems friendly, when she doesn't immediately ask him why he's calling.

His mind cycles through all the things he doesn't think he can say—*I just wanted to hear the sound of your voice, I have been thinking about you all day, I feel it's time we had a talk but only if that talk leads to us being back together without question.*

Finally he lands on, "Hi. Do you remember Andreas? The antique dealer?"

"Yes. What a sweet man. Please don't tell me he's dead."

"No! He's getting married. An instant wedding. He wants me to play."

"Of course he does."

*Don't say it like that. Why do you have to say it like that?*

"I talked to the couple today—I think you'd like her. Now I have about seventeen hours to write them a song."

"So you called me for inspiration?"

*I don't need to call you for that. Right now you're underneath every thought I have about love.*

"I called because it's been over a week since we talked."

*I miss you.*

"It's been so busy here. I can't explain it to you—I'm not even sure I can explain it to myself. At any given moment, there are a hundred things to do, and I'm lucky if I get to one of them each day. It's a barrage, and the scary part is that everyone thinks I know what I'm doing, and I sense that if they knew how out of my zone I am, everything would fall apart."

"That sounds very stressful."

"You could say that."

*Don't fight. Please, let's not fight.*

"It was wonderful to see Andreas so happy. After the disaster of the cake wedding, it's a relief to see two people who only care about each other, and not how everyone else will see them. Because no one else will be there. Well, except for the officiant and me."

"Why are you telling me this?"

"I'm just telling you something that happened today. Are we not doing that anymore?"

There is a long pause. He can hear V take a deep breath, then exhale.

"No. I'm sorry. I'm just feeling very burned out right now. I am a puddle of wax and the ashy remains of the wick."

"Whatever's happening between us," J ventures, "I still want us to talk. Talking to each other is our thing."

As he says this, it rings true, and it rings false. True because they do love to talk. False because they love to talk face-to-face. They are crap at everything else.

V surprises him by saying, "It is our thing. And, believe me, I wish I had that in me right now. Which leaves us at the same impasse."

"Okay. I'll stop."

There's another pause, as if V is checking the clock, or maybe changing the channel on the TV in the background.

"So," she says, finally, "Andreas is getting married. Is that why you called?"

*I need to see you.*

*I need us to be in the same place.*

"No," J says. "I actually called to tell you I'm coming to New York."

It feels right to say this, even if it surprises him as much as it (hopefully?) surprises her.

"When?"

"In two weeks."

"No," V replies. "That's not a good idea."

"It's not for you. I've been asked to sing at a wedding in Brooklyn. Though of course I want to see you as well."

"Whose wedding?"

"No one you know. It's a secret wedding."

"A secret wedding? What does that even mean?"

J has no idea what it means.

"It's . . . They want it to be a surprise. Something semi-spontaneous that seems entirely spontaneous. I think at least one of their parents disapproves of the match. So it's like an elopement, in terms of family. But their friends will be there."

"You realize you're not asking me if you should visit—you're telling me you're going to visit. I know you mean well, but I also have to point that out to you."

"I'm sorry. How would you feel about me visiting? If you don't want to see me, that's fine. But I hope you will."

"*Of course* I want to see you. How could I not see you? I'm only worried it will make things more confusing. I am trying to get my footing here. And . . . I'm also enjoying coming home at night and being alone. No, *enjoying* isn't the right word. It feels necessary for me to come home and be alone. My mind needs that space."

"I don't need to stay with you," J proposes. "I can find somewhere else to stay. I know how busy you are."

Another pause. Then: "If you don't mind, I think that would make things much easier for me. There is so much going on, I'm not sure two weeks is enough for me to get into the headspace of having you here. I mean, in this apartment. I do appreciate you offering. And if we just see what happens. I don't want it to become a big deal. Do you understand?"

J says he'll keep her posted as it develops, no pressure either way.

"I'm not sure there's such a thing as 'no pressure' these days," V says. "But I suppose without some pressure we'd all just float off, no?" She yawns. "I don't even know what I'm saying—it's late, and I am more exhausted than I thought was possible. I just want . . . I guess I just want you to know I have no idea what I want. If that makes any sense."

"It's nice to hear your voice, even if it's exhausted," J replies.

V laughs tiredly. "I hear your voice all the time; Thor has you on half the office playlists. I'm almost used to it by now."

This information is a jolt to J. It has to mean that she hasn't told her coworkers they're through . . . doesn't it? And what reason would she have to keep such news from them . . . unless she herself didn't believe it.

"V, I—"

"No more talking. Really, I need to go to bed. Good luck with Andreas's wedding. I hope he's very happy."

"Goodnight," J offers.

"You too, darling J," V says, then disconnects.

It's time to reckon with the song. He must block out V's voice—or, more accurately, push it below the surface, since there's no way to be truly rid of it, not right now. He must forget about the fact that he's just invented a wedding in New York and will need to find a real wedding to save face. He must forget about V, which really means forgetting about himself.

J finds an instrumental track on his computer and decides to use it as his foundation. He studies the few scribbles he made in the café. He closes his eyes. He walks into the theater. The dancers, too many of them, are waiting for him on the stage . . .

It is a good thing that Andreas has sent coordinates, because Ramberget is, for all practical purposes, a mountain overlooking Gothenburg, although guidebooks like to call it a "hill," because that sounds more pastoral, less intimidating.

Andreas and Kerstin have been blessed by a warm, cloudless day. J is less blessed; he thought it would be too childish to text Andreas to ask what to wear, so he is in a suit and tie, carrying a rucksack and his guitar. Already he is hot. He's misjudged the coordinates and parked in the wrong lot.

To get to the spot where the couple and the officiant wait, J must walk through Keillers Park. From a panoramic perspective, it makes sense for Andreas and Kerstin to have chosen a spot called "the view point" on the east side of the mountain. The problem is that J walks the winding road for minutes without feeling he's getting much closer to it. By the time he is, in fact, closer, he has sweat through his shirt and into his eyes.

He is fifteen minutes late, but nobody mentions the lateness, or seems to care. He is, by a stretch, the most formally dressed person in their party; Andreas is wearing a loose blue shirt, buttoned at least one station lower than J thought Andreas would go. Kerstin is wearing a white summer dress covered with blue and yellow flowers. Her sister, the officiant, is wearing a red t-shirt, jeans, and sandals.

Undeterred by the sweat or the strain in J's breathing, Andreas gives him a hearty hug of welcome. Kerstin introduces her sister, Elin, who shakes J's hand and says, "Shall we?"

There is enough of an outcropping for her to stand with space for Andreas and Kerstin to face each other in front of her, the city and everything around it spreading out at her back. Andreas and Kerstin take each other's hands.

"Would you like me to take a picture?" J offers.

"It's okay," Andreas says. "We'll remember."

J lifts his guitar out of its case, stands to the side.

Elin begins. "It is my honor and my pleasure to be here to recognize the love of these two people as they garner legal recognition for a love that goes far beyond this ceremony. Andreas and Kerstin will first regard each other, and then each of them will reflect. This regarding and these reflections will act as their vows."

Elin then closes her eyes, as if leaving the room they're all in.

For a minute, maybe two minutes, Andreas and Kerstin hold hands and look at each other. J doesn't know whether he is supposed to close his eyes or not, but the couple doesn't seem aware of him at all, so he keeps watching. On Andreas's face he sees many emotions unfold: A smile of recognition; an intensity of purpose; a sigh of admiration. A wonder. And tears, tears in his eyes. Gratitude.

Without any discernable cue, Kerstin says, "This is it. You and me."

"You and me," Andreas echoes tenderly. "Near and far."

"High and low."

"Easy and hard."
"Good and bad."
"Old and new."
Kerstin smiles. "You and me."
Andreas smiles back. "Yes, you and me."
Without having to be told, they kiss.
Elin opens her eyes and applauds. J applauds, too.
The kiss doesn't end as much as it pauses. The couple turns to J.
"I believe you have a song?" Elin prompts.
"Oh, yes," J says.
He sings.

> Everyone I tried to love
> Sang the same old song
> A choir of "why don't you love me's"
> Drowned out my own voice until it was gone
> Every "I love you" was a question
> It was loaded like a shotgun
>
> But with you
> With you I can hear my own voice
> With you I can hear my own heart
> With you I can hear what it wants
>
> With you I hear its response
> Its complete renaissance
> What used to be so mute
> Now speaks in tongues
> Now when I've learned how to use it
> Every syllable is music
>
> Oh with you . . .
> With you I can hear my own voice

> With you I can hear my own heart
> With you I can hear what it wants
>
> So thank you
> Thank you for listening
> Thank you
> Thank you for listening
> For letting me take the lead
> While you gently harmonize with me

What does J feel as he sings this song?

He feels gratitude to be singing in the open air, gratitude to be part of the sunshine, part of the day.

He feels hope that this song is the right gift for the two lovers in front of him.

He feels sadness to have fallen into the gap between singing about himself and singing about them.

He feels worry that this is only a song, only a moment, and that no couple is truly prepared for near and far, high and low, easy and hard, good and bad.

He feels fullness in knowing what he's singing is true.

He feels emptiness in his uncertainty that what he's singing is true for him.

He feels power, because this song is, in fact, what he wants to put into the world.

As soon as he is done, Andreas lets out a huge cheer, while Elin and Kerstin applaud. Somewhere, a car honks its approval.

Andreas corrals everyone into a group hug. The car honks again.

"That must be the cab!" Andreas says. "Wondering where we are."

"Thank you so much," Kerstin says to J. "That was perfect. The only gift we could possibly want."

"In that case, I'll take my towels back," Elin says.

"We're off!" Andreas exclaims, hugging J one last time. "I'll be in touch when we return!"

Laughing, Andreas and Kerstin join hands and run down the hill like schoolchildren at the end of the school day. The taxi waits just out of view.

"Do you need a ride?" Elin asks J.

"No, I'm good."

"Well, it's been nice to meet you."

"Where are they going?"

Elin shrugs. "I have no idea."

With that, she heads to her car, at a safe distance behind the married couple.

J packs up his guitar, pulls a water bottle from his rucksack, and takes in the view as he drinks.

The wedding is over so quickly, it would be easy to wonder if it actually happened.

But J senses Andreas is right—this is indeed something they will all remember.

Now that it's done, now that he doesn't have a song to retreat into, all J's other cares seem to rise from the city and reenter his thoughts.

He can hear his own heart, but V can't.

He needs to find a way to talk to her.

And he needs, right away, to start planning a fake wedding in Brooklyn.

# THE FIFTH WEDDING

It is surprisingly easy to plan a fake wedding in Brooklyn.

J texts Julia, a guitarist in New York who plays in his band when he tours America. He knows she is a creature of Brooklyn, and also trusts her to keep the secret from V, who she's only met in passing.

*On it*, she replies.

Five hours later, there's a plan.

J's desperation is so loud that it drowns out any possible alarms. So when Julia explains that the couple, Skye and Detroit, are polyamorous performance artists who are willing to donate the night they've reserved at a Brooklyn performance space in order to "perform" a wedding, the only response J has is "That's great!" There isn't anything inherently alarming about polyamorous performance artists in Brooklyn performance spaces—it's just that in this case, had J bothered to check their joint Instagram, he would have noticed that the word *disruptors* comes up a lot in their self-description, and the only recent review they've quoted (not from an actual reviewer, but from someone else's Instagram) calls them "a mess so hot it's *steaming*!"

Skye is J's point of contact, and when they refer to the event as a "wedding-slash-wedding deconstruction," J doesn't stop to ask what they mean by that. Instead, he focuses on the fact that Skye and Detroit have asked for two songs rather than one—one for each of them, "because otherwise we'll feel overly defined as a couple." J replies that he'll do anything they'd like, as long as it looks like a wedding to anyone who isn't in on the joke.

Julia will be away for J's sudden visit and is happy to offer her apartment for his lodgings. This is a huge relief to J—New York City is many adjectives, but more than any other, it's *expensive*. He also likes that if he ends up staying with V for at least part of the time, he won't feel like he's paying for somewhere he isn't sleeping.

He texts V to share his flight information and the details of the wedding. He sends this information at the start of her day, before work hours, in the hopes this will enable the quickest response. But it's still two hours and three minutes before he receives a noncommittal *thank u for letting me know*.

J tells himself to play it cool, but he's far too hot to do this effectively. In less than a minute, he's replied, *will I get to see you?*

This time her response is instant.

*I hope so. We'll see when you get here. My days are not my own.*

It's that last sentence that J feels opens the door. The implication is clear, isn't it? If her days *were* her own, she would be making plans to see him.

That's what he wants to believe, and since there's no reason to do otherwise, he believes it.

When V sends her text, she is standing in a bathroom stall in her office, because it's the best chance she has for uninterrupted privacy. She doesn't exactly know why she feels she needs to make such a retreat from her coworkers; it's not about them, and more that this is the way she's always been, looking for corners when the world gets a little too personal. As a girl, talking to her friends on the phone at night, it wasn't enough for her to be behind her closed bedroom door. No, she needed to crawl under her bed, to hide there and talk.

It is not quite right to say that all these weeks, J has felt more theoretical to her than real. His presence *has* been real—just at a remove. And in that remove, she's felt she's been slowly building, for the first time ever, a life of her own making. It reminds her of when she was a teenager and discovered how swimming would make her feel. Suddenly, she had a new kind of body, and that body had power. Now she has a new kind of life, and she's still waiting to see if the result will be power or simply exhaustion.

She is not used to the notion of J coming to visit her. The farthest he's ever had to travel to be with her was the distance between his apartment and hers. He has always been the one with the far-off destinations, the tour stops that she might hop on a plane to join him at. It was a strange way of being away together—they rarely had evening plans, because for other people, J *was* the evening plan. V never shed the self-consciousness of being a perpetual plus-one, knowing that everyone else in the room knew she was only there because he was there. Especially when they were staying with his friends, the vagabond network of people in different cities that he'd now visited long enough for it to feel like a familiar route—she felt a constant pressure (from herself, never from him) to justify her own presence. She would clean every dish in the sink, even though her own dishes often stayed sink-bound for days. She would be sure to make every bed they slept in, even though she knew the sheets were likely to be thrown in the laundry as soon as they left. Hotel rooms were better, were more neutral territory, to a degree that she almost suggested that J get a hotel room for this trip. Which V knows is ridiculous; whatever they are to each other right now, he should be staying with her. But instinctively she knows that would be too much, too soon.

She would be trying to justify her presence again, in her own temporary apartment.

*My days are not my own.* She half expects him to challenge her on this. To type back, *Then whose days are they?* She is grateful that he doesn't, but that in itself is tricky—because gratitude is one of the ingredients in a relationship that needs to be provided in just the right amount.

She wants him here, but she doesn't. She doesn't want him here, but she does. He's often told her that he loves how decisive she is, how straightforward their communication styles are. But now she feels that casual directness is hiding something else underneath. She is not able to be entirely honest, and that doesn't feel right.

She wants him here; she doesn't want him here—ultimately it doesn't matter, because one way or another, he will be here soon, and she will see him, and there won't be any corners to hide in anymore.

The week before J leaves is one of the most productive he's had in ages. Knowing that he will soon be in the same city as V allows him to stop thinking about her constantly and deal with other things. The pause works because he's the one declaring it.

He waits until the last possible minute to text her from the plane. The cabin door will soon be closing. Liftoff is imminent.

*Flight is on time*, he tells her. *In seven hours, we'll be back on the same clock.*

He turns off his phone, and when he revives it upon landing, there is a brief hiccup where it recalibrates to the new hour. It reaches out for a signal, and once J has signed his life away to get one from an American carrier, a message from V appears.

*I can meet for lunch tomorrow. I'm afraid I'll only have an hour. ☹ I'll meet you here.*

There's a link to her office address.

J smiles.

The door has opened wider.

After freshening up at Julia's apartment, J figures out how to take the subway to where Skye and Detroit live. He feels his usual discombobulation, the excitement of travel deeply tempered by the fact that his body thinks it's midnight well before the sun has begun to set. When he was younger, it was much easier to adapt. Now, the discombobulation only underscores that he's no longer younger.

The door to Skye and Detroit's apartment is answered by the fresh-faced friendliness of a twenty-six-year-old, who turns out to be Skye. They are wearing a striking light blue silk shirt that's scattered with small birds and a small diamond nose ring that glints against their dark skin. Even though they and Detroit are the ones doing the favor, Skye welcomes J in as if J is the bestower and Skye is the recipient.

"This is so surreal," Skye says. (As with most twenty-six-year-olds, this is a preferred adjective, because it covers oh so much.) "When Julia mentioned the idea . . . I just thought, *what*? But Detroit thought it sounded like a blast, and when I started to listen to your music, I thought, sure, let's go with the universe here."

The thing that makes this charming rather than simply bearable is the fact that Skye is so transparently sincere. It's also very clear when they take J inside to what they call "the sitting room" that the apartment is usually a complete mess, and that they have spent much of the day trying to tame it for their visitor.

"I hope you're not allergic to cats?" they say. "If you are, I have some Benadryl. It's not likely that Veneno will come out while you're here—she's not very social. But she definitely sheds."

"I'll be fine," J says, taking a seat on the lime-green couch. He doesn't see any cat hair.

"Can I get you something to drink? Are you just off the plane? Do you need coffee? I put on a fresh pot an hour ago. Or—where are my manners?—I could also brew a new pot. I'm not sure how picky you are."

"I'm good."

"Water? Diet Coke? Whiskey?"

"Water would be good."

"One sec!"

J grows more and more curious as he looks around. This apartment has clearly been lived in longer than Skye has been alive... or it's the home of two young people nostalgic for a time before they were born, a time when showgirls and speakeasies were ascendant. J senses that the sitting room is the only room in the apartment that isn't the kitchen, bedroom, or bathroom. In one corner, there's a sewing machine and a basket of fabrics that seem like they were gathered hastily.

Skye returns with two glasses of water, then looks to the front door. "Detroit should be here any moment. I texted him and he promised me he was on his way. He's excited to meet you, too."

"I really appreciate you doing this," J says.

"Well, I can't remember the last time anyone *appreciated* something I did!" Skye says, bemused. Then they add, "That was a joke. I swear."

J isn't sure. He senses that, for all their open demeanor, there are things Skye doesn't want him to see. Which, of course, makes perfect sense. They've just met.

"How long have you lived here?" J asks.

"Almost two years! That's when I moved in. Detroit's been here longer. Much longer. It's really more his house than mine."

J waits to see if Skye is going to say that's a joke, too. They don't.

"How long have the two of you been together?"

Skye smiles tensely. "Oh, I probably shouldn't answer that until Detroit gets here."

J has plenty of follow-up questions to that statement—but also takes the statement to mean that follow-up questions should be avoided. This isn't that unusual for the interview process—he's certainly been with couples who always wanted to answer together, partly out of fear that one of them would give a "wrong" answer that the other one would take the wrong way. Still, he doesn't want the time to be wasted, so he decides to press on . . . but gently. He takes out his notebook and brings up the recording app on his phone.

"Do you mind if I . . . ?"

This time, Skye's smile seems warmer. "Who doesn't love posterity? Go right ahead."

"Do the two of you make your living as performers?"

Skye lets out a big laugh and paces a little. "Um . . . no. I mean, we have a following—I promise there will be people there on Friday night. But having a following doesn't necessarily pay the bills."

"Please—sit down," J says, as if he's the host.

"You're sweet," Skye says, taking a chair close to the couch. "And cute."

"For an old man," J replies.

"Yeah, right. I've seen old men, and you are *not* one of them."

Again, the sincerity of this comment gets to J.

"Now you're the one being sweet," he points out.

"It's nice to have the chance," Skye replies. Then, before J can think of a new question, Skye asks, "Have you always performed solo?"

"I have a band. You know Julia—"

"No, I mean, it's always been you in the spotlight, right? You've never had to share it?"

"I guess. The whole singer-songwriter thing."

"I've never done that. I bet it's nice."

J isn't quite sure what constitutes "nice" here. So he asks, "Have you always been part of a group?"

"Duos, mostly. Ironically enough."

"Why is that ironic?"

"I mean, right now polyamory is a big part of what Detroit wants in our . . . I don't know what to call it. Our relationship? Our act? Our lives? At a certain point, they're all the same thing, you know?"

*You're so lonely*, J thinks. That's part of Skye's sincerity—its desire to connect to someone else's sincerity, to be seen for what it is.

It's at this moment that a key fumbles in the door. Skye reflexively stands and smooths the front of their shirt, as if crumbs had fallen there simply from talking.

Detroit enters the room and makes sure the room is paying good attention. He's wearing a black turtleneck and designer jeans, topped with a phalanx of scarves. He bears a strange resemblance to Meryl Streep playing Ian McKellen. Possibly Ian McKellen playing Meryl Streep. Instead of apologizing for being late, he says, "Oh, good—you're already here."

J stands too, now. "It's great to meet you," he offers.

"Yes, it is, isn't it? Detroit says with a devilish smile. "In all my years, I've never been asked to be in a fake wedding before. Fake dates, for sure. Fake orgasms, more than I can count. But a fake wedding? I'm just so glad we now have the constitutional right to pretend to get married. Until it gets taken away by Clarence Thomas's wife."

For a moment, J forgets Skye is also in the room . . . and then, when he remembers, he feels immediately guilty. For their part, Skye falls as silent as the furniture.

"Now, how does this work?" Detroit asks, unraveling a scarf and draping it over the sewing machine while keeping at least a half dozen other scarves on. "I can't say you'll be the first person to ever write a song about me, but you'll definitely be the first person who's ever asked first."

"I ask you a few questions, get a sense of you for the wedding. I mean, we should call it a wedding, even though it's obviously not a wedding."

"Yes, don't get this one's hopes up," Detroit warns. It's only after he lowers himself onto the couch that J sits. Skye remains hovering until Detroit shoots them a glance. Then they, too, sit.

"So . . . how did the two of you meet?"

"Oh, lord, *no*," Detroit answers immediately. "That is the least interesting, most obvious question. How do you expect to get *art* out of *that*?"

J looks to Skye for help, but Skye just looks to their feet.

"Okay," J says. "We can skip that one. I understand that the two of you are polyamorous?"

Detroit likes this line of conversation more. "We are," he says, leaning toward J. "There's a very stringent application process to join us. But don't worry—you're already on the fifth page of the application, at least."

J can dismiss this flirtation because it is in no way sincere. It's simply the way Detroit talks.

"Is it exclusive polyamory?"

"What do you mean by that?"

"Sorry. I mean, is it the two of you with the same other partners or do you . . . go your separate ways?"

Detroit laughs. "Such binary thinking! Can't it be both?"

J feels himself blush. "Of course."

"Sometimes we play together. But we're also free to see other people."

Now it's Skye who laughs. Not an open, wanting-to-be-heard laugh. A private laugh that's spilled over to public.

Detroit swings his focus to Skye and asks, "Do you find that funny?"

"No . . . it's just that phrase. *Seeing other people*."

"What about it?"

"It's actually the opposite of what it means, isn't it? You're not just *seeing* them. We all *see* other people—it's a question of what we do when we see another person and want them. Yes, you and I see other people. But we also do much more than see them. You more than me." Skye turns to J. "You understand what I mean, don't you? I'm just making a point about how silly that phrase is."

"I'm sorry," Detroit tells J. "I had no idea this was show-off time! Suddenly my partner has become a lexicogitator."

"A lexicographer," Skye corrects.

"Yes, *I know the word*," Detroit seethes. "I was just playing with it for our guest."

Skye goes back to looking at the floor. "You're right."

"And let's keep it that way!" Detroit says with an attempt at a lighthearted air. "Now—I've already forgotten your question. Did we answer your question?"

The interview continues on a path that can only be called circuitous.

When J asks them how they spend their days, Skye says they work in costuming, and when they start to say what Detroit does, Detroit shushes them and says, "I want to be a mystery. You can write that down in your notebook. *Detroit is a mystery.*"

J asks about their names.

"I was conceived in the city of that name. But I won't tell you by whom."

"My mom was a hippie. My brother is named Oak."

J asks about their performance art.

"I really think of us as *sensation artists*. It doesn't have to be a *pleasant* sensation, mind you. I am more thrilled by a revulsed audience than a quote-satisfied-unquote one."

"I think it's a fun excuse for our friends to get together. Some groups do Dungeons and Dragons. We do performance art."

J asks the secret to the longevity of their relationship.

"Honesty," Skye says.

"Sharing!" Detroit replies. "Which, in our case, is the same as honesty."

Detroit is now comfortable, in his element. Even though there are no cocktails present, Detroit talks as if to the whole bar. J is reminded of the missing cat, hiding somewhere in the apartment. Perhaps Skye, too, would feel better in another room.

J turns to address only Skye. "What's the most romantic thing Detroit has done for you?"

Skye looks at him, startled for a second. Then, to J's dismay, Skye bursts into tears, soon followed by apologies.

Detroit doesn't move from the couch. J offers up a tissue from a box on the side table.

"Thank you," Skye says. "I guess I wasn't prepared for that one. I just—it's almost impossible to explain. I don't know if you've ever been in a bad place—I mean, a really bad, dark place. The kind of place where you wake up and you have no money, no pride, no possibilities, and you realize you gave up your dreams so long ago that all they can do now is taunt you. That's where I was. Stuck in a basement apartment with a guy I hated so much, hating myself even more. I had this panic attack—I just woke up and my heart was pounding and the only thing I could think was, *This is it. You are going to die here.* But something in me pushed back and said, no, that would just be too sad, too much of a waste. So I got up—I'd been sleeping through the days—and I put on my favorite outfit and I left. I had no idea where I was going, or even if I was ever going to come back. I went to a bar, because of course I went to a bar. And right there onstage is this foul-mouthed bruiser, this defiant motherfucker, and he is taking on the whole crowd. Like, ripping right through it mercilessly. Making fun of their clothes, their laughter, their drinks. But then Detroit gets to me, really sees me and where I am, and he holds back. Even if it ruins all the momentum. Even if it makes people uneasy. The crowd is waiting for the punchline, you know? But instead Detroit says to me, 'This too shall pass. Because you and me—we're going to send it on its way.' And that . . . well, that was the most romantic thing that's ever happened to me.

From anyone. I stayed around until the bar closed that night. And I moved in here the next day." Skye stops for a second, takes a deep breath, composes themself. "I'm sorry again about the tears. I still think about it all the time."

"Because lord knows I haven't said a romantic word since!" Detroit chimes in. Not as caustic as before. A little gentler.

"And how about you?" J asks. "What's the most romantic thing Skye has done for you?"

"Skye humors me," Detroit answers. "They make me feel both adored *and* adorned. I mean, look at me—they've made me so many scarves, I can't bear to go out without at least five of them on. One wouldn't be enough. I want as much of them with me as possible!"

J often follows this question by asking the couple what their greatest fear is. But he's afraid he will only make Skye feel worse. So instead he asks to see more of Skye's creations, and this ends up being the right path to take. Both Detroit and Skye get to their feet, and soon there's a parade of garments, from scarves to coats, silk shirts that flow like dresses and capes that would make even the stampedest bull stop and admire the handiwork before charging. When they're done, the room has been returned to what J imagines is its usual state of chaos. Skye looks around and is mildly horrified, but before they can say anything, J tells them this has been a remarkably helpful afternoon.

J yawns, then rushes to assure his hosts that the yawn is from the jet lag, not the company.

Skye walks him to the door, and they arrange a meeting time for a walk-through of the performance space the next afternoon. J is surprised when Skye gives him a full hug goodbye—surprised to have deserved it, and also surprised by how nice it feels, because once again, it seems led by Skye's sincerity.

It's only later in the evening, when J's body can't decide which time zone's rules it wants to play by, that his mind unspools everything from the interview. Skye was right about "seeing other people," and with a tremor, J wonders if that will come up in his conversation with V. He also steps back and observes Skye and Detroit's overall dynamic; clearly, theirs is a relationship based on Detroit having "saved" Skye. J wonders whether any relationship built on rescue can work in the long run. This is not, luckily, a problem he and V have. They've helped each other, yes. Supported each other. But saved? Hardly.

J does not wonder if this is because neither of them has needed saving . . . or if it's because they each lack the capacity to save anyone besides themselves.

J is up before dawn.

Not for the first time, he wishes he were a runner, because these excess mornings that come from traveling westward would be perfect for sprinting through foreign cities, pounding the pavement while it is still free and clear.

Running would also distract him, because he is nervous about seeing V, nervous about whatever circuitous route their own conversation may take. He is not a fool, and he doesn't expect that V will take one look at him and melt into his arms, telling him that his presence has made her realize how wrong her distance has been. V would never reduce herself to that puddle, and that is—trickily enough—one of the reasons he likes her so much. The best he can hope for here is not capitulation, but détente. "Here's to a warming of our relations" is not a lyric he's ever written, but it wouldn't be entirely out of place in his oeuvre. But V isn't going to be won over by song or wordplay. No, she'll be won over by . . . well, he's not exactly sure what, really.

And not *won over*, he reminds himself. Détente.

He goes out for coffee, but none of the coffee shops are open yet. He settles for an all-hour bodega's lukewarm brew. Back in Julia's apartment, he starts to work on the songs for Detroit and Skye, happy to lose himself in other people's stories, not understanding (or not wanting to understand) that working on other people's stories will inevitably bring him back to his own, even in something as short as a song.

By the time the clock tells him to get ready to meet V, he's ready for a nap. Instead, he rallies, and follows his phone as it tells him how to get to the subway station and which subway to take. Then he follows his phone some more, from the station to the front of V's Midtown office, a place so anonymous he forgets it even as he's looking at it. He texts her to say he's here; he's three minutes early and she says she'll be down in seven.

In this case, seven means ten, which results in J having ten minutes to imagine each burst of elevator release will contain V in its midst. He begins to speculate on what the first moment of their reunion will be like. A hug? A kiss? Speechless wonder? Whether because of jet lag or recent events, his imagination is acting as if they are young lovers being reunited after years apart, even though neither of them is that young, and it's only been two months.

Also, it's questionable whether they're still lovers.

When she finally appears, something is decidedly different about her. He can't pinpoint it, but it's drawn from a combination of the fact that he rarely thinks of her with makeup on and the presence of a new wardrobe she bought for herself in New York, having only packed for a stay of a couple of weeks. Even her jacket, thrown over her arm, is new.

He wants her to smile when she sees him. Cut to the swell of the soundtrack, the small tear in the audience's eye. Even a subtle gasp, a tremor of recognition, would be satisfying. But instead, she looks like he's a deliveryman, here to hand her the salad she's ordered.

She kisses him, but it's quick, too quick. "We only have an hour, so I booked a table in a place nearby," she says as she pulls away. "It's Greek—I hope that's okay."

"That's wonderful," J tells her. "And it's wonderful to see you."

"It's good to see you, too," V replies hurriedly. "It's this way—follow me."

The place she's chosen is named Iris; the man at the front desk speaks to her with such familiarity that J supposes V eats here often. The waiter is equally friendly, although in this case J thinks he just happens to be a very friendly person.

"The moussaka is very good," V says, barely looking at her menu.

J can't help but feel this is a passive-aggressive move on her part. Surely she remembers that he dislikes moussaka?

"You look nice," J says after deciding on an eggplant dish.

"I'm a shell right now. An exhausted shell. So you're basically complimenting the shell. I'm glad to hear it doesn't look like it's cracking yet."

"Things are busy?"

Oh, yes, things are busy. V spends the next ten minutes talking about how busy things are, what with investors and logistics and Thor being too in love with Meta to do all the management he needs to be doing. Even the friendly waiter stays away, since no break is provided for him to swoop in and take their orders. Only when V pauses for water can he make his move.

J is not uninterested in V's work, but he's much more interested in their relationship and its imperilment. But, as with the waiter, she isn't giving him any port to dock in.

It's possible she's nervous. It's possible she's as at-sea as he is.

The frustrating part is that he can't tell.

Not until she finally takes a rest from talking about her job and asks him how his flight was and where he's staying. She is asking about his itinerary, his geography, his transit experiences. She isn't asking about *him*.

Polite. Not sincere.

Her interest might even be genuine. It's just that she's interested in hearing about the least important things.

Polite. Not sincere.

Once his head notices this as a refrain, he can't shake it. And it feels like a worst-case scenario. V can be a bald-faced liar sometimes, a queen of bullshit. But the twist is that the lies are sincere, the bullshit is sincere, in that they always have a force of conviction behind them. Negative conviction, perhaps, but not the neutered neutrality of politeness.

The polite thing would be for J to go along with it. Lord knows he is guilty of retreating into politeness all the time.

But, Jesus—not with V.

"What are you doing?" he asks her.

"What do you mean, what am I doing? I'm asking you questions." Her immediate defensiveness is, at the very least, sincere.

"You just asked me about my subway ride here. On what possible plane of existence would you care about my subway ride? How is that even remotely relevant to the conversation we should be having?"

The waiter takes this moment to deliver a mezze plate, compliments of the house.

"Please thank the house for us," J says. The pita looks fantastic, still hot and inflated from the oven. He rips some off and sweeps up some hummus, making it clear he will not speak until V gives him some kind of response.

She holds the moment hostage with a long sip of water, then sets it free with a sigh. "What is it you want? If you want to cut to the chase, so be it. What would you like to be happening right now?"

"I want us to be the young lovers who haven't seen each other in years!" he says, perhaps a little too loudly. (There are looks.) "I know a lot has been happening for you, and I know I'm walking in right in the middle of it . . . but I've come all this way, and I thought I would get more of a greeting than being told we only have an hour. I'm not so naïve that I expected you to fall into my arms. But we've shared our lives for a while, haven't we? At the very least, I would have thought there'd be some recognition of that. Even if it's over, even if we're truly through, isn't what we had worth more than idle conversation?"

"Wow," V says. "I'm not sure I would have asked that question if I'd known that would be the answer. I didn't come here to disappoint you. I thought we could just have lunch. We used to be very good at lunch."

J tries another dip and can't help himself. He says, "This tzatziki is really good. You should try it."

V breaks off some pita but goes for the hummus.

"You told me you didn't fly here for me," she says. "You told me you flew out here for a wedding."

"I did," J says between bites. "I sent you the invitation. It's tomorrow night."

"Then why are you acting like someone who flew here for me?"

"I am acting like someone who still sees your toothbrush every night as he washes up, and still puts out two towels even though I don't know when or if you'll be back. I know you've been living without any trace of me, but I've been living with so many traces of you. I want to know what they mean."

"I told you, Thor loves playing your music in the office. So I'm not entirely without traces of you."

"How gratifying."

"Just trying to support you with the fraction of a cent you get every time it streams."

"Now look who's paying attention."

V shakes her head.

"What?" J asks.

"This is exactly how I was afraid it would go."

"And how is that?"

"*Infuriating.*"

J allows himself a small grin. "Nice to know I can still infuriate you."

He thinks they are falling back into their groove, their banter. A good sign.

Then she pushes her chair back and stands up.

"I honestly don't think I can do this right now," she says.

And now it's doubly frustrating. Because the artifice is gone. The politeness has been put back in a drawer. This is her raw, trembling self. And he still doesn't understand it.

"Please," he says. "Sit down. Let's talk."

She is still holding her napkin, and looks around as if she doesn't know what to do with it. Finally, she puts it over her plate.

"I keep telling you, and you just don't listen," she says. "I'm hanging by a thread here. And you want to throw your weight on me, see if the thread will hold. But I'm telling you, it won't. I can't deal with you and everything else at the same time. I know you think this means I'm choosing here over you. And maybe I am right now. But I'm in it so deep that nothing feels like a choice. And I don't think I can get you to respect that, or even comprehend it. You know how much I hated not having a job, when there was so much uncertainty. You know that nothing has ever been given to me, not by my parents, not by anyone. You know that I wasn't expecting this job to become what it's become. You know these things, but you can't connect them to where I am right now, and what it means. One of the things I've loved about being with you is that you never get in my way. But I also feel I never really tested that. I think you want to be my top priority, and right now I can't do that. When you said you were coming here, I should have simply said *don't*. Because, believe it or not, I didn't want us to do this. This is exactly what I didn't want. I was hoping I'd see you and something else would happen, that it would be casual, low-pressure. But I don't think you're going to let us do anything other than this, so I need to go. I need to pretend you're still over there."

"Look," J replies, "let's just have lunch. You need to have lunch anyway, right?"

V takes her wallet from her purse, opens it, and laughs. "I don't even have cash to leave you for the bill. I'm totally stiffing you here."

"I don't care about the bill. Please. Stay."

But no. Instead of sitting back down, she reaches down and squeeze his hand. Once. Then she lets go.

Infuriating.

"For the record," J says, "I very much would like to chase after you, but I don't want to leave without paying, and I also think you would only hate me for following you."

"For the record," V says, "you are absolutely making the right call."

She kisses him on the top of his head (*infuriating!*) and leaves.

J sits there for a moment, stunned.

Then the friendly waiter comes over, looking concerned.

"Is everything alright?" he asks.

"No," J says. "How can it be?"

The waiter looks at a loss for words, and J decides to let him off the hook.

"Everything will be fine," he says. "Just please, although I'm sure it's very good, don't bring out the moussaka."

J finishes the meal. Of course he finishes the meal. When he gets the check, he sees the waiter has taken the moussaka off.

As if V had never been there.

He knows it won't work to show up at her office with flowers.

He knows it won't work to text her and ask if she'll meet for a drink after she's done for the day.

He knows it won't work to follow her and see if she's meeting anyone else.

He knows it won't work to find the last boom box in Manhattan, hold it over his head, and blast the love songs he's written for her until she comes down to the lobby and lets him take her away from it all.

He knows all the things that won't work.

He just can't find the one that will.

*I still want to see you*, he texts.

She reads it, but doesn't reply.

He should go back to the apartment, work on the songs. But instead he goes to the Museum of Modern Art and walks around. He wishes he could get lost in the paintings, but they too fall out of reach. He feels like he is an exhibit himself, for all the tourists to see. *Man with Failed Reunion*, a collage of worthless words and deeds, a gift of the artist.

*You know that nothing has ever been given to me, not by my parents, not by anyone.*

V feels this, more than any other, is the sentence that J should be focusing on. While his own parents were certainly concerned when he decided to try supporting himself with his music, they never removed the safety net that had been underneath him his whole life. V's family was far more fraught—her father perpetually drunk and perpetually underemployed, her mother a locked box of oddly shaped resentments. When V left home at sixteen, there was no going back and no map forward. She made mistakes and then had to live with those mistakes. J has heard stories of these times, but none of it was visible to him. The woman he met, the woman he fell for, was built from a girl he would barely recognize. She is proud of this evolution, but she doesn't think it would take much to undo it. Like all smart people, she is petrified of making a stupid choice. And when a golden opportunity comes along—and what she's doing with Secret Project is that elusive golden opportunity—that fear is so large that it can influence everything else. J has never felt this way about anything. V knows he hasn't. And now, when this is the sentence he should be focusing on, she's sure he's hearing others instead, the ones more directly involving him. It's human for him to react that way. But that's why humans are such messy creatures.

She doesn't even have the energy to hide in a bathroom stall. When Meta walks into her ramshackle office, V is staring at a calendar pinned to the wall. It shows March of last year, but V's kept it up, because she likes the owl that illustrates it.

"Am I interrupting?" Meta asks, so flatly that V can't tell whether she's being sarcastic or not.

"No," V says, sitting up in her chair, all business.

But Meta doesn't take the hint. Or pushes it away.

"Bad lunch?" she asks.

"Difficult lunch," V says.

"Your boyfriend's in town, right?"

V doesn't remember telling Meta about J's arrival. She realizes she has to start assuming if she tells something to Thor, Meta will end up knowing it.

"Yes. That's who I had lunch with. Even though I ended up missing lunch."

Meta clocks this and pulls out her phone.

"You have to have lunch," Meta says. "I'm ordering you lunch."

Meta is talking to V like they're friends, like they are in Meta's dorm room at NYU commiserating over a bad date. V doesn't know what to do with this.

"Thank you," V says. Then, "Do you know what I want?"

"Yeah," Meta replies. "I pay attention. Just like you. Someone has to around here."

Now the girl is offering even more than friendship. It feels like . . . respect. And that's exactly what V needs right now.

Meta hits her screen a few more times, then says, "There. All set. Fifteen minutes."

"Thank you," V says again.

"I'm honestly not sure how you do it," Meta tells her.

*What?* V wants to know. But the moment for asking passes. As Meta leaves, not sharing why she arrived in the first place, she adds, "Also, I really like your haircut."

This almost undoes V.

J, who's known her for so long, didn't seem to notice.

But this girl, who she's only known for a few weeks, did.

J is early to meet Skye at the performance space, but Skye is even earlier.

Skye takes one look at J and knows something's wrong.

"Wedding jitters?" Skye asks. The space is basically the back room of a bar that's a little too fancy to be a dive and a little too much of a dive to be fancy.

"No, I'm good," J says,

Skye raises an eyebrow. "If this is good, I'd really hate to see bad."

"Did Julia tell you the reason I wanted to spontaneously create a wedding?"

"Oh," Skye answers, in a tone that makes it clear Julia provided the gist. "Reunion didn't go as planned."

J shakes his head.

"Look," Skye says, "we don't have to do any of this. If you're feeling like you just want to get into bed for the weekend and not see another living soul, we can cancel the fake wedding. It would be easy—probably too easy—for me and Detroit to stage a big fight, post it online, and make a big to-do about the ceremony being called off. Your girlfriend will never know the difference. Because, if I may be a little presumptuous, I know full well that heartbreak isn't a noun, it's a verb, and it's also one of the harder verbs to replace with other verbs, like *perform* or *socialize* or, I don't know, *exist*."

J hasn't been thinking of anything that's happened in terms of heartbreak, per se. But now that Skye mentions it . . . well, he feels worse.

"Do you want some whiskey?" Skye offers. "Or a hug? I'm a firm believer in hugging it out."

J wavers, because from yesterday he knows that Skye does give really good hugs. But he also wants to change the subject, wants to create something else to focus on.

"If you don't mind," he says, "I'd like to talk about the wedding. I'd still like to do it. Otherwise . . . I *will* go to sleep for the weekend. And that's not what I should be doing."

"Okay. Detroit should be here any minute . . . but I can start giving you the tour. There ain't much to see."

There's an okay AV setup, and a stage that's maybe two feet off the floor. Not a lot, but enough. There are also poles on the stage. ("There's a pole-dancing class on Wednesdays," Skye explains. "It's strangely popular with people my age who aren't paid very much.") The décor is hardly wedding-friendly—just a few framed posters from fifties and sixties biker movies, which could have just as easily been purchased at IKEA as at a vintage shop.

"I'm sure this isn't what you're used to," Skye says. "You're so nice to do this."

"No, you're nice for letting me do this."

"You know what would be fun? If we got into a total fight over who's being nicer." Skye smiles, and J is charmed. The two of them smile at each other for a beat longer than either would consider normal. Then Skye, a little flustered, checks their phone.

"I'm sure I told Detroit the time," they say. "Let me just text him." They type something quickly, then stare at the phone. Waiting. Waiting. "His phone might be off. We have *that* fight all the time. I say, what good is a phone if people can't reach you? He says, 'It's okay, the answering machine will pick it up.' I swear, that's what Detroit calls it. The answering machine."

"I'm in no rush," J says, feeling much more rooted in Detroit's generation than Skye's.

"Do you want to sit down?"

There are a few chairs at the side of the room ("for when the pole dancers need a break, presumably"). J sits down and Skye turns their chair around so they can straddle it and lean on its back, putting J and Skye face-to-face in a strangely intimate way.

Skye can't hide how glum they're feeling.

"If history's any indication, Detroit's blowing us off. Not deliberately. But I'm sure he got caught up in something—or someone—else, and when he loses track, there's no point in waiting for the train to arrive."

"It's not a big deal. We can just talk about how it'll go, and you can pass it on."

"I know, I know," Skye says. "I just thought maybe Detroit would show up for, you know, our wedding rehearsal."

"I mean, it's not a real wedding rehearsal."

Skye stands up, swings the chair around, and sits back down. "Oh, I'm very aware of that."

"Do you want it to be a real wedding rehearsal?"

Skye leans back and laughs. Then they lean forward and touch J gently on the knee.

"Thank you. You are the only person who's actually asked me that, Detroit included. And the simple answer is, unfortunately, very complicated. Do I wish we were getting married tomorrow? No, I do not. But do I wish that our relationship was in a place where it would make sense for us to get married tomorrow? Well then, yes, I do."

"You want to be monogamous?"

"Hell no! But I do want to be that important to Detroit. Or someone. I would like to have the confidence to say to someone else, 'You. You're the one I want in my life for the rest of my life.' Doesn't mean there can't be anyone else. But as much as I believe in an open relationship, I also believe in constants. Is Detroit the closest thing I have to a constant right now? Absolutely. But does that make Detroit an actual constant, an absolute, enthusiastic constant? Well . . ."

"You've only been together two years, no?"

"I know. But shouldn't it be long enough to at least know whether there's the potential?"

J thinks of V. "Maybe. But even if you feel the potential . . . that's no guarantee that you'll arrive there. Life gets in the way. Or maybe you get in the way."

"Would you fight for her?"

"What do you mean? Like a fistfight?"

"Just answer the question. Would you fight for her?"

"Yes. But I'm not sure it would matter."

"I think Detroit would fight for me. But only if I found a way to make him realize he needed to."

"It sounds like neither of us is in an ideal relationship."

"Come on," Skye says, reaching for J's arm. "I'd settle for something really good."

Skye's hand lingers a little, then goes back to their own lap. It again occurs to J that there might be some flirting going on. But it also could just be the way Skye is, the affection not held back by any self-consciousness.

"Okay," J says, trying to bring it back to business, "let's talk the run of show."

"Sure," Skye replies, sitting up as if they're about to take dictation.

It's pretty basic, really. There will be about seventy "guests" if they're lucky, bribed into attending with drink tickets, Detroit's treat. A friend of theirs who goes by the name Sarah Burnheart will be the officiant. When the time comes, she'll welcome guests (i.e., tell everyone to shut up and listen), give a brief comment on the present state of matrimony (spoiler: not great), and then ask Detroit and Skye to share their vows. This, Skye says, is the true performance art part, because they've been working on them separate from one another, "like a real married couple," and the vows could take two minutes or twenty. No telling. ("Mine will probably take three, tops," Skye promises.) Then Sarah Burnheart will introduce J, who will play his songs. Once he's done, Sarah will ask if anyone objects, and there should be at least a half dozen plants in the audience who will do so, strenuously. Chaos will ensue. The wedding will be called off, and then everyone will drink a little more and go home.

"We have the place until midnight," Skye concludes. "But I'm guessing we'll be done by eleven. Detroit often invites people to the apartment after. You're more than welcome to join, although I can't predict what we will be doing with those people. Could be an orgy, could be a spirited game of Charades. It's hard to say."

J can't tell if Skye is joking or not and errs on the side of believing they aren't.

"Any questions?" Skye continues. "Anything I missed?"

"No, I don't think so. Do you have any questions?"

Skye suddenly looks bashful. But doesn't say a word.

"What?" J asks.

"I mean, the only question that comes to mind is . . . what are you doing after this? I mean, do you want to get dinner or something?"

It's sweet. And sincere. And for those reasons, J knows he has to say no.

"I'm so sorry, but the jet lag is due to kick in any moment now—the second day is always the hardest. Plus, I have some songs to write by tomorrow! You don't want me phoning it in."

If Skye feels rebuffed, their expression doesn't show it.

"Of course," they say. "The songs! I hope we've given you enough to go on. If you end up needing more, you have my number, right? Just text me, any hour. Odds are, I'll be up."

"I promise I will," J says.

They both stand up and chitchat while they walk to the street. They're going in opposite directions—J has no place to go but back to the apartment, and Skye is doing the same. J wonders if Detroit is there or somewhere else.

"Thank you," Skye says.

"No," J corrects, "thank *you*."

"Good lord," Skye replies, "*come here.*"

For a second, J thinks Skye is going to kiss him goodbye. But then their arms open, and here it is, the hug.

And damned if it doesn't feel great again, to be held for a few long seconds. Held, then freed.

The jet lag doesn't come, nor does a text from V. J spends the night grabbing at words. He tries not to be too negative about Detroit, to see things through Detroit's eyes. What has Detroit lost over their life? What have they found in Skye? What makes a person want to reach for the world, even when there's someone right there in their home, in their bed?

J wonders.

V is aware that right now, J is somewhere in this city. Lying in bed, she stares at her phone on the bedside table. She knows that all she has to do is type *Come over* and he will. She has not had sex in two months . . . and who better to break the cycle than the person who she is supposed to be sleeping with in the first place? She wishes, somewhat, that she were the kind of person who could slide into casual without it feeling like a casualty. She can't imagine asking J over without also asking him to stay the night. Which would lead to lying awake beside him. Which would lead to the next morning, and figuring out how he fit into her day. Or days.

Sleep is the easy way out, and she takes it.

Perversely, because of the body clock, J sleeps late. Checks his phone. Doesn't see anything he wants to find.

He has a late lunch with his friend Eric and then drags Eric back to Julia's apartment to play the two wedding songs for him. Then he video calls Julia and plays them for her; she is amused to have a concert coming to her live from her own bedroom. Finally, it's time for him to change into the charcoal suit he brought for the occasion. Guitar in tow, he walks through Brooklyn to the performance space.

Before he steps inside, he texts V, to remind her the address.

Three dots appear. Then they go away.

He steps inside.

The bar is packed; J can't tell whether it's usually a busy bar on Friday nights, or if people are here for the wedding. He's the only one dressed for a wedding, or at least traditionally so. He catches some glances at his suit and guitar case and makes his way to the room in the back. Once there, he breathes a sigh of relief; wedding bell streamers have been hung across the ceiling, and Skye is waiting by the door—waiting for J. When Skye sees him, their face lights with delight; the reaction, J realizes, he'd hoped to get from V the day before.

"The man who made it all possible!" Skye announces to no one in particular. "And looking so dapper."

For their part, Skye is wearing a stylish blazer over an even more stylish silk shirt. Is it a blouse? A pajama top? A really expensive piece of formal wear? J isn't sure, but he *is* sure that it looks fantastic on Skye. J now feels underdressed in comparison.

"How are you doing?" Skye asks, serious now. "Any word?"

J shakes his head.

"Do you think she still might show?"

"Doubtful."

"Well, as our most honored guest, you get unlimited drink tickets. Or I could offer you some of this."

Skye takes a silver flask out of their blazer and tilts it J's way.

J decides to go for the flask over the tickets. He uncaps it, and takes a long swig.

"Honey whiskey," Skye says. "I save it for weddings."

J takes another gulp, then hands the flask back.

"If you need it later, you know where to find it," Skye tells him. Then they head to the stage for set up.

"Do you want to rehearse?" Skye asks. "If you don't want me to hear the songs, I could wait outside."

"No," J says. "I rehearsed earlier."

With that, the door from the bar opens, and Detroit strides in. He's not wearing a wedding dress so much as a demolition of a wedding dress—the white and the lace are there, but they're at all the wrong angles. It's cleverly made (by Skye, J assumes), but Detroit doesn't quite pull it off.

"Our beloved songbird!" Detroit cries. J is relieved to be on the stage so there's a small remove between them. Otherwise, he suspects he'd be subjected to a bombastic embrace to match Detroit's bombastic tone. "Are we ready to start the festivities? Sarah's out there taking Skittles shots. We should probably start before she goes into vodka-drenched sugar shock."

"Sounds good," J says.

Detroit strides back out. Skye removes the flask from their blazer and takes a fortifying dose.

"Here, pass that over," J says.

"Gladly."

Like most alcohol, honey whiskey gets better the more you drink it.

As Skye takes back the flask, they say, "Since this is probably the last time we'll be alone together, I just want to say . . . I'm really glad this happened."

The doors reopen and people begin to shuffle in. Skye jumps from the stage to greet everyone. (Detroit, J notices, remains by the bar.) There are no wings to wait in, and J feels a little too obvious standing by his guitar, so he stations himself in the darkest corner. One last time, he checks his phone. No messages. He turns it off.

The crowd grows thicker—J isn't sure if it's because more people have shown up than expected, or if the room is just smaller than he imagined. Detroit is the last to come in, guiding a woman by the back of her neck over to J. The woman's physique is not unlike that of a turkey—her head is small and thin, her middle is round and wide, and her legs look like twigs. When she opens her mouth to speak, though, she sounds more like a duck—a duck that has smoked two packs a day since infancy.

"So you're the singer, eh?" she says, offering her hand and then squeezing J's with all she's got, which isn't a whole lot. "I always wondered what it would take to get this rascal to tie the knot. Didn't know it'd be some random Swedish guy. Life is just so fucked up, am I right?"

J assumes Sarah knows the wedding isn't real.

"Okay, okay," she continues, looking at everyone milling around. "No one likes to wait for weddings to start. It's always such bullshit—tell you to be there at seven and then you have to sit there like a dumbass for an hour before things actually begin. It would be one thing if they gave you something to read, but those programs, man—they're the worst. It's like, let's tell you what's going to happen just so you can see how fucking long it's going to take, right? People have no idea. They really don't."

With that, she walks up to the stage, turns on the mic, and bellows, "Alright, folks! Let's do this, okay? My name is Sarah Burnheart and you better fucking treat me like a priestess before this night is through. You understand? We're here for an extremely special occasion. How often do you get to see two good people make a huge mistake? All the time, right? Well, tonight we're going to see Detroit and Skye make a *colossal* mistake. It is my honor to help them do this. Now shut up so we can get started."

Skye has quietly stepped beside J.

"I wasn't nervous before," they whisper. "Now I am."

J pats Skye on the back, then lets his hand stay there, to give Skye some support.

"It's a performance," he says. "Just keep telling yourself: It's only a performance."

"Just like every other wedding," Skye replies. Then it's clear they don't like that reply, because they add, "No. That's not fair. I just didn't realize how much it would hurt, to have it be fake."

J wishes he could say, *We can stop it*. But he suspects that there's no way Sarah would let them. The audience is here for a show.

"Can the wedded couple please take the stage?" she intones.

J puts down his hand. Skye squeezes his shoulder as they pass.

"Gaydies and lentlemen, let's hear it for Detroit and Skye!"

The crowd whoops. Some sound more caustic than enthusiastic.

"I am so happy to be joining these two in holy matricide!" Sarah proclaims, then stops for a second to cough. "In our humble community of artists, it's always especially touching when two of our own pair up. Because you know the saying: There's nothing more stable than two artists dating, unless you count nuclear war. But I don't mean to be the golden shower on this parade. No, anyone who's ever seen Detroit and Skye together knows it's meant to be . . . especially if other people are involved! No, no—oh, I see some of you in the audience nodding. Pretty good, huh? But wait—the law has decreed that there can only be two of them in this union. So the rest of you will have to wait for the after party, okay?"

J studies the couple as Sarah talks. Detroit is laughing, a good sport. Skye looks like they want to disappear.

"I want you to know, I got ordained by the Church of the Internet for this! It's true—I got the paperwork and everything. You should see the Church of the Internet's Sunday services. Eighty percent of it is porn. At least."

A few laughs, but probably not as many as Sarah Burnheart had hoped.

"Alright, you're not here for me." ("We're not!" someone in the back yells.) "Didn't you get the memo about *worshipping me*? Don't fuck with the Church of the Internet, bro. We can absolve hit-men just as easily as we can marry a pair of queers."

Now Skye looks to Detroit, who nods and moves forward to get the mic.

"I see the wedded couple is eager to exchange their vows. Is it going to be youth before beauty or beauty before youth?"

"I'll go first," Skye says.

"Eager to get it over with, eh? Believe me, I felt that way with Detroit, too. But don't worry—that was before you were born!"

J wants Detroit to tell Sarah to stop, but instead Detroit laughs and gestures for Skye to take the spotlight.

J notices that Skye does not thank Sarah Burnheart when she passes over the mic. They reach into their blazer, and for a moment J thinks they're going to drain the rest of the whiskey from the flask. Instead they pull out a stack of index cards.

"Detroit," Skye begins. But Detroit stays behind, doesn't step up to stand next to Skye. Undeterred, Skye pivots, turns their back on the audience to speak directly to the person they are supposed to be marrying. They take a deep breath . . . "I vow to be there when you need me and to stay out of your way when you need me to stay out of your way. I vow to help you move the boulders that life throws in the road, and vow to turn those boulders into planters, so we can grow from our misfortunes. I vow to keep bringing colors into your days and nights, colors you can wear, colors you can feel, colors that decorate every piece of our life together. I vow to try harder to squeeze the toothpaste from the bottom, because I know how much it annoys you when I don't. I also vow to put the cap back on. Neither of these are metaphors or sexual references. I'm really talking about toothpaste here. I vow to let you into my bad moods as well as my good ones. I vow to try, and try harder, and try even more, even when all I can feel is the strain. I vow to be a source of brightness. I vow to rub your feet and massage your back and take the things off your mind that hurt you the most. I vow to be honest. I vow to be with you so long that we can't remember what happened in what year. I vow to never listen to you when you say you're giving up sugar. And I vow, more than anything else, to be yours. Not exclusively, but primarily. Not lightly, but purposefully. With joy and gratitude."

The crowd has grown quiet as Skye has spoken, and now they cheer. From the side, J can see Skye try to catch their breath. Detroit, meanwhile, looks moved for the first time this evening.

Skye holds the microphone out, and Detroit takes it. They face each other in front of the audience, just like at a real wedding.

"Damn it, Skye," Detroit says. "I wrote something down, too. I have it folded here in my cleavage. But it's . . . it's not what you just said. I just—you caught me off guard. I mean, I vowed things like fucking with the patriarchy and making sure to never wake you up when I get in after you're already asleep. I just—what is it you want me to say? You know how I am with vows. They always seem like a good idea at the time, but that time passes pretty quickly. When I was your age, one of my deepest vows was to never get married, to never give in to the madness that strikes everyone else. When my sister got married, it cost as much as a year of school for me. I mean, that's madness, right? And I thought that tonight wouldn't be like that, obviously. But those vows. Those are serious vows. Mine aren't serious. And I guess the one vow I can keep is to not disrespect you by reading them. I thought it was a jest. Honestly, I did. Now I feel on the spot, and my brain just isn't getting where it needs to be. I love you. Let's be clear about that—I love you. I don't have to vow to love you, because it's already there, and I don't think it's going anywhere. You talk about gratitude; well, I'm nothing but grateful to have you in my life. You're young and talented—you could do better than me. But no, I'm the person you come home to. I appreciate that. As for the rest, the being only with each other forever part—you and most people in this room know how I feel about that. How *we* feel about that. But, yeah . . . I guess that's my vow. I vow to keep it like it is. Because it really works, as far as I'm concerned. Cheers to that."

Detroit goes to embrace Skye, but Sarah intercedes, putting out her arms like a boxing referee. "Not yet!" she hollers, even without the mic. "Not 'til I say so!"

Skye's back is now entirely to J, so he can't really tell how they're taking all this. The crowd, too, is milling uncertainly. There aren't cheers like there were for Skye's vows.

Sarah takes the mic back from Detroit and says, "Alright, folks. We've had the vows. Or at least one set. So now it's time for you all to be serenaded by our wedding singer. He's here all the way from Sweden, which I'm told is even farther away than New Jersey, if such a thing is possible. Take it away, wedding singer. I apologize I can't remember your name."

J takes the stage to polite applause. He puts the mic in its stand, plugs in his guitar, tunes for a second. Sarah, Detroit, and Skye line up on one side of the stage.

The honey whiskey provides a nice undertone.

"I'm so happy to be here to celebrate Skye and Detroit's big day. They've asked me for two songs, one for each of them. Unusual . . . but I can see how it makes sense here. We'll start with Detroit's song."

There's a single, blinding spotlight, so J is relieved he has a reason to look to the side of the stage, to sing to the subject of the song.

> He enters the room like a spoon
> enters a bowl of soup
> He'll look at you like a tasty crouton
> a crispy bamboo shoot
> He'll let you have a taste if you want
> He believes in sharing the stew

> And because he holds this to be true
> he'll always stay true to you
>
> You have to try everything once
> and then you have to try it again
> Don't bother to knock or ring the bell
> his door is always open
> Know that if this makes you insecure
> if this is something that bothers—
> That he'll always stay true to you
> (and his fourteen other lovers)

There are some drunken cheers when J is done, and one person laughingly yelling out, "I'm always true to you—in my fashion, baby!" Detroit hams it up, bowing as if he's been given a medal. Skye remains in the eye of the storm, observing without reacting.

"Okay," J says. "Now, fair being fair, it's time for Skye's song. I have really enjoyed the time I've spent with them, and really hope they feel this song in some way captures them and how they exist in the world."

> Skye
> What does it mean to be kind?
> The things they taught us as a child?
> To say thank you and to smile
> And to send a birthday card
> to the weird kid
> who no one liked?
>
> Sometimes
> I've found those gestures to be lies
> But then I've found myself on trial
> Walking the loneliest of miles

And how much it means
just to be seen
in those times

Skye
You must have X-ray eyes
You saw right through my fake smiles
You know how kids wait to cry
Until they have permission
A safe haven
Where it's alright

Do the world a favor and come out tonight
Do the world a favor and come out tonight
Everybody wants to see
Skye
We want to see
Skye

Skye
Love letters want replies
If you keep sending them despite
getting no answer
from the other
mail your hopes
to another

Skye
I wanna get you drunk and high
I want to hear your heart sigh
Get on the dance floor
What do you long for
in your life?

> Oh
> Do the world a favor and come out tonight
> Do the world a favor and come out tonight
> Everybody wants to see
> Skye
> We want to see
> Skye

As J sings, the rest of the room doesn't exactly fall away, but Skye's response is the only one that matters. To J, this is the first song in a long time that actually feels like a gift. Maybe because it's only for one person instead of two. Maybe because he knows Skye needs it more than most people would on a real wedding day.

When the song is over, he's barely had time to take his hand from the guitar strings when Skye comes over to him. There are tears in their eyes.

There is such power in being seen, in seeing yourself in a song.

"Thank you," Skye says. "Truly, thank you. I can't—I just can't—"

Words failing, Skye reaches out and goes to hug J, then sees the guitar. So instead they raise their hands up, take each side of J's face, and kiss him.

J is not expecting this. And there is such appreciation, such need in that kiss . . . he is not not-kissing Skye back. Because whose need is it? Whose appreciation? Then Skye pulls away and J feels his body being shifted, and all of a sudden it's Detroit kissing him, kissing him hard, and then Skye eases J away from Detroit and takes control of kissing J again. This time, when Skye's done, they hold out a hand to block Detroit.

There are more cheers from the crowd than ever before. J tries to laugh himself out of it, retreat from the mic, retreat from the wedded couple.

"Well, well, well!" Sarah Burnheart quacks into the mic. "I'll bet your sister's wedding wasn't like *that*, Detroit!"

J puts his guitar back in its case. He walks off the stage.

He wonders if anyone even remembers the songs.

Except Skye. He's pretty sure Skye does.

"Now, if there's any objection to these two tying the knot, now's the time to object. Because if you don't, I'm going to be sure to use the powers vested in me by the Church of the Internet."

J is trying to avoid eye contact with the crowd, but he looks up when nobody speaks out. He's sure Skye said there were a bunch of people prompted to derail the wedding.

But none of them are saying anything.

Sarah Burnheart looks like this is the best thing that's ever happened to her. "No one?"

J looks at Skye, who seems about to pass out.

They don't want this to happen. But they aren't fearless enough to object.

*Come on, people*, J thinks.

Detroit finds it hysterical. He takes a ring out of his pocket. Not a wedding ring.

"Just something I had hanging around," he tells the crowd. "From my days performing as Pubic Zirconia."

The crowd whoops.

"Going once!" Sarah calls.

Skye's eyes meet J's again.

The message is clear: *Help*.

"Going twice!"

Nothing. No one.

*Fuck it*, J thinks. Then he calls out, "I object!"

The crowd turns to him. They are not happy.

"The wedding singer objects!" Sarah Burnheart is incredulous. "Why do you object? You want back in on the action?"

*Skye deserves someone who will truly love them*, he wants to say.

But how can he say that?

So instead he says, "This whole thing is a sham. My sham. You're all here so I could debut two new songs. This is something my record company likes us to do, surprising strangers to launch new music. It's huge on Swedish TikTok. Detroit and Skye are just playing along. They have no desire to get married. There's no such thing as the Church of the Internet."

(There actually is, but J doesn't know that.)

J has faced some tough crowds, but actual booing is rare. The Brooklyn performance art community does not like being scammed. At least not by a singer-songwriter.

"I think you need to leave," Sarah Burnheart says into the mic. This gets some applause.

J doesn't have to be asked twice. He takes his guitar, and the crowd parts for him. People say, "Are you for real?" and, "There's no way those songs get traction on TikTok, not even in Sweden," and, "Well, the kiss was a nice touch—c'mon, it *was*."

Out on the sidewalk, he reaches into his pocket to check his phone for directions. As he does, he hears someone call his name and turns to see Skye coming out the door of the bar, alone.

"Hi," they say.

"Hello," J replies. "That was . . . something."

"I don't even know how to begin to thank you."

"I got you into this mess in the first place."

Skye shakes their head. "The mess was already there. You just managed to find a reason for it to be on a stage tonight. Which was, in retrospect, maybe a mistake."

"I'm the last person to give relationship advice, but . . . you should be with someone whose vows match yours. They don't have to be the same. But they should match."

"I know. But I think the important thing for tonight was . . . well, not getting married."

"Mission accomplished."

"I know, I know." The two of them hang there for a moment; there's either a lot more to say or nothing more to say, and both instinctually retreat to the latter. Skye goes on, "I suppose I should get back in and make sure Sarah doesn't forge my signature on whatever paperwork she printed out from the internet. But . . . I hope you don't mind, but can I ask you one more favor?"

"Sure," J says. He knows it's not going to be an invitation to the after party.

"Can you send me the song? I just . . . it would mean a lot to me to be able to listen to it. Just a little life raft I can keep with me at all times."

"Of course," J tells them.

"One last hug," Skye says. J obliges. They hold for as long as Skye needs. Then they say goodbye and Skye heads back into the bar.

J genuinely has no memory of how to get back to Julia's apartment. He hates that he is so dependent on his phone, but it's either that or catch a cab. Except the address . . . is also on his phone.

He powers it back up, and while he's on the maps app, he gets a notification of a text message from V. He quickly swipes over to read it. He's expecting an excuse, or maybe to be told to stop texting her.

Instead she's written:

*The three of you make such a beautiful throuple.*
*Best wedding I've been to in years.*

## THE SIXTH WEDDING

J writes back: *But what did you think of the songs?*

To his surprise, V replies immediately. *I think it's clear who your favorite was. It was sweet to see you inspired by such sweetness.*

J ventures, *Is it the kind of song you'd want to hear again? Or perhaps you have other requests?*

V volleys, *A private performance?*

J looks at the Brooklyn storefronts around him, their eyes closed for the evening. How long ago did V leave the venue? He curses himself for not paying more attention to the crowd . . . and is disturbed that he didn't notice her. He doesn't want to make the same mistake twice. Could she be hiding in a doorway, watching him text?

*Yes*, he replies. *A very intimate performance.*

A month ago, this wouldn't have felt like a risk. But now it does. Flirtation is always a wave between two people, and it used to be that he knew its rhythms with V. Now he feels unsure about when it's going to crest.

He's even more unsure after getting V's response: *I see.*

Surely, he thinks, there will be more.

He waits.

And waits.

Okay, so it's his turn. He types, *I happen to have my guitar with me, so am available now for an engagement.*

The three dots appear and stay for a while. Is she typing something lengthy, or merely rewriting the same sentence over and over?

Finally, more words arrive:

*It's not that I forgot what it was like to see you perform . . . but I don't think I was prepared for how it would feel to be standing there, watching. I was sure you didn't know I was there, because I was sure if you saw me, I'd see the change. I would see your awareness. I liked getting to see you without me in the room. But I also missed being in the room, because it made me realize how much you share it with me when I'm there.*

A group of boisterous late-night teenagers passes J as he reads. One of them jostles his arm, but he barely notices. His obliviousness makes some of the teens laugh. Only their laughter makes him look up, and when he looks up, the teen who jostled him stops laughing and shoots him a look that says, *Oh, dude, you're going through some deep shit, aren't you?*

J types, *Where are you right now? Are you still in Brooklyn?*

She replies, *I'm in transit. Though that statement will still apply when I get home.*

*Would you like me to follow?*

*I would like you to follow. And I wouldn't like you to follow. I feel both things at once. I don't know how to decide between them. Or if I should decide anything right now.*

*I would like to be there with you.*

*I hope I don't sound presumptuous if I say I know that. I know what you want. I don't take that for granted. Or maybe I do. I don't know what's fair anymore. To you, to me, to us. I imagine you've picked up on that.*

*That may have come across at lunch.*

*Yes, sorry about that.*

*I'm sorry too.*

*For what?*

*I don't know*, J types. Then he knows he has to do better, so he adds, *For coming here, I guess. For putting you on the spot. The not-knowing was growing too invasive, too persistent. I had to do something to know for sure what was happening.*

V replies, *But there's only one answer you want . . . and I don't know that I can give it to you. Not without it being a lie.*

*A lie?*

*I'm not saying it would be a lie to answer that I want to be with you. I'm saying it would be a lie to give any answer, to say I know what I want right now.*

*So there's hope.*

*You're putting me on the spot again. I don't know how to answer that without either getting your hopes up or knocking them down.*

Now it's J who types *I see*, without realizing it's an echo of V's earlier remark.

There's another pause. J has almost reached the subway. He needs to know what to do, where to go.

*What was the line in the Skye song about being a kid?* V asks.

Instead of typing it out, J hits the microphone button and sends it as a voice message.

> You know how kids wait to cry
> Until they have permission
> A safe haven
> Where it's alright

V must listen to it a couple of times, because it's a full minute before she writes anything back.

*Yes, those lines. I wasn't expecting them, especially after the first song. They really hit me.*

J responds, *I can definitely include the song in our private performance. I won't even make you wait until the encore. I'm at the subway station now . . . where should I go?*

Another pause. J looks at the electronic board beyond the turnstiles and sees the next train is arriving in three minutes.

V texts, *I think you should go back to where you're staying. Can we rain check the private concert?*

*But it's not raining.*

*I'm the rain in this scenario.*

*Got it.*

*Let's talk tomorrow.*

*Please.*

*Goodnight.*

*Goodnight.*

*PS—I really did like the sky song.*

*Thank you.*

When J gets back to the apartment, he doesn't want to feel lonely, so he checks his Instagram. It is not particularly surprising to learn that Skye and Detroit's friends document every single moment they experience and then tag it within an inch of its life. There are hundreds of photos of J at the fake wedding, especially during the group kiss.

J sighs and feels old.

He dodges all the comments and sees there are a few direct messages in his inbox. Some are from fans, cheering his "experimentation." Two are from people he knows—one a guitarist who he often gets a drink with when he's in New York, and one a woman named Tara, with whom he has a less straightforward relationship.

Roughly a dozen years ago, J met Tara at a party (possibly Julia's?) and then made plans to go on a date with her the following night. The next afternoon, J was walking through the city and realized they hadn't pinned down the particulars of where and when they'd meet. The good news was that he'd written her number down on a piece of paper, and he still had the piece of paper in his jacket pocket. The bad news was that his phone was dead. The search for a way to call her inspired a song called "Increasingly Obsolete," which has since proven to be a popular obscurity for listeners willing to dig deep enough to find it:

> I'm calling from the last payphone in New York
> After looking for quarters on the ground
> I don't have much time, I'll cut it short
> Since you're probably hearing more static than sound

At the end of the song, whatever connection they've had is thrown into the junkyard of obsolescence, like so many *E.T.* Atari games and Garfield phones.

> I've emptied my pockets for nickels and dimes.
> All my hope has been put in the slot.
> But just when I think I've reached you, a voice cuts in
> And says the connection's been lost

Tara had been amused to receive a collect call, but the date itself hadn't really transcended amusement. J honestly can't remember whether they kissed or not. He would have forgotten her entirely, except for the song. And she might have forgotten him entirely . . . except for the song. At some point on the date, he must have mentioned the payphone idea, because when the song first came out, he heard from her again. She emailed to ask if, ha ha, the song was about her. J didn't have the heart to make the distinction that the song was about a circumstance that arose because of her, but it wasn't particularly about her. So he (generously, he thought) told her that the song wouldn't have existed without her, and in her account it became her song. A few weeks later, she emailed again to say she was going to be at one of his shows. (In Boston, maybe?) At that show, he dedicated the song to her. That cemented it. In her mind, she was his orange-feeding Suzanne, his envisioned Johanna, his Emily whenever he may find her or his Emma forever ago.

Now she is messaging to say she's seen he's in New York City—which, small world, is where she's living now! And not just that! She's getting married next weekend, and she *knows* he likes to play at weddings. It's short notice, but doesn't it all seem so serendipitous? How can she resist asking if he'd be willing to play *her song* as part of the ceremony? Wouldn't that be *amazing*?!?!?!

It is now late at night after a long, emotionally twisted day, which means the best course of action (always) is to get some sleep and figure it out in the morning. But, paradoxically, one of the side effects of it being late at night after a long, emotionally twisted day is that best course of action is profoundly illegible to the mind's eye. So other courses are taken instead.

*That's wonderful!* J types. *I'll be there!*

(The best course of action at this hour never ever involves two consecutive exclamation marks.)

J feels a brief satisfaction from giving a person he owes nothing something she wants. Then, five minutes later, he wonders what the hell he's doing and gets angry with himself. Five minutes after that, he turns philosophical, wondering if there is, in fact, a difference between a moment of weakness and a moment of generosity.

What he doesn't admit to himself—not while he's philosophical, not while he's brushing his teeth, not while he's trying to make a pleasing sleeping arrangement with the available pillows—is that by saying yes to this wedding, he's given himself at least one more week in New York. And that has nothing to do with Tara or generosity.

Whether it has anything to do with weakness . . . that is still to be determined. So he will stay in New York longer to determine it.

The next morning, J wakes to find a response from Tara that has the appropriate number of exclamation marks for the situation, plus a few heart emojis thrown in for emphasis. She provides him the time and place for the wedding and tells him he shouldn't go to any trouble to dress up, get a band, etc. His appearance is already guaranteed to be a highlight of the wedding. (J appreciates that he will be *a* highlight but not *the* highlight.)

Ten minutes after her first message, there is a second one.

*Oh! The man I'm marrying is named Hugh. After years of online dating, I ended up meeting someone by joining a runners' club! I figured if anyone could find me charming after running 10K, I'd be a fool to let him go! It's his second marriage. It's my first (which I think you know ☺). We've been together for two years now, which might seem a little soon—it does to my mom!—but we're both more than ready for the step. On one of our first dates I told him about the song you wrote for me, and one of the first things he did after we moved in together—I still can't believe he did this!—was he somehow found an old payphone that still works (?!?!?) and he had it installed in our kitchen. His daughter (a handful!) thought it was super weird, but it's one of my favorite things about our apartment. And I guess I have you to thank for that! Anyway, let me know if you have any questions. And (oh, the awkward part!) if there's a fee or anything else we can do (charity?) to thank you for doing this, please let me know. I am sure you have hundreds of other ways to spend a Saturday night. (And of course if you want to bring a guest and stay for the reception, please feel free . . . but don't feel any obligation. As I said, I know you probably have plenty of other places to be!)*

There is also an earlier message from Skye, from four in the morning (the tail end of *their* long, emotionally twisted day):

*I couldn't go to sleep without thanking you again for your song. A lot of my friends have sent me videos of you singing it, and so far I haven't been able to watch it without crying. There's something about it that makes me very happy and also something about it that makes me very sad, because I don't know how someone I don't know can see these things while people much closer to me can't. But my point is that it's very special to me, and I would love to get your address so I can sew you a little something as a thank you.*

No messages from V, but J isn't particularly expecting any. It is still very early for a Sunday; J's body is still clinging to Swedish time, but V hasn't been living that way for a while now.

J goes for a walk, gets breakfast. He messages Tara to thank her for the details and to tell her that Hugh sounds great. He messages Skye with his address, but also adds that he'll be in New York for at least another week. Finally, once the clock ticks past ten, he messages V a simple *Good morning*. He figures it will apply whenever she's awake. (Assuming it's before noon.)

When this is done, he sits back down on his bed and stares at his hands without realizing he's staring at his hands. His thoughts have borrowed the energy from the rest of his senses, molding them into a profound indecisiveness. Being in New York, in someone else's apartment, feels like limbo. He's not on vacation—not really. He's not on tour. But he's also not home. He knows he could launch himself into his emails; nobody he's answering needs to know where he is, especially at a moment when the wakefulness of the time zones overlaps. Except the placeless place of cyberspace also feels like limbo, perhaps more so than anywhere else.

An hour and ten minutes after he sent his morning greetings, V replies and forces his mind to moor itself again.

*Thor and Meta have taken a helicopter ride upstate—I don't even know what that means, except that I'm free for a few hours. Have you eaten?*

Since it's eleven thirty, J isn't entirely sure which meal he is or isn't supposed to have eaten. Either way, the answer is: *I'd love to meet up.*

*I promise to stay for the full meal this time*, V replies. Then she sends him a link to a café in Brooklyn.

J wonders what it means, that she's coming to his borough.

He remembers how nervous he was, the first few times they dated. (Dated? Mated? Which was the primary instinct?) Partly he was nervous because of the way they'd met, with her as Tom's date. But mostly it was the twofold intimidation that comes from wanting to be with someone you find to be spectacular. Their spectacular nature is itself intimidating, and you wonder how you could possibly measure up, because you feel they are inherently (pick any that apply) smarter/more beautiful/more comfortable in their skin/more popular/happier/saner/sexier than you. And then there is the intimidation of the wanting itself—it is so much easier to date or mate when you don't particularly care about the results. The more you care, the more you worry you will fuck it up. And the more you worry you will fuck it up, the more intimidating it gets.

At the start of the relationship, J was certain that he was a better musician than V, and he soon discovered he was also much better at keeping his apartment clean. But other than that . . . he was willing to concede that V might be his better in all other regards. It was only when he got to know her more than it got more complicated, and the more complicated it got, the less intimidating it was. It wasn't that she became any less smart or sexy; it was just that these qualities were wedded to her more vulnerable qualities, her own bouts of doubt. Comparison became situational, not empirical, and their relationship became a relationship, not a contest or a puzzle.

He liked that part.

It hasn't gone back to the start now, but a new kind of intimidation has crept in. He handed her such power over his happiness, over his plans, without even realizing he had done so. Now, he has no idea how she will use this power . . . or if she will choose to relinquish it entirely.

He doesn't want it back. He still wants her to have it. He also wonders if he's a fool to feel that way.

Maybe V chose this place so they wouldn't have the intermediary of a waiter. They order at the counter, get their premade sandwiches handed over on white plates alongside their coffee. As they walk to a table, they make small talk about the wedding. V is wearing a casual purple dress that J remembers well; he takes some comfort that there's a kind of continuity with her Swedish self, even if this New York City self seems like a more tired version.

"I wish I'd seen you there yesterday," J tells V when they sit down. "I would have very happily escaped with you after the vows were done."

"Yes, those vows." V shakes her head. "The whole thing made me sad. I'm not even sure why."

"The imbalance between them?" J asks, thinking of poor Skye.

"Maybe that. But honestly, they didn't seem to mind the imbalance too much. At least not in the beginning. I think that can be navigated, if both sides know what they're doing. It was just so . . . performative. And, look, I know all weddings are performative, and that you're a wedding performer. But now everybody is performing all the time, aren't they? I think it would be hard to be an actual performer during the mass performance our culture is becoming. There are so many times when I'm sitting in meetings about Secret Project, thinking about how people are going to use it, and I have to tell you—it exhausts me. All of it exhausts me. How performative we've all become. But it's not like I'm going to bring that up with Thor or the investors. It's the whole reason we're there. To monetize people's desire to control how they're seen, to get gratification from how their words and images are received. To give them the platform to exploit themselves . . . at least until the next platform comes along and makes ours a relic, a floating vessel of dead profiles lost in a sea no one sails anymore."

"Those certainly sound like the words of an exhausted individual," J ventures. "You seem tired."

V grunts at the obviousness of this observation, then says, "You think?"

"You need your sleep."

This isn't just an adage on J's part. It's something he and V have talked about. While he has the ability to be both a night owl and an early bird, she grows shakier the less sleep she has. Many nights he would come home very late from a gig and he'd crash on the couch, knowing that even the slightest noise in the bedroom might cause a ripple effect through her day.

V seems to understand that J's words aren't empty, that they are being offered by someone who knows her. She doesn't have a sarcastic response. Just more tiredness.

"I've been trying to sleep," she says. "Honestly, I have. And Thor is good about that—the workdays are long, but when they're over, they're over. The problem is more with the days themselves, and what they take out of me. That's what it feels like at this point; the taking is outpacing the giving."

"Can't you get a few days off to recharge?"

"No. Not now. I have to see it through . . . and then, who knows? I used to wonder about those people who left Facebook or Google early in the ride. *How ridiculous!* I thought. *Cashing in before the real cash came to town.* But I'm starting to get it. You have to get to a point where you're compensated for all you've done . . . and then you can step away before it takes over more of your life. I don't know yet if I'm looking to get to that point or not. It's a day-by-day thing. And in the meantime, I perform."

"Do you enjoy it at all?"

"Sure. It feels great when we're winning. But I get the whole shark tank thing now."

"Shark tank?" J asks.

"I'm in with the sharks, and they all see me as a fellow shark. But my secret is that I know I'm not a shark at all, and I have to keep up the shark pose so they'll let me keep swimming with them. Otherwise, best-case scenario, I'm left behind. Worst-case, they eat me alive."

"And where do I fit into this shark tank?" J can't help but ask.

"That's exactly it," V says. "You're on the other side of the glass. I know you're there. I know you can see I'm not a shark. But there's nothing you can do to help me. If I think too much about you out there watching me, I will lose my place."

"Is that what this is about? Is it *work* that's separating us?"

V takes a sip of coffee before replying. "I don't know how to explain this without hurting you. In a way, yes, it's the work. I have no doubt that if I'd never met Thor, if the company hadn't gotten the attention it's gotten, I'd still be back home with you. That *has* separated us. But when I think about the end of my time in New York, when I think about what my next step should be . . . going back to you feels like going backward. It feels like trying to squeeze myself into clothes I've outgrown. I know you want to know why, and I can't tell you why. Last night . . . it would have been so easy to invite you over. And enjoyable. But I am super conscious of not misleading you. Or myself."

J feels there is something he should be able to say here, some bridge he can create for her to use to cross back to him. But he can't find his way to those words. He understands she is in the shark tank without him. He knows he can't break the glass between them, that there isn't any safety for either of them in doing that. This isn't intimidation, really. It's more like the perils of self-awareness, the inability to wrestle the situation into a form that can be pinned down.

"I am here for you," he tells her. "I can stay here for you as long as you might need me. If you want me to come over, I'll come over. If that doesn't feel right, I understand."

Something has shifted, because she doesn't push this offer away.

"I appreciate that. But I don't want you sitting around waiting for me. Here or anywhere else."

"It's okay for me to stay longer," J assures her. "I have another wedding to play next weekend."

As they eat their sandwiches, he tells her about Tara; somehow, V has never heard the story behind the payphone song. She doesn't even seem familiar with the song itself. (J is not offended; it's a *very* deep cut.)

When he's done telling her the story, V says, "Her husband-to-be can't possibly want you to play that song at their wedding."

"Why do you say that?" J asks. He explains about the payphone Hugh bought for her.

"He was trying to neutralize your influence, take some of your territory. Why would anyone want to hear another man's song about his wife at their wedding?"

"It's not about her, really."

"That's not how he sees it, I'm sure. At the very least, he thinks you slept together, and that it's your night of passion, as much of the song, that Tara remembers."

"I don't even think we slept together!"

"You can't remember?"

"I'm sure of it," J says. (He's not.)

"What I'd suggest is that you turn it into a wedding song. Change the last verse or something. Take yourself out of it. Make it about them."

"That's not what she asked me to do."

"Trust me. It will be better for her if Hugh doesn't think you're serenading her with your lost romance on their wedding day."

"It wasn't a lost romance!"

"To you. You have no idea what it was to her. People rarely connect in identical ways. You cannot determine how much a moment matters for the other person."

J wonders how this applies to whole relationships, if what V is saying is also about the two of them. But she doesn't extend the statement in their own direction, and instead changes the subject and asks about some friends back home. They spend the rest of the meal like that, in the safer harbors of other people's shores. At the end of lunch, he asks if they can meet up again, and he decides to take it as a good sign that she doesn't say no or that she isn't sure, and instead says they can figure out a date once she sees how the work week is going to play out. She assumes J will be free whenever, and he doesn't challenge this assumption, because they both know it's true.

"Look," V says as they're leaving, "about that song for the wedding. I still don't think you get it, but I think I can help. You see, at first, even for me, when you wrote a song and I knew that it was about us, or inspired by us, I made the mistake of thinking that it was only about us, that it was basically a message from you to me. It took time for me to realize that it wasn't only about us, that even if I was an element and you were an element to it, the song wouldn't work unless it tapped into larger elements. If anything, by trying to figure out you and me, you were also trying to figure out bigger things, more often than not love. It was still interesting for me to hear the songs and to try to figure them out myself. But I knew that even if I was inside the song, it was never really mine. Now, I'm not saying you had the same kind of relationship with this woman; I know you didn't. But odds are, she's never been a part of any other person's song. So she will want to think it's more hers than it really is. And you don't need to correct her, if it means something to her. You just need to shift it a little to be less about her and more about her and her husband, for their wedding. You see what I'm saying?"

J wants to ask her more, wants to ask what she hears in his songs. What does she find about herself? What does she find about him?

But she's already leaving; their conversation is already over. So he simply nods, and they say goodbye. Later that afternoon, J decides maybe he should play around with Tara's song a little bit.

It does seem that time has proven the song right, at least in terms of payphones: They have completely disappeared from the streets of New York. J can even spy some of the alcoves they once called home; now only the metal shells remain, sometimes with a cord dangling out like a dead creature's tail. J is struck by this aspect of time, how you never know exactly what is going to disappear, and when. Things that work can still become obsolete. The only way to avoid this fate is to be the beneficiary of a sentimental connection—there's no other real explanation for why vinyl records remain. Our attachments carry a value. With relationships as well as curios.

It's not too much of a stretch to think that, theoretically, in a year or two, couples won't even need him anymore. If they want a personalized wedding song in the style of Ed Sheeran, or Taylor Swift, or the Beastie Boys, all they'll have to do is type their request into an AI and something will spew out. But will that song really know them, the way a human can know them?

J wanders too far, too much. He realizes he needs to add some structure to his days if he's going to stay here and not rely on V's availability. He scrolls down the contacts in his phone and texts a few who live in New York, including the drinking buddy who messaged him earlier. He also messages Skye again and asks if they want to get coffee or take a walk in a park.

The only way out of limbo is to make plans. So he makes plans.

He and skye meet at a Van Leeuwen and, cones in hand, find a bench in Tompkins Square Park. J feels strangely suggestive as he licks his salted caramel ice cream, futilely trying to prevent the melt from trailing down his fingers. Somehow Skye manages to keep their cone intact without flashing too much tongue.

When they first saw each other, Skye repeated what they'd said in their message about how much J's song had meant to them, what a special evening it had been, and so on. But underneath all the happy words, J could easily spot a restlessness, a sleeplessness beneath. If anything, the exhaustion seems even more pronounced than V's; J is starting to wonder if he is the only person in New York who gets a good night's sleep.

Once the two of them take the last bites of their cones and sit down on the bench, J intends to ask about Detroit and where things stand after the fake wedding. But before he can, Skye asks how things are going with V, and J finds himself explaining that she'd been at the wedding, and that just when he thought she was going to shut off from him completely, she seems to have turned on a backup generator.

"The problem is, she seems to think I'm a figure from her past, not her future. I don't know what to do about that," J confesses.

"Don't take this the wrong way," Skye says, "but I'm starting to think that I know how she feels. Even if what she feels is wrong, in terms of you, it might be right for me, in terms of Detroit."

"Did you have a fight?"

"Have you ever gotten to the point in a relationship where you're not even sure what counts as a fight anymore?"

"Of course."

"Well, I think Detroit and I have been fighting for a long time now. I've gotten so used to it that I don't even notice. Then, after the party . . . he was so triumphant, like a baby king basking in a parade that had been thrown in his honor—confirmation that he *is* the center of the world, as he'd always assumed. I was upset, and he was just *up*. And it would be one thing if he was oblivious, if he was so high that he couldn't see my low. But he saw it, alright. Saw it and made fun of me for it. Told me to lighten up, make out with some of our guests. But this voice inside me that Detroit always drowns out . . . well, I heard it, and it was saying, *I don't want to do this. I don't want to do any of this right now.* So for once, I didn't."

"That's good. You should listen to that voice."

"I knew you'd heard it. When you sang your song . . . I just had the strangest feeling, that somehow you, this person who doesn't know me at all, managed to hear that voice inside me and treat it like it's the best part of me. Which it might be. I don't know."

"It's not as hidden as you think it is. That kindness is a very clear part of who you are."

Skye looks away. "Stop. Please, stop."

"Stop?"

"It's just . . . some things are clearer, but others are more confusing. I—oh, never mind."

"What?"

Skye looks at J again. "I felt more when I was kissing you last night than when I was kissing Detroit. Please don't read too much into that—I'm trying not to. But at the end of the night, you were the person I wanted to be going home with."

J has not anticipated this proclamation. He respects it and doesn't want to react in any way that will make Skye feel bad. But he also doesn't know if there's a way he can react that will make Skye feel better.

He pauses too long. Skye shrinks back, says, "Please forget I ever said that."

"No, no," J says. "It's very kind of you to say. And if I'm being honest, I will tell you that for me it was much nicer kissing you than it was kissing Detroit, as well. But I don't think it's really me you wanted to go home with. I think maybe it was the song. And the way you saw yourself in the song."

Skye smiles. "Sure, it was the song. But I think it was at least a little bit you."

"I'm flattered, really. It's just—"

"It's okay. Please, let's just leave it there. I shouldn't have said anything, because I don't want you to think I'm expecting anything in return. I'm not. Honestly. This really isn't about you and me. It's about me and Detroit."

A little relieved, J asks, "What will you do?"

"I think I'll leave him. Not tomorrow. Not the next day. But soon. Which is many things: scary, heartbreaking, necessary, probably inevitable. Most of all, it's disappointing." Skye doesn't try to hide their sadness, in a way J admires. "I really wanted to live without labels, to have a relationship where things didn't need to be defined. Philosophically, I believe in that. But when it comes to my heart? I'm not sure I can subsist on a casual kind of love. I don't need it to be formal, either. But I need to know what it is, and I need to know that it understands who I am and what I need. I don't think that's what Detroit wants. I think Detroit wants to enjoy himself, and I think he loves me most when I'm enjoyable to him. I was okay with that, because if that was his definition of affection, that meant he did, in fact, feel affection for me. I let my own definition get erased. I didn't even know I was doing it. But now I see I was."

"I wonder if that's part of my problem with V," J says. "Or if she believes that's part of the problem."

Skye looks thoughtful for a moment, then asks, "Do you think it's possible to have a relationship without defining it?"

J wants to dismiss this as a young person's question; Skye is, indeed, a young person, and the way they're asking the question, it's like they actually believe there can be a decisive answer. It's this decisiveness they desire.

J says, "Maybe it is possible for other people to have a relationship without defining it—who knows? But I don't think it's possible for me. Or, perhaps, for you. I think relationships are about definitions, and about constantly talking over and revising and questioning and navigating those definitions. They have to be. Because the words that relationships are based on never have inherent definitions. You and the other person have to define them for yourselves."

"How so?"

"What does *love* mean? What does *trust* mean? *Friendship? Companionship? Desire?* These are all too vast for us to pin down in a word or a sentence or a paragraph. They require a constant conversation, and that's what a relationship is—that constant conversation. It can be arduous and cruel and confusing. But when it works, you hear yourself better than you ever have before. You learn more and more about the complex definitions of all these things, like love and trust, even as you understand you will never be able to articulate them fully."

"I think I'm having more of a conversation with you, right now, than I've had with Detroit in months. Maybe ever."

"But isn't that part of it, too?" J wonders aloud. "The constant conversation isn't something you can have with only one other person. You need to have it with lots of people, to varying degrees. You need to learn things outside the relationship in order to learn things inside the relationship. Random encounters like ours are part of the conversation. Songs can be part of the conversation. Movies. A line of poetry that says something you've always known but never knew how to say."

"Even that tree could be part of the conversation."

"No, I'm not that zen. Fuck that tree. It doesn't talk. It only gives us some shade so we can have our conversation."

"Got it. But, yes, here's to random encounters that lead to conversations that might end up changing your life."

"I'd drink to that, only I don't have anything to drink."

"How 'bout we blink to that?" Skye suggests.

"Blink?"

"Yeah. Let's make that a thing. I'll blink to that!"

"Okay. I'll blink to that."

They look into each other's eyes. They blink a few times, at long intervals. There is a concentration to it, a focus that everyday interaction rarely allows anymore. J sees creases and marks on Skye's face that he hadn't noticed before, and he is sure Skye sees the same in him.

Blink.

(Breath.)

Blink.

(Breath.)

Blink.

"That was strangely intense," Skye says.

"It was," J agrees.

"I liked it."

"I'm not sure how I feel about it. It's much more direct than drinking."

"I think that's why I liked it."

J knows that V would like it, too. Celebrating not by raising a glass but by recognizing the other person for a collection of silent seconds.

"How long are you in the city?" Skye asks.

"Well, I have this other wedding now," J answers, then explains the history.

"It's interesting, what you do," Skye says when he's done.

"How so?"

"Well, you use your songs to connect to people. And then you have to figure out what to do with those connections."

"It's different. The song I wrote for you was about you. The song I wrote for her was about calling someone on a payphone."

"But that's the tricky part, isn't it? Once you connect with a person, you only have so much control over how long it lasts, and in what way."

"What do you mean?"

"I don't want to get *all zen* on you, but I just think that once you connect with someone, it makes an imprint, and that imprint is always there. You might not notice it. You might forget about it. But it's there. And there's always a possibility the connection will continue, even if you think it's over. Like, you hook up with someone and assume it's just a one-night thing. Maybe two years later, you bump into each other and it happens again. Or you bump into each other and it's awkward and he doesn't even acknowledge you when he sees you on the subway platform. Either way, that imprint surfaces. Same with exes. Same with people who've passed. Any reminder can cause a reconnection. I like that about being human. I like that we feel our lives have this one storyline, but there are all these tiny subplots—microplots—that we carry, never knowing when they'll connect, and if they connect, what they'll spark. You say your girlfriend thinks that being with you will only take her backwards?"

"Yes, that's what she told me."

"Well, tell her that's not possible. Time doesn't work that way. There is no backwards. There's not even an over."

"But you're about to end things with Detroit, aren't you?"

"I am. And I'm sure that the end will be messy, and hardly an end, only he will be mostly in the past, because I won't spend any of my present with him. Not anymore. But that's not going on with you and her, is it? You're still here. She's still here. You're in the present, waist-deep in the constant conversation."

Yes, J thinks, but what if, after all the talking, their definitions are still unreconciled?

He knows the answer: He will go home alone. He will lose the connection. He will try to make a new start.

He doesn't want that. He is sure he doesn't want that.

He shifts the conversation back to Skye, to what Skye will do next. Skye doesn't come right out and say, "I'd still like to kiss you again," but the vibe is there. It is not, however, the prevalent vibe. What's more important is what Skye said about how this random encounter could end up changing their life. J can see that, because J believes Skye will leave Detroit, will find their own place, their own footing. It would have probably happened anyway, but it's happening now because J needed a fake wedding and wrote a real song.

He has a hard time wrapping his head around how this works. He thinks about it after he says goodbye to Skye and walks over to the East River, just to get some skyline into his afternoon, even if it's just Brooklyn he's seeing (or maybe Queens—he has no idea). How is his connection with Skye different from his connection to Tara? How is his connection to them different from his connection to V, or at least his initial connection to her? Isn't anytime you meet someone new a random encounter, even if there's every reason for you both to be there? Why do some encounters flourish and others fade? And if things with V don't work out, as things with previous girlfriends didn't work out, does that mean there's some kind of limit on how much connection he can share with another person? What if, despite all his efforts, everyone else in his life is merely passing through? What does that leave him with? And what would it mean if the answer is that it leaves him with more than enough?

He texts V. *How is your day?*

He just wants to keep the conversation going.

In his head, it is still constant. But he knows that's only one side of it.

He and V have lunch on Thursday. This time he's offered to bring the meal to her office. Caught off guard, she agrees.

When J hands his identification to the security officer, she raises an eyebrow and says, "Oh, so you're *that guy*." J immediately wonders what V has told her about him . . . until she laughs and says, "Just joking with you! Here's your pass—sign in on the fourteenth floor."

The receptionist on the fourteenth floor's knowledge of him seems a little more informed, though not to the degree of bias.

"You're the musician, aren't you?" the immaculately coiffed man says. "Thor plays your music all the time. Let me give V a buzz."

The reception area is a ramshackle affair. While it's not full of boxes and crates, J wouldn't say it contains furniture, either. Or at least not permanent furniture; there are two folding chairs, one open, one folded. And there's something that might be a table or a tipped-over shelf.

"I know it looks dire," V says, appearing from a side door. "We haven't had much time to decorate. One of our advisors had the space available, so we took it furnished. Or semi-furnished. I think there was a massive layoff in the last company that was here, and I suspect the employees took the good furniture with them as a kiss-off to the bosses."

J holds up the bag he's brought. "There happen to be seven different salad places in a two-block radius, so I got a salad from each of them and had them mixed together into a super salad. Only the best for you."

"Did you remember to get forks?"

J blanches. "I'm sure they put some in there."

"Don't worry. I have forks."

The inner sanctum of the office isn't as bare-boned as the lobby. It looks like someone made an inebriated, homesick dash through an IKEA; there is even a Swedish flag hanging on a door. V takes J to what she calls a "small conference room"—J thinks it might be more similar to a holding cell, containing a round wood table with, strangely, a box of tissues at its center. (For sneezes? Tears?) As he unpacks the salads (from a place called Just Salad, since J felt more comfortable in the hands of a specialist), V goes to retrieve some forks from her desk.

J begins to wonder if this is one of those American buildings that skips the thirteenth floor, meaning that the fourteenth floor is really the thirteenth. He wishes he'd paid closer attention in the elevator . . .

"Our superstar! It's so good to see you!"

Thor is standing the doorway, grinning with sincere enthusiasm.

"Thor!" J stands, and there is an awkward pause (on J's part) where J tries to determine whether a handshake or a hug would be more appropriate. Thor, however, doesn't deliberate, and wraps his arms around J like they are reunited fraternity brothers.

"It's so good to see you," Thor says. In truth, J and Thor have only met a handful of times, mostly in passing as J picked V up or dropped V off. Thor seems a little more put together now, a little fitter. It is rare for a nineteen-year-old boy to have clothing that looks deliberately chosen to impress, but Thor, who at home seemed to subsist on sweatpants and t-shirts, now looks like his button-down has been starched and pressed for maximum effect.

J guesses the new look comes from the professionalism that has been thrust upon him . . . but then he guesses again as Thor says, eyes alight, "You have to meet Meta!"

A wraith of a girl emerges from behind him dressed in a three-hundred-dollar t-shirt that J thinks is a ten-dollar t-shirt and a skirt that would not be out of place at a Renaissance fair.

She doesn't quite muster a smile, but she does offer her hand for J to shake.

"It's so good to meet you," she says. "We listen to you all the time."

J can't help but note the lack of compliment here. He suspects that she is not in charge of the playlist when his songs are playing.

"We have J to thank for Secret Project's name!" Thor reminds Meta. "As well as so many other things. Honestly, when I think of the couple I want us to be, I often think of J and V. The two of you are so inspiring."

J wants to ask, *Are we?* But he also is aware he's treading on V's territory, and thus he should not be the one to correct any of the markings.

The doorway isn't big enough for V to come through with Thor and Meta standing there; only J can see that she's arrived and probably heard the last minute of conversation. It isn't until she says "I found the forks!" that Thor and Meta part to let her squeeze into the conference room.

"Are you here to do a show?" Thor asks. "If so, we'd love to come."

Before J can answer, V steps in with "I told you I'd let you know the next time he's playing! Don't you trust me, Thor?"

Thor laughs. Meta, notably, doesn't.

"Fair," Thor says. J senses this is a common dynamic—V is the older sister who knows the rules a little better, so he defers to her.

"I'm here to sing at two weddings," J tells him.

"Weddings are more about taxes than they are about love," Meta states.

The other three people in the room turn to her for explanation. But all she says is "What? They *are*."

Thor looks at his watch, then says, "We'll leave you two alone now. But, J, we should talk soon—I would love to get your take on the sonic modalities we're employing to create a more hyperconscious user experience. You know?"

J does not know, but he nods. He is reminded that this nineteen-year-old in front of him has managed to conjure up his own virtual universe, which requires knowledge that J can't even begin to fathom.

Meta says again how good it was to meet him, and Thor gives him another hug before they depart.

It's only after the door is closed and he and V are alone in the conference room with their salads that J says, "Well, she's . . ."

"Young," V finishes. "They're both young. And extremely smart. I actually think she's as smart as he is, just with a different set of skills. I just wish I knew more about her. Her last name, to start."

"You don't know her full name?"

V shakes her head. "I don't know anything about her, besides what she's told Thor. She's definitely a student at NYU, and on social media she presents herself as just plain Meta. But beyond that, it's like her history has been scrubbed clean. I don't know many college students who know how to do that."

"Steal a peek at her driver's license."

"This is New York—no one has a driver's license. And her student ID only has Meta on it. No last name. Apparently NYU is the kind of school that lets you do that."

"I love that you checked."

"Of course I checked. She's either an heiress who's ashamed of being an heiress, a killer who's smart about being a killer, or some combination of the two."

"Seems like a lot for Thor to handle."

"I don't know that he's questioning it. He's just enjoying it. As I said . . . they're young."

J wants to ask her about what Thor said about them being a perfect couple; the implication is that V is clearly painting a rosy picture among her colleagues. But he also doesn't want to disrupt the rapport that's returned between them. So instead they talk about her job, and life in New York, and where J is staying. About anything but the two of them, and what the two of them might mean.

Still, it's close quarters in the conference room, and the proximity of their bodies can't be denied. It's easy enough to deny while they're eating salads, because it's impossible to be sexy while eating a salad. But when the salads are finished and pushed aside, J feels his leg moving over to touch V's, because it is there and his desire to do so is undeniable. She doesn't move her leg away. Instead, she moves her other leg so it's touching his other leg. They hold in that position for a moment, neither of them attempting anything more than this simple touch.

"I *have* missed you," V says.

"I've missed you, too," J says. He wants to lean over to touch her hand, her face. But that would mean shifting his legs away to get the right angle.

Then he sees it: V deciding that this a bad idea, to be touching him, to be saying she's missing him. Sure enough, she pulls back in her chair, disengages their legs. She starts to gather the trash from the table.

"You don't have to do that," J says.

"I'm not leaving out salad bowls for the cleaning staff!"

"I meant pull away. You don't have to pull away."

Now he's standing. Putting his hand on hers, as it holds a salad container.

The room now smells more like salad dressing than it does of either of them. He tries to find her perfume underneath.

"This is why it's hard to see you," V says. "This is what I mean. I'm going to throw these out in the kitchen." She pulls away, then leaves.

She is back quickly but stays in the doorway and then leads him back to the elevator. She asks again if he's made sure Tara's husband-to-be is okay with him singing the song that Tara thinks is hers, and he tells her he'll do it this afternoon. She doesn't ask him for any more details about any other plans he may have.

As they walk back to the elevator, J can hear one of his own songs blasting from an office—no doubt Thor's. It's a song from thirteen years ago, a happy song that sprung from his own sadness. A silly lifeboat of a song that other people ended up wanting to climb aboard.

V hears it, too.

"I promise, he's not just playing it because you're here. This is one of his favorites."

"Does it drive you crazy, him playing my music all the time?"

"No," V says. "I like it."

And she leaves it at that.

About ten minutes after J leaves, Meta checks up on V.

V is not expecting this. She is at her desk, trying to return to the monotony of her emails, her equivalent of being on a factory floor. Meta comes into the office and closes the door behind her.

"How are you doing?" she asks.

V isn't sure why Meta thinks she has the standing to ask this particular question in this particular tone. Is it because they are two of the only women in the office? Is it because of V's vulnerable exchange with her last time? The way Meta asks, it makes V think of her best friend, Glenda, at home. They talk every few days, and Glenda is always asking her how she's doing. But somehow it's different when it's face-to-face.

"I'm okay," V replies.

Meta continues to watch her in the space after, knowing V will have to fill that space with more words.

V continues, "It was weird seeing him here, in the office. I never imagined him here, and suddenly, there he was. With salad. I kept asking myself, *Would this be any less weird if we were back home, if he was bringing me salad there?* And I think the answer is it would have been weird there, too."

"Do you think it's strange that I'm here?" Meta asks, in a perfectly neutral tone.

V is not expecting this. She hadn't been thinking of Meta and Thor at all. But she also understands that Meta can only see things through that lens at this stage.

"No," V replies. "I think the two of you have a connection, and Thor is better for it."

Meta nods, but doesn't change her inquisitive stare. "Do you love him?" she asks.

"I do," V says. "I think he's wonderful and flawed, and when I see him, it's definitely love I feel, not hate or indifference. But the thing is, while all love is made out of the same material, it comes in different shapes and sizes. And what I need to figure out now is what shape and size my love for him is. It might not be the shape and size that fits him anymore. Or fits us—I should have said *fits us*."

If this were a conversation with Glenda, she'd have a dozen follow-up questions. But Meta seems satisfied.

"He seems decent," she says. "But that can also be a drag, you know?"

"Believe me, there are far worse things than nice," V tells her. "Far, far worse things."

"I get it. I just thought, you know, you looked a little tense before."

"I'm okay now. I promise."

Glenda would say, *I'm here for you anytime.* Or, *Let me know if you want to talk more.* Maybe even, *Don't worry—things will work themselves out.*

Meta doesn't have this kind of vocabulary—at least, not for V. She just says she'll see V at the three o'clock meeting. Then as she's leaving the room, she adds almost as an afterthought, "You know I really love Thor, right?" Her voice climbs out of neutrality, to a mix of defensiveness and concern.

V doesn't think Meta is fishing for her to say "I'm sure Thor loves you, too"—because how would V know? Instead V says, "I think you make a very good couple," which is true enough.

Meta surprises her by saying, "Thanks," softly. Then she leaves the room.

V picks up the phone, tempted to call Glenda to tell her what just happened. Then she puts the phone down. All of this—J's presence, Meta's sympathy, the pressure of the afternoon's meeting—is something she wants to navigate herself. She wants to prove that she has her bearings.

Once J gets back to the apartment, he texts Tara.
*Have you told Hugh about my appearance?* he asks.
*No. It's a surprise!* ☺ she replies.
*Are you sure that's a good idea?*
*He surprises me all the time . . . it'll be fun to have a surprise for once! I asked his sister Lori (my maid of honor) and she agreed. Lori's the only one who knows, besides the wedding planner and the priest!*
J feels reassured by Lori's opinion.
*Looking forward to it!* he types.

V calls that night, to make sure he did as he promised. They end up talking for twenty minutes, mostly about her day. He asks her if she wants to come to the wedding with him, and she says no. Not a *no, because I already have plans* or a *no, I don't want to be doing that with you again.* Just an unambiguous-in-decision, ambiguous-in-cause *no.* J thinks it's a little strange to be lying in bed in the same city (albeit a different borough) and talking on the phone. He makes what are (to him) the slightest of hints that maybe they should hang up and continue in person, but she passes them by, signs for exits she's not taking.

He is happy to have her be the last voice he hears before he goes to sleep. And at the same time, he wishes he could reach out and find her there in the bed, to fall asleep to the sound of her breathing.

J takes some time on Friday to rework the payphone song. It's like going back to a house where he once lived and rearranging the furniture; it might end up being an improvement, but it will still seem unfamiliar.

By the time the sun sets, he's pretty much done with the song. He messages V to see what she's up to. She replies, *Work,* and that's that.

Next he messages Skye, to ask how they're doing. *Messy* is their reply. *Want to talk?* J offers, thinking it would be nice to see Skye again. He's disappointed when Skye responds, *Had to go out of town for the weekend to think things through. Sorry. Are you still around next week?*

*I think so?* J replies. There is another wedding on the horizon that will require travel, but if he doesn't stop at home first, he might be able to get another week here.

Tara and Hugh's wedding is at a hotel in Jersey City, overlooking the Manhattan skyline. J arrives an hour early, partly to situate himself and partly because he thought New Jersey was much farther away than it really is (a mistake most people make; the Hudson River isn't *that* wide).

He realizes too late that Tara hasn't given him instructions. He is already a little self-conscious because he is wearing the same suit he wore to the fake wedding, although he is fairly certain that nobody from that wedding will be attending this one . . . and even if they do, what he wore was the least memorable part of that wedding. He also has his guitar case, which always garners looks when striding through a hotel lobby or into a ballroom where a wedding has been set up.

As he walks in, he sees a cluster of old men in tuxedos talking in a corner. Their talking stops when he enters the room, and almost immediately he feels like a trespasser and hopes he has picked the right wedding in the right ballroom; he imagines any hotel with a skyline view will be packed to bursting with weddings on a Saturday night. One of the older men says something to his cohorts, then strides over. From his age and genteel bearing, J imagines this is Tara's or Hugh's father.

J is expecting a *Can I help you?* But what he gets instead is a blunter, "What are you doing here?"

"I'm looking for Tara," J replies. "Can you tell me where she is? Or maybe the wedding planner?"

"Christ, you've got a lot of nerve," the man replies.

"Tara invited me," J says, taken aback by the father's vitriol. "This is Tara's wedding, isn't it?"

"This is *our* wedding," the man says. "And I guarantee, you're not on the guest list."

"Hugh?" J asks, confused. "I'm J—"

"I know exactly who you are. And if you think you can waltz in here and make trouble . . ."

This completely breaks the tension for J, because it's so ridiculous.

He laughs. "I'm not here to make trouble. I'm just here to sing a song as part of the wedding. It was supposed to be a surprise for you. Please, just ask Tara. Or the wedding planner. Or Lori."

"Like I'd trust Lori!"

"The wedding planner, then."

"Fine," Hugh says. Then he turns to his cohort and yells, "Will one of you go get Maria? The planner? She's probably in with the girls." As one of the men runs off, Hugh tells J, "You wait here."

J is relieved that when the wedding planner arrives, she does not seem at all disturbed by his presence.

"You knew about this?" Hugh accuses.

"Yes," Maria replies calmly. "This was meant to be a surprise."

"Some surprise!" Hugh says to Maria. Then he turns again on J. "Have you and my wife been talking all this time? That would be one helluva fucking surprise."

J resists pointing out that Tara isn't Hugh's wife yet. Instead he says, "I only heard from her last weekend. She saw I was in town from Sweden. It's been years since we last spoke. She asked me to sing in the ceremony and invited me and my girlfriend to the reception afterwards."

J is hoping the mention of a girlfriend will satisfy a man like Hugh . . . and in this case, it's the right call.

"I see," Hugh says. "So where's your girlfriend now?"

"On her way," J bluffs. "I'm here early to see the stage—I mean, the venue. Amp my guitar if that's possible. See where I'm supposed to stand."

"I have all of that information for you," Maria says. "Why don't you come with me? I'll introduce you to the priest performing the ceremony, and he can tell you when you'll be singing."

Hugh calls out to his groomsmen, "It's a *surprise*. From Tara. I swear . . ." The groomsmen murmur in response, nod.

J can see Hugh reading the room, understanding the situation and his options within it. He can't quite muster an apology, but he does say to J, "Look—no hard feelings."

J echoes this: "No hard feelings." Even as he does, he thinks there are two ways to take the phrase. He's always heard it with *hard* meaning *not soft*—you shouldn't carry around feelings you aren't able to swallow or digest. But right now the other meaning of *hard* comes to the fore, and he realizes people like Hugh who say "no hard feelings" are actually asking for all their feelings to be easy ones. They resent having to deal with any complications.

It's Maria who says "I'm sorry about that" as they leave the larger ballroom and step out onto the sweeping balcony where the ceremony will be held, with the skyscrapers of Manhattan looking on. "I told her I don't like surprises at this stage. But she was so excited to have you here, and to have you perform the song. It's a great song, by the way. She had me stand there and listen to it as she played it on her phone. Anyway, will you and your girlfriend be staying for the reception? I don't think we planned for that."

"No," J says. "I think we'll make our exit after the ceremony."

"Yes, I think that's for the best."

Maria heads off to find the priest, and J places a quick call to V.

"Hello?" she answers.

"What are you doing right now?"

"I was washing the dishes until I had to answer the phone."

"Look—I need you to come to this wedding."

"Has something happened?"

J fills her in.

"I told you!" V laughs. J can't say he's particularly missed this brand of self-satisfaction in her voice.

"Just come for the ceremony. Meet Hugh. And then we'll run off. There's a great view here."

"Where are you?"

He tells her the name of the hotel and where it is.

"You want me to come to New Jersey?!?"

"It's not like *The Sopranos*. Much less gunfire. Possibly less therapy."

"And you need me there in an hour?"

"Ideally. I can order you an Uber."

"How do I let myself be dragged into these things?"

"Because of your love for chaos. I promise, this is a chaos site. And also, I need you."

He makes the *I need you* sound site-specific, although as he says it, it feels bigger than that.

V says, "I'll send the address. Order that Uber and screenshot the driver info for me. If you need me right away, I'm not going to change for the event. What I'm wearing is nice enough."

J does not see Tara until her father (around the same age as Hugh) walks her down the aisle. V, sitting next to J at the extreme left of the front row, whispers, "She's not what I pictured," and J wants to ask her why she bothered picturing anything at all. And with the veil, how can V tell what Tara looks like? J isn't sure himself . . .

although in this case the vague sense of Tara under the veil matches his blurred memory perfectly.

The ceremony itself is so traditional that J wonders whether he should have rewritten his song in Latin. The vows have been composed with a hand so heavy it might as well be God's—*you are my possession and I am yours, and nothing will ever stop this chain of mutual ownership.* Or something like that.

The veil is lifted, and Tara comes a little more in focus, both in person and in memory. For all J knows, she *is* the one who got away. But probably not. Almost certainly not.

The priest admonishes Tara and Hugh to be kind to one another, to be beacons for their children, and to live a good life together.

"Before we conclude," the priest says, "we have a special treat. One of Tara's dear friends will now immortalize this moment in song."

This is not the cue J would have written, but it's the cue he's been given. Tara beams and actually waves as he walks up to the microphone and plugs in his guitar. Hugh keeps his hand on Tara's back and tries his best not to grimace. J does not make any opening remarks this time. He just plunges into the song, which has a new, happier ending that the original version.

> I'm calling from the last payphone in New York
> After looking for quarters on the ground
> I don't have much time, I'll cut it short
> Since you're probably hearing more static than sound
>
> Can you hear the music from the subway doors
> As it's swooshing by our platform
> They don't stop at our stop anymore
>
> Baby soon we'll be
> On the junkyard of history

> About to be forgotten and obsolete
> The world is picking up speed
> At a pace that I can't keep
> But time stood still when you were here with me
>
> Slowly we slide out of existence
> Like trilobites, old satellites, and rotary phones
> They stopped making upgrades for our systems
> So listen
> You and me
> We are version 1.0
>
> Baby we are telefax and paper maps
> We're Betamax. We're personal ads
> The incandescent light that shines through the cracks
>
> Why don't you meet me
> On the junkyard of history
> We're about to be forgotten and obsolete
> The world is picking up speed
> At a pace that I can't keep
> But time stands still when you are here with me

When the song is over, Tara begins the applause. When the applause is over, J bows in the couple's direction, then returns to his seat and takes V's hand. He has no idea if she's letting him do this to keep up the façade or whether she is enjoying having her hand held.

After the wedding ceremony concludes, Tara and Hugh are whisked away to some secret location to prepare for the reception.

J is sorry to stand, because that means letting go of V again. He is hoping, now that they can speak, that she'll say something about what she heard in the song. When he sang the line about wanting time to stand still, did it mean anything to her?

The truth is, V did notice that line. And she thought to herself that, as lovely as it is, she's spent too much time standing still. She wants to get to the next part. Not with J, but with her own life. J didn't mean to, but he's managed to articulate to V something that was wrong with them. She knows how happy it made him to hit Pause. And she agrees with him in the fear of Fast Forward.

But right now? It's not Pause she wants.

She wants Play.

J finds Maria, introduces her to V, then says they're going to go.

Once again, Maria says, "I think that's for the best."

J and V find a pier on the Hudson and walk as far out as they can go. It feels as if only a few more steps would take them into Manhattan; the skyline feels that close.

"Thank you again," J says. "I saw Hugh taking note of your presence. You probably saved their marriage."

"Is that a good thing or a bad thing?" V asks.

"None of our business."

"Agreed."

They look out at the water, the lights. There is so much they aren't saying.

"That song makes me melancholy," V says, because she knows J will want her to say *something* about the song. "The older I get, the harder it hits me. We all want to think evolution ends with us, but the world has other ideas, doesn't it?"

"You're hardly obsolete."

"I mentioned *Groundhog Day* to Thor and Meta the other day and they had no idea what I was talking about."

"How is that possible?"

"It'll happen to them, too, someday. Some assistant will ask them, 'What was *Survivor*?'"

"'To everything, turn turn turn.'"

"Exactly."

Somewhere above them, the wedding band strikes up some entrance music for the bride and groom.

J watches V and the way the night breeze makes her hair move. She is staring into the distance . . . but then she turns to him and asks, "What?"

Instinct kicks in, and he says, "Nothing."

"It's something. What?"

"I keep think about what you said, and about where we are. I can't help wondering . . . if you don't want to go backwards to find me where we were, why can't I go forwards with you? Why can't I be your future, too?"

V looks at him sadly. "I wish I had an answer for you. For me, too. But it's not going to appear right now. You called me, and I showed up for you. That's the best I can do, and even that . . . I can't do it that often."

J feels suddenly defensive, says, "I don't plan on asking you to do it too often. I'm sorry I got myself in that situation."

"Don't get angry."

"I'm not angry. I'm frustrated."

"I can tell."

"Please."

The tenderness in his voice throws a blanket on the fire.

"I don't know what to tell you," V says gently.

"The truth."

"Okay. I'm going to tell you how I see it, and then I am going to walk back to the hotel and order my own car home. We are not going to resolve this tonight. So let me just say what I'm going to say, and we'll talk about it again tomorrow. Agreed?"

J agrees. He doesn't think he has much of a choice.

"The way I'm thinking of it is this. You keep asking me whether the door is closed or open. Are we together or aren't we? But what I'm trying to tell you is this: The door is open, but I don't want you to walk through it."

"How is that fair?" J asks. "We're not a couple that's just met. We've been together for *two years*. And while I understand what an opportunity this is for you, I don't think you understand what a loss it's been for me. In fact, I don't think you see it as a loss at all for yourself. Being told to not walk through an open door—how is that different from a closed door? In your mind, it might be. But for me . . . it leaves me in the same place, doesn't it?"

"I'm sorry. It does. I don't know what to tell you."

"Tell me you love me. Tell me you want me to be with you."

"What if I can tell you the first and not the second?"

It hits J then. Really hits him.

This is not a fight he can win right now.

A tear falls out of V's eye, and she quickly wipes it off. The city looms behind her.

"I'm so sorry," she says. "I know you won't believe me, but it's not about you. It's about me, my life. I wish I could imagine you here with me, but I can't. It's like this new life is forming around me, and it feels right. I'm not leaving you. I'm just arriving somewhere else."

"What if I'd come with you? What if, when you'd gotten the news, I'd said, 'Let's move to New York together'?"

"But you didn't, did you? You have a life there, much more of a life than I had. You have family, all these people who care about you. You've always had the chance to leave, but you never have. This is my first chance. And I'm taking it. I think if you weren't dating me, if I were just someone telling you my story, you'd understand it. Because one of the things I love about you is your capacity to be by yourself, to make connections where you go but not get tied down by them. That's where I am right now."

"I hate this."

"I do, too."

J shakes his head. "No, you don't. If you hated it, it wouldn't be happening."

Now he starts to cry, and the two of them look at each other with a sadness they've never shared before.

"Is this it?" J asks.

He expects a yes. Instead he gets an "I don't know." And then an "I have to go."

V hugs him goodbye and lets him hug her goodbye. Then she walks down the dock, to order her own car. She leaves him with the city, just out of reach.

He knows her "I don't know" is genuine. He knows she believes the door is still open.

For the first time, he wonders if he should be the one to walk away from it. But even as he thinks that, there's the hope that if he started to walk away, she'd call him back.

# THE SEVENTH WEDDING

J's next wedding is at St. Thomas Church, an eight-hundred-year-old Gothic establishment in Leipzig, Germany, with a frankly intimidating musical lineage. Bach was choir director there for almost three decades and is buried there. Wagner was baptized in its waters. Mendelssohn often dropped by. The groom, who J has never met, is a Bach scholar, and J suspects this is his dream wedding venue. The bride, who was the one to reach out to J, is a British flight attendant. The groom comes from money. The bride is glad she didn't know the groom had money when they met. She'd assumed that a Bach scholar wouldn't have a large nest egg. She hadn't realized that the only reason he could be a Bach scholar was because he had a large nest egg.

The bride, Imogen, emailed J well over a year ago to ask him to sing at the wedding. It would be a paid gig and he would do a DJ set to close the reception as well as a song in the ceremony. It was good money, and J had a good feeling about Imogen from her email, so he'd agreed.

About six months ago, he'd been in London and they'd had a chance to meet up so she could give him the background he needed for his song. (Carl, her fiancé, was off in Thuringia, doing research.) Imogen and Carl had not, alas, met on an airplane, but instead had been set up by Carl's sister, who had a flat in the same building as Imogen's. It had not been an instant match—while Imogen knew her Bach from her Beethoven, she didn't necessarily know her *St. Matthew's Passion* from her *St. John's Passion*. Carl vowed to properly introduce her, and she'd been taken by how sincere his joy was as he shared each cantata and concerto. When he'd told her his dream of being married at St. Thomas mere moments after she'd accepted his proposal, she said that if he could somehow make it happen, she would be there.

He made it happen. And his parents made all the other arrangements happen. In terms of the music, Carl had been understandably particular. Plenty of Bach. Some Mendelssohn. Some Mozart. (He'd played at St. Thomas, too.) A snatch of Wagner. ("Nothing too heavy," Imogen said. "If that's possible with Wagner.")

The way Imogen put it to J was this: "You are the one chance I have to bring my own music to my wedding." Perhaps understanding how this sounded, she quickly added, "Not that I don't love Bach. I truly love Bach. I don't think I'd be able to marry Carl if I didn't. It's just that . . . have you ever been to St. Thomas?"

J admitted he hadn't.

"Well, it's awe-inspiring. The architecture. The fact that it's been there for so long without burning down or being bombed. It's a place that's full of God, in the most exalted sense. But whenever I'm in a space like that . . . I can get lost in my own insignificance. God's there . . . but I want to be there, too, you know? Especially at my own wedding. Carl's music will be the voice of God. And you . . . well, I want you to be the reminder that we're here, too. A song that only lasts a day means just as much as all the songs that stand the test of time, if you're the person whose day it is. Does that make sense?"

J told her it did. Later, he let this conversation guide him as he crafted the song. He felt like his job was to help Imogen stand up to Bach. Which was a ridiculous task . . . but it helped that she wasn't expecting him to be equal to Bach. Instead she wanted him to be her side of the story, her space in the church.

Because the wedding was so long in planning, he'd had plenty of time to work on the song, to shift it around from time to time. Now, after Tara's wedding is over and he is in New York with little to do, he takes the song back out and makes it into what it's meant to be.

J flies with enough frequency that he is subject to the following truth: Good flights are always forgotten as soon as you land. Nobody ever tells the story of this really great flight they had, not unless they met their future spouse or got to sleep for the first time in one of those seats that turns into a bed.

Bad flights, however, can linger for years, and become the stuff of legend.

J's flight back to Sweden is one of those bad flights.

There is a delay getting on board. Then a delay once on board that lasts long enough for the pilot to need to be switched, which means going off board, only to board again an hour later. Once in the air, there is turbulence that makes the plane seem like a yo-yo at best and a yo-yo with its string cut at worst. The monitor at J's seat malfunctions so the only channel he can watch shows instructional meditation videos. The man next to him practically dares him to contest the arm rest, then gets irate when the flight attendant cuts him off at four vodka tonics.

By the time J lands, the ten-hour layover has evaporated to just under four hours, which isn't enough time to go through customs, get home, and return to the airport to go through it all again. J desperately wants to leave the no-man's-land of the travelopolis, but he knows more chaos will be unleashed if he misses his next flight. So instead J arrives early at the gate of his next departure.

He needs a shower, to make him feel more living than dead. He wants to text V about all his flight misfortunes, then wonders, *What's the point?* He'd only be doing it to make himself feel better, and ultimately, he won't feel any better. Just alone at the hell of an airport gate.

His spirits go up a notch when a dog in a service-dog vest comes over and sniffs him in a friendly manner, then starts barking. J isn't sure he's supposed to pet a dog in a vest, but the dog nuzzles in close and gives him a raised-head look that all but coos, *There . . . don't you feel better?* Then the dog sniffs him and starts to bark again, with an unnerving insistence. People in the seats around J are starting to react to the disturbance, not positively.

The dog's owner comes over and J instinctively apologizes.

"Don't worry about it," the man says in a thick German accent. He's probably J's age, with a beard that looks more figurative than literal. "C'mon, boy."

He tries to shush the dog, but the dog continues to bark.

The German laughs and says, "Oh, no—that's not good. Mona is being trained to detect cancer, and she's signaling that she's smelling something on you."

J has heard of dogs sniffing out drugs. Tracking down fugitives. But . . . "Cancer?"

"Yeah, cancer."

"So the dog thinks I have cancer? Do I have cancer?"

"I don't know . . . do you?"

"No!"

"Do you have any candy in your pockets? That could be it."

"No."

"Huh. Any food?"

"Nope."

"Maybe you have a dog yourself? She could be picking up on that."

"I don't."

The man is pulling Mona back now, leading her away.

"That's strange. She's usually pretty accurate. Apologies for bothering you. Have a good flight."

The dog owner walks away as if they're not on the same flight. Mona looks back at J and barks one final time.

J has no idea whether the man is joking with him or not.

Germans are very hard to read.

On the flight to Frankfurt, J is seated in front of someone who kicks his seat incessantly. He assumes it's a young child, but when he finally gets a look, he finds it's a surly teenager. He feels he cannot ask the girl's mother to calm her daughter down at that age. So he lets himself be kicked, and he is frustrated that the plane doesn't have wi-fi, because how else is he supposed to look up whether dogs can actually be taught to smell cancer? He tries to distract himself by assembling tomorrow night's DJ set on his laptop. These songs are supposed to put him in the mood for love, not despair, but at this point he's not sure the two are separable.

There is a note waiting on his bed when he gets into his hotel room in Leipzig. Absurdly, he hopes it's from V—every now and then when he was on tour, she'd consult his itinerary and do that, ask the hotel to leave a message on his pillow. Usually it was something remarkably embarrassing, which would cause him to get no shortage of strange looks when he checked in—*Darling, I thought you were going to bury the body before you left. It's not fair that I have to do it.* Or *I seem to have lost my diaphragm—you didn't take it again, did you? I keep telling you—it's not a coaster.* Or *I'm the woman you met last night at the show. My husband would like to have a few words with you.*

Of course, the only person who knows where he's staying is Imogen, and that's exactly who the note is from. She apologizes that she won't get to see him before the wedding—she and Carl are doing things "the old-fashioned way" and she won't be getting to the church until the last possible moment. She says the priest will tell him when he'll be playing the song and says that there will be an area in the sacristy for him to change and set up, away from the choir.

*You'll be the final song on the program*, she writes. *Think of it as us having the last word.*

J finds it hard to sleep that night. It is like that dog is still barking at him. Barking and barking and barking.

He wakes up disoriented, out of sorts. The sun has risen, but the sky hasn't fully caught on to the fact. It is going to be a dreary, dismal day.

Just past noon, J puts on his suit and walks to the church. It is only as he nears it that he fully appreciates that he's about to play at a site where Bach and Mozart once played. Of course, if you count the choir, tens of thousands of other people have also sung there over the centuries. But how many have played their own songs?

The church itself more than lives up to its history. On the outside, it looks like an alpine lighthouse has fallen into a more traditional cathedral from time immemorial. The sanctuary inside is striking in its simplicity—a white skeleton of pillars ribbed in red at the top as the ceiling soars. *Toccata and Fugue in D Minor* is playing as he walks up, as if to remind everyone of all that the walls have absorbed over the years.

A crowd has already gathered, speaking both British-inflected English and German. J feels a little silly flagging down an usher and asking to be directed to the priest . . . but that's what he's been instructed to do. The usher just shakes his head, and at first J thinks it's a refusal, but then the usher points to another usher who explains after J introduces himself that the first usher doesn't speak English. J is then ushered into the back corridors of the church, ultimately landing in the sacristy. In the rooms around him, J can hear the choir gathering, tuning themselves. A string quartet bows in the distance.

About twenty minutes before the service begins, a man who has to be the priest comes into the sacristy and nods at J. J nods back, and wonders if the priest, too, only speaks German (as well as Latin, presumably). He is an older man, very serious looking, with sharp features and small round glasses.

"You must be the singer," the priest finally says, almost dismissively.

"I am, yes," J confirms.

The priest calls out a name, and another man pops into the doorway.

"This is the organ player," the priest says.

"Hello," J greets.

The organ player nods back, then looks to his boss.

With as few words as possible, the priest says that he will signal J when it is his time to sing. There will be no mic, no amplification. J's song will see the wedded couple out of the church at the end of the service; J must keep singing until the last person has filed out.

The priest doesn't ask J if he has any questions. Instead, he dismisses the organ player, then turns away from J and puts on his vestments.

"So why did you become a priest?" J asks. In a sacristy, he imagines this amounts to small talk.

"For the love of God," the priest answers. He almost sounds sarcastic, but because the priest is German, J can't tell if he's being mocked, if the concept of religion is being mocked, or if this is just a very straightforward answer.

The answer is so fiercely punctuated that J figures this will be the end of their exchange. But then the priest, with his back still to J, asks, "Why do you sing at weddings?"

J has a usual answer to this, but he tries to make it more elaborate for the priest.

"Singing at weddings make me feel like a kind of midwife," J replies. "It's like I'm delivering these people, like babies, into the next phase of their lives."

He has to imagine neither Bach nor Wagner gave this particular answer. But, in fairness, he's not sure they ever played weddings.

At first, J doesn't think the priest has heard, since his answer gets such a lack of response. But then, fully vestmented, the priest turns and says, "Yes . . . and like a midwife you stand at the middle of life, but still on the side. You observe and study but you don't really participate."

When J finds himself at a loss for a response, the priest humorlessly nods once and leaves the room. About two minutes before the start of the service, an altar boy comes over and leads J to the spot where he'll wait. Not in the middle of the service, but on the side.

Carl and the rest of the wedding party are waiting at the front, by the altar. Then a pipe organ begins to play Mendelssohn's *Wedding March*.

J has never heard this piece played at a wedding before, and if it weren't for the setting, he might think it's a joke. It sounds like a Transylvanian circus processional, delivered with perfect solemnity. V would absolutely love it, for its garish audacity. But V is not around to appreciate it, and when J looks around to see if there's anyone else he can share a smile with, he sees only the choir members, who have clearly been trained to match their expressions to that of the priest.

The ceremony continues along these somber tones, with Imogen walked down the aisle by her father and conveyed to the space next to Carl. Bach is evoked far more often than love. The priest speaks of Imogen and Carl's holy union, but he seems more interested in the holy part than the union. It feels to J as if they've all been sucked into a much earlier century, and that the marriage has been arranged to shore up a lineage or acquire a dowry. There's no mention of how Imogen and Carl met, or indeed why they've chosen to be married. It's all very by-the-book, and there's no question which book it is.

J figured he'd be the grand finale, but now he realizes he's meant to be the afterthought, the outro, not even the first song after the movie ends, but the second one, playing as the names of the prop handlers and finance executives are listed. For a moment, after Imogen and Carl exchange their vows and are pronounced man and wife, J thinks the priest has forgotten him entirely. When Imogen and Carl kiss, a cheer rings out from a few people and is quickly swallowed by the silence of the rest. It's only as they turn to leave the church that the priest shoots his steely glance J's way. There will be no introduction here. J is meant to simply step out of the shadows. Which is exactly what he does.

> In a cave in Lascaux
> Before Lascaux was called Lascaux
> Scribbled on the cold cave wall
> "We were in love"
> Shades of hematite
> Manganese oxide
> Memories lost forever
> Captured in a drop of amber
> We were here at the same time
> And what a time to be alive
> We were here at the same time
> It was a time to be alive

It is such a peculiar feeling, to sing in a cathedral. As he sings, it is as if he's also following his words as they travel into the air, as if he can feel the heights they reach and the emptiness they move through.

> In a men's room stall
> Scribbled on the bathroom wall
> For a good time call
> Imogen and Carl

> Longtime listener, first-time call
> A trucker with a southern drawl
> Breathing hard over the line
> Said I can't believe that we are
> On Earth at the same time
> And what a time to be alive
> We are here at the same time
> What a time to be alive

J closes his eyes and keeps singing. He can sense everyone else moving away from him, the space they leave behind. His voice echoes back to him, reverberates through the eaves.

> Carved into an old oak tree
> A rugged heart. I + C
> You find an old guitar
> and you play Bach's *Suite no. 1 in G*
> We leave it in the canopy
> and over time the guitar's body
> is swallowed up by the tree
> performing the slowest melody
> as each string snaps successively
> Stretched out over a century
> An automated music piece
> no music sheet, the title simply reads:
> We were here at the same time
> It was a time to be alive
> We were here at the same time
> It was a time to be alive

When he opens his eyes, he is alone.

Does he have the church to himself, or does the church have him to itself? Is it possible for the answer to be both at once, and for his aloneness to be in such equal balance as well? Having omniscience over the moment, and the feeling of power that comes from that. And also having the moment completely unshared, completely solitary, and the feeling of isolation that comes from that. Both feelings sublimely coexisting—as they always do, but not usually in such stark relief against the rest of life.

J keeps singing. Not for anyone else. Not for the pillars or all the centuries they represent. He takes the moment and sings for himself, to hear his voice as he's never heard it before.

> **We were there at the same time**
> **It was a time to be alive**
>
> **We are here at the same time**
> **It is a time to be alive**

His voice lifts on the final note, and then he watches to see where it goes. Like Bach's, like Wagner's, like Mendelssohn's, his work is invisible, and yet it has a chance to endure.

You don't have to believe in any particular deity to feel gratitude. J lingers in the silence for a moment and bows his head, grateful for this unexpected gift of time and place. Then he returns to the sacristy before anyone else can step into the scene and make it any less his.

There is an afternoon's pause between the ceremony and the reception. J calls V to tell her about what happened, but the call goes to voicemail, and he doesn't want to say anything about it there. In his room, he starts to think about the ceremony in terms of a song, and he begins to free-write in his notebook. Then he fiddles around with his DJ set some more and checks his email. One address catches his eye—it's not a name that he knows, but the email address is from *The New Yorker*. Normally, he would figure it was just a solicitation from the subscription office, but the subject line reads: *Friend of Skye's, curious about doing a piece.*

It ends up that Nick Andrews, the reporter, is indeed a friend of Skye's, but wasn't at the wedding because of his "conscientious objector status." In other words, he wasn't there because he's never liked the way Detroit treated Skye, and that means he's one of the people Skye has turned to now. Meanwhile, they told Nick about J's wedding-singer gigs, and about how helpful J has been, and Nick, a staff writer at *The New Yorker*, got the idea of pitching a story about J to Talk of the Town. *You have the right profile—obscure enough, but not too obscure*, Nick writes. *And the weddings are a great hook. Will you be back in town in the next couple of weeks? And would you be up for doing something if my pitch lands?*

J has appeared in *The New Yorker* before, but always as a listing, never a subject. He writes the reporter back and says he'll be back in New York in a few days. Then he writes Skye to thank them (and also to make sure Nick's email isn't a prank).

He is eager to tell someone else the news—but there's no one in Leipzig, or in the entirety of Germany, really, for him to tell.

So he calls V again.

And again it goes to voicemail.

This time he leaves a message. "I know how much you love *The New Yorker*. Well, guess who they want to talk to. I'll give you a hint: You've slept with him repeatedly, and I sleep with him every night. Call me back."

It's a weekend, and even if she's working, she should be able to check her voicemail and call him back.

J is left to wait in a hotel room, which is second only to a hospital in terms of worst places to wait for someone to call back.

V does not call back.

J can think of a hundred things she could be doing instead of checking her phone. Driving! (Except she doesn't have a US license.) Hiking! (He checks the weather in New York, and it's not great for hiking.) Napping alone! (Possible.) "Napping" with someone else! (J doesn't want to think about this option.) Perhaps she's stuck underground in a subway car, delayed by a jumper on the tracks.

*Just call me*, J thinks. *I want you to call me.*

But this appeal backfires, because it makes him even lonelier when it doesn't work.

It doesn't take long for J to fall into the pit—the one that's even worse because he feels he dug it himself, then forgot it was there. It's not a big pit—it is, in fact, the perfect shape of his own body. He wonders, is this all his life will ever be—moving from hotel room to hotel room, singing about love without ever making it work for himself? The priest's unfair words about midwives come back to him—what if he is nothing but a romantic bystander, a charlatan who convinces couples he knows more than he really does? What if it's this, more than anything else, that V has recognized? What if she was his best shot, and he missed?

He thinks all these thoughts, and the pit doesn't give them any room to dissipate. They are incessant. And behind them, a dog is barking, barking, barking.

J loses hours this way. The thing that could free him from the pit is a call from V, even a text.

But his phone remains silent.

Any power he felt in the church is gone now. The balance of the aloneness has tipped, and he feels separate from the rest of the world, separate from the place he should be.

J's DJ set will be after the meal at the reception, so he receives a table card just like any other guest. Before he goes to Table 23, he stops off the spot by the dance floor where his laptop will be set up. Everything seems in order.

Table 23 is near the dance floor, but not particularly near the bride and groom's table—this is the Pluto of wedding tables, at such an orbit that guests may debate whether they're part of the wedding at all. It is a table for ten, and four people are seated when J arrives. One is a very, very old man who stares off into the distance like he's waiting for a steamship; when he breathes, which is infrequently, his lungs sound like a broken whistle. Next to him are two women in their fifties or early sixties who are clearly sisters, if not twins. And then there is a slightly older man, who is walrus-like in both his shape and demeanor, seated at a one-chair remove from the closest woman.

"Welcome to the Losers' Table," the man says when J has taken a seat.

"Don't listen to him," one of the sisters says.

"It's true. I checked every single place card. We are the only adults here who don't have dates."

"Pam is my date," the second sister says.

"Will you listen to yourself?" Walrus Man spits out. "Did you take your sister to your dances in high school, too?"

J introduces himself, aiming the introduction more at the sisters than at the man. The sisters, Pam and Sam, introduce themselves back. The elderly man nods, then returns to seeking his steamship. The more garrulous man focuses on buttering a roll.

"Elgar here is Carl's great rival," Sam explains, gesturing to the butterer.

"Regarding scholarship and Bach," Elgar huffs. "I was not his rival for Imogen. He can have her."

"Don't listen to him," Sam says. "Most people don't."

"I thought your song this morning was lovely," Pam adds. "I mean, we had to leave halfway through. But I wanted to hear the rest of it!"

A server comes bearing salads.

"Do you know if there will be others joining you?" the server asks.

"Those seats are extra," Elgar replies. "Just in case anyone becomes single during the reception. There's got to be a place for them to be banished."

"Is he always like this?" Pam asks Sam.

"Believe me," Sam says, "it's worse when he's flirty." Then she gestures to the seat next to Pam and tells J, "Join us."

At first it feels awkward to J to ignore Elgar throughout the meal, as he, Sam, and Pam turn to talk to each other and, occasionally, the older man, who appears to be an old friend of either Imogen or Carl's now-deceased grandparents. This conversational avoidance doesn't stop Elgar from ridiculing the proceedings, from the bride and groom's entrance ("I guess she finally wore him down") to her father's toast ("I hear he's been married four times, so he'd know how to do this") to the choice of music the string quartet is playing during the meal ("Ask not for whom the Pachelbel tolls, because it might just toll for you"). J has encountered men like this for years, usually in all-male spaces—men for whom a lack of love has turned malignant, with side effects of blame and hostility.

Pam and Sam are better at tuning Elgar out. They ask J about his singing, and after a digression about his career that gives him the opportunity to mention the *New Yorker* email ("Their crossword is a joke"—Elgar), the discussion turns to love stories, and how everyone has a favorite story about love. It doesn't take much prodding for Pam to volunteer her own.

"This was in the nineties, when I was a young doctor working for Médecins Sans Frontières. We were in Bosnia, and it was relentless work. Most rewarding work I've ever done, but relentless. There was such a shortage of doctors that we worked in shifts, and since I had always been a night owl, I always took the night shift. We all shared quarters, so while I was at the hospital, someone else would sleep in my bed. And then when that person went off to the day shift, I'd go and crash.

"I always went to the same bed, and when it was time to leave, I'd take my sheets and fold them into a box underneath. An hour or so later, the second person would come, take out their own sheets, and go to sleep. We never saw each other."

"Of course you didn't," Elgar grumbles.

"Shush. I know this sounds like something I'm making up, but I swear it happened. From offhand comments by other people, I knew the man I shared the bed with was Belgian, and from the way the bed smelled when I returned, I knew he smoked. It wasn't a fancy mattress, and sometimes I'd come back and his shape would still be there. It was like I was sleeping in his shadow. Naturally, I was intrigued.

"One day, probably three weeks in, I came back and his sheets were still on the bed. While I was folding them, the scent was enticing—I wasn't much of a smoker, but the times I'd smoked had been memorable, and at that moment, I felt an actual craving. Lo and behold, when I went to put the sheets in his box, I found a pack of cigarettes there. At first, I felt he owed me a cigarette, because of the sheets. So I nicked one and had the best time smoking it. It was only after, when I was trying to fall asleep, that I felt a little guilty, like I had broken some kind of pact by going into his things. I wrote him this note, saying 'I couldn't resist taking one—I hope that was okay.' When I got back from my shift there was a cigarette waiting for me, with a note that said, 'Figuring you might need this.' The next morning I left an apple on our pillow as a thank you and a note saying I hoped he'd had a good night, all things considered. He left me chocolate the next time, and more cigarettes.

"It went back and forth like this for about two weeks. It would have been so easy for us to find each other—all we'd have to do was slip out on break and go back to the house—but neither of us did that. We just left each other presents and notes, until one morning I came back and there was a whole pack of cigarettes, and a note that said goodbye. It's probably the sweetest, most passionate relationship I've ever had."

"God, I love that story," Sam says with a sigh.

Elgar just laughs.

J figures they'll ignore him, but Pam says, "What? Say what you want to say, Elgar."

"Well, *of course* it's the most romance you've ever had. You two never had to look at each other. Nothing will kill a romance like seeing what the other person looks like!"

"This is why you don't have any friends," Sam says.

"I'm talking about myself as much as I'm talking about you or him! Women look at me, they run. Because, let me tell you, you feminists like to say it's men who objectify women, but women are just as bad."

"You know as much about feminism as Bach did," Sam says. "Probably less."

Elgar is about to say something else, but he looks over J's shoulder and stops. A few seconds later, the newly married couple is at the table.

"We're so glad you're here!" Imogen says to everyone.

"Even you," Carl says to Elgar.

Small talk is made. When it's done, Imogen asks J if she can talk to him for a second. Once they're off in a corner, she tells him the few remaining things that will happen before the DJ set begins and confirms the first few songs J will play for the married couple. Once that's settled, Imogen says, "I'm so sorry about your table. You are such a good sport. Carl had to invite them, for professional reasons. We didn't think they'd actually come."

"I'm enjoying Pam and Sam's company," J says.

"Well, that's a first. But I'm glad to hear it."

"Are we really the only single people at this wedding?"

"What a thing to say! I mean, you're not . . . if you count the children. Unless I'm forgetting someone. Oh! Carl's great-aunt! Her husband passed away before I met him. She never remarried."

*Don't you have any single friends?* J wants to ask. But it's clear what the answer is. At this point, J doesn't know if this is odd, or merely to be expected.

If V were here, she'd know.

When the time comes, J excuses himself from the table to DJ.

"Would one of you ladies like to dance?" Elgar asks the sisters.

In response, Sam hails the server for more wine. The old man looks up for the first time in an hour or so, mutters excuses, and steps away.

J loves being a DJ. If performing a wedding song is like midwifery, DJing a reception is like air-traffic control, trying to keep everything in seamless motion and spirits lifted. He starts with a favorite opening salvo, D Train's "You're the One for Me," which jumps quickly into Diana Ross's "My Own Piano." Everything he puts into the air lands beautifully, and the dance floor becomes energetic.

A few people come over and make requests. A teen asks for some Kraftwerk, and J tells him that, lamentably, this doesn't feel like a Kraftwerk crowd. To his surprise, the next request comes from a noticeably intoxicated Sam, who says she wants him to play "Dancing Queen."

"Always a hit," J says, moving it up on his playlist. "Makes people happy."

"But it's such a sad song!" Sam protests. "A tragedy!"

"How so?"

"The song isn't told by the dancing queen. It's told by someone standing on the sidelines." (Her words make J think of the priest for a second.) "Look, I used to be a dancing queen. When I was younger, you couldn't keep me off the dance floor. Those were wild times. But then your friends start to get busy. Don't want to stay out as late. And you try to go alone, but it's like your friends have been replaced by all these strangers. Younger strangers. First you disappear from the spotlight, then you disappear from the dance floor altogether. You watch your glory pass to someone else. And that, my new friend, is what 'Dancing Queen' is about. She's having the time of her life, sure. But she has no idea how soon that will end."

"And you want me to play it?"

"Maybe I'm no better than Elgar. I like to see young people dance to it. Because they have *no idea*."

Sam returns to their table, and when J puts the song on, he looks over to her and she gives him a thumbs up. As predicted, young people throng to the dance floor—this is the first ABBA song of the night. More unexpected, Elgar also leaves their table for the first time and steps onto the dance floor.

J wonders at first if he'll start throwing dinner rolls at the crowd. But, no—Elgar is plunging in, not quite singing along, but clearly under the sway of the song. He looks painfully aware of the crowd around him, his expression daring them to say he doesn't belong here. But nobody seems to mind his presence. Some look to see who he's with, and then just shrug when they realize he's on his own. Then, unbelievably, he starts to strike that pose where you wrap your arms around yourself so it looks from the back like you're making out with someone. From the smoothness with which he does it, J can tell Elgar's danced this dance before. It could even be his signature move.

J is debating whether he should let the ABBA wave crest now, or whether he should prolong it with "SOS" when suddenly there are screams from the dance floor. People stop dancing, many turning to look at something happening at the center. J sees Pam run to this hole that's forming and realizes that there is a body collapsed at the center of it—the body of the ancient man from his table, who must have attempted a dance. J does not have a DJ mic, but there is an emcee mic, and Carl is suddenly on it, telling everyone to remain calm. An ambulance has been called. In the meantime, a doctor is doing what she can. Please give them room.

Now J has a clear sightline to Pam doing heart compressions. Then she stops, and he can see the old, anonymous man's hand move. Guests are murmuring "heart attack" in at least four languages, though nobody knows for sure what's going on. J has stopped the music, doesn't know what to do. Like everyone else, he waits for the paramedics to arrive, watches as they take the man away. Nobody else joins him; he is alone on the ambulance journey, in a way that pierces something within J. Carl gets back on the emcee mic to tell everyone it's going to be okay. He says that "the old man"—that's what he calls him—"overexerted" himself.

Imogen's mom is now at the DJ station.

"Play something," she hisses. "We can't let this ruin their big day. You have to play something good to get the dance floor going again."

"SOS" is clearly out of the question. J skips to the next song on his playlist—Kylie Minogue's "Hand on Your Heart."

Also not a good choice.

Nor the next song, "Heart of Glass."

Or the next, "I Think I Need a New Heart."

"Stop playing around!" the bride's mother chides. J half expects her to grab the laptop. Is it too soon for "Dancing on My Own," he wonders?

"Just play 'Celebration'! Everyone loves 'Celebration'!"

J does not love "Celebration" and doesn't have it on his laptop. Finally, he lands on Diana Ross's "Coming Out" and hits play.

Imogen's mom gives him a strange look. But it gets some people on the dance floor.

J closes his set with Foreigner's "I Want to Know What Love Is"—and almost stops to dedicate it to the old man, who everyone's been told is recovering well in a nearby hospital. It's an odd choice for a last song, but it's Imogen's choice, and J respects that. The wedding party is now intoxicated enough to sing along with near-gospel fervor, and J tries not to listen to the words too closely. He feels the deep impulse to leave before the song is over, because he can imagine the scene from the service playing out, although in this case instead of filing out pew by pew, the guests will file out two by two, couple after couple after couple, until J is the only one left.

J doesn't leave first; he can't abandon his laptop. Enough couples—and they are all couples—stay until the last dance that J doesn't feel so alone. At the end of the song, there's a half-hearted cheer, and the messy dispersal begins. Imogen comes over, thanks J for coming all this way, and tells him she hopes he'll send his song from the ceremony so she and Carl can hear all of it.

J tells her of course, of course, and makes as graceful an exit as he can.

As soon as he's by himself, he checks his phone. Then he does the math—it is unquestionably a waking hour in New York City.

He texts V.

*Why haven't you responded? Is everything okay?*

To which he gets . . . no response.

He is angry at her for the silence, and angry at himself for not being able to give her the space she so clearly wants. He feels like he needs to apologize for liking her so much, for how inconvenient that is. Which is ridiculous. And it hurts.

Just after midnight, Leipzig time, Nick Andrews emails, saying he's so happy to have heard from J, and he will try to pitch the Talk of the Town piece on Monday. This calms J down a little; it's nice that *someone* is excited to hear from him.

Plus now he has a reason to go back to New York. Let V wonder if it's really about her or not.

*If she wants there to be games, two can play*, he thinks. Then he feels even more depressed, because in his head, that sounds a lot like something Elgar would say. And he doesn't want to sound like Elgar. Ever.

He knows he has to let go a little in order to ultimately keep hold.

But that's hard. So hard.

He's not sure he can pull it off.

That night, he's awakened by more barking. It's anyone's guess whether it's a real dog outside or just too many thoughts demanding to be heard.

## THE EIGHTH WEDDING

"Are we monogamous?"

This question had come from V about seven months into the relationship. They had woken up amorous, coupled, and were luxuriating in the lazy sunrise afterglow.

J had known this question would come up, but was still surprised that it arrived so abruptly, and at this particular moment.

"I don't know," he said. "Are we?"

He hadn't been with anyone else for months, and V hadn't told him about extracurricular exploits. So his big, immediate concern was whether the question was theoretical or logistical.

V didn't show her cards. Instead, she cuddled into him and said, "I'm curious what you think."

"I love being with you, and I'm happy being only with you."

V kissed him then, for long enough that J had time to wonder what lay at the other side of it.

When V pulled back, she was smiling.

"Good," she said. "That's how I feel, too. So I guess the answer is, we're monogamous."

"I'll prepare the press release," J told her.

"Yes, we'll send it to all our exes."

"And our more attractive colleagues."

"And baristas. We need to send it to all the baristas. They're always asking me what my name is, and we know what that leads to."

"I love you," J said to V then. It wasn't the first time, but it still felt like an event when it was said this way.

"I love you, too," V said back. Then she shifted away and asked, "Do you mind if I take the first shower?"

No, J didn't mind at all.

"This is how it will go," Nick Andrews says to J at a Starbucks across from Borough Hall, ten days after their initial contact. "The judge officiating today happens to be a big fan, so she's down with you and me being in the chapel for the weddings, and you playing your quick tune—emphasis on the word *quick*. Now of course we don't want to be wedding crashers, so I've got two amazing interns, Dylan and Mike, asking each of the couples if they would like a serenade, no additional cost, courtesy of *The New Yorker*. I'm guessing half will be takers, half will tell us to scram. But the judge performs four or five weddings an hour, so even if half say yes, we'll have enough for the story."

"It's nice that the judge is a fan," J observes. "When I imagine my audience, it's rarely the judiciary."

"Oh," Nick responds, looking momentarily at his shoes. "I meant she's a fan of *The New Yorker*. She hasn't heard of you. But she was intrigued!"

It had taken V three days to respond to J's messages. In that time, he'd left Leipzig, returned home, and booked a new ticket to New York.

*Sorry*, she texted. *I keep running out of time. I hope the wedding went well.*

The text arrived at seven in the morning, J's time. Which meant he was still asleep, and when he woke, he assumed V was already lost to work. He knew it was unlikely that V had planned the message to fall into this time-zone limbo.

If it had been three hours, and not three days, he would have texted back, *It's okay. No problem.* But since it had been three days, and it struck him that she didn't have any idea where in the world he was, he messaged back:

*I'm in my apartment. Just woke up. The wedding was interesting. Someone almost died. You would have loved it.*

He was satisfied with his tone as he typed, then dissatisfied as soon as he sent the words on their way.

What he really wanted to ask was, *Do you miss it here?* Because back in the apartment, all he felt was its emptiness of her. But could she feel that emptiness from so far away? He knew it was possible—he often missed that home-shaped space while he was on the road. But as he once again waited for the passing hours to bring him a reply, he wondered if, without talking about it, their relationship had slid into something that had happened in the past, once upon a time, in a place she no longer brought to mind.

J isn't sure exactly what to expect on a Thursday mid-morning at the Brooklyn courthouse. He has never performed at a city hall wedding before. At receptions afterward (sometimes long afterward), sure. But not at the event itself. He understands the impulse to separate the legality from the celebration, to take away some of the suspense before the big performance. He also, frankly, prefers to think of marriage in terms of the law and not in terms of a higher power needing to be pleased. But that, of course, is just his opinion.

The courthouse exterior is monumental enough, but once you get inside, it quickly devolves into the architecture of bureaucracy, circa 1960. J half expects men in gray flannel suits to be popping in and out of the office doors, with colorful secretaries glimpsed inside, pitter-patting away on their typewriters. The hall leading to the marriage office is the same as any other hall, and when you step inside the office, it looks like any other municipal office, with a check-in counter that would not be out of place at a department of motor vehicles. The people behind the counter could be working anywhere, dressed respectably but not reflecting the supposed joy of the occasion.

The thing that's different is the waiting area, and the dynamic of the people within it. Here, every party is at least a party of two. A few smile at J and his guitar, and he doesn't know if this is because the interns have already asked if they want him to join their weddings, or if it's simply the sight of a man in a suit with a guitar in this particular lobby that makes them happy.

Nick sees J looking around. "My husband and I got married here," he says. "I know it's pretty drab, but in a way, that makes it more incredible to me. Like in a fantasy novel, when the most boring building imaginable houses a ministry of spellcasters. You have each other, you have your friends and family, if they can make it. Nothing big. But the building tells you that's all you need. A marriage is about a lot of people, sure. But at its heart, it's about two people. And here, you're stepping right into the heart."

*Someone almost died at the wedding?* V wrote back ten hours after J's message. *You didn't try to hit any high notes, did you?*

The line made J smile, and the smile made him hurt. When things are falling apart, isn't it easier when you're not getting along? When you no longer have access to the things about the other person that once brought you pleasure? For J, the fact that V could ricochet any of his remarks back to him with equal precision (if not speed) has always been part of the thrill of the pairing.

*What can I say?* he responded. *You weren't there to prevent me from doing my "Ave Maria."*

*How do you solve a problem like "Ave Maria"?*

*That's what I need you to teach me.*

There was a pause. Those excruciating three dots. Then:

*How's home?* V asked.

J hated how hopeful this simple question made him. And hated even more that he immediately replied, *It misses you.* Because it only set him up for the disappointment of what she wrote next:

*My apartment here misses me too. Or at least the awake version of me.*

*It's considerate of your apartment not to wake you, just to play. Good thing I got an apartment and not a puppy.*

*Exactly.*

Sitting alone in his room, approximately 3,750 miles away from her, J could sense V about to end the conversation, and felt a spur of fear that it would be another few days before he could re-engage her. Quickly, he threw something else into the breach:

*I'm going back to New York in four days. To be interviewed by The New Yorker.*

(He knew "interviewed" wasn't entirely accurate, but it was close enough.)

*Oh, wow. The New Yorker thing came through.*

*I'm very excited.* (Somehow, this obvious statement felt like a confession, as if sharing any emotion with her had implications.)

*Are you staying at Julia's again?*

That was the plan. But J was curious if V would offer her forlorn apartment. So he answered, *Not sure. Might need to find somewhere else.*

*You always liked the Ace Hotel, didn't you? It's off season, so there might be a deal.*

It could conceivably be some consolation that her memory of his hotel preference is accurate. But at that moment, it wasn't a consolation at all. Or, at best, it was a condescending consolation.

*I'll let you know where I end up*, J typed.

*Great. I do want to hear more. But I have to go now. I suppose you can catch me up in person in a few days. Message me when you get here.*

The judge's name is Anna Pao, and she spells it twice for Nick even though there is a nameplate right on her desk. It is clear to J that Nick wasn't kidding—even more than J, Judge Pao is excited to be in *The New Yorker*.

They meet in the room where all the ceremonies occur. It looks like it was created in 1962 by an architect who wanted to stretch his stained-glass budget as far as it could go, by choosing abstract shards of color rather than any coherent representation. The swath of colored shape is either countered or complimented by a whole lot of wood paneling. On the plus side, it definitely looks like they've left the municipal vibe behind. On the minus side, they've left it for a nondenominational, windowless rec room.

There is a slightly elevated platform for Judge Pao and the couples getting married, and then a wide area for chosen spectators. The judge gestures to a space to the side of the platform where J can stand.

"This way you'll only be in the photos if they want you to be," Judge Pao says.

"Makes sense," J tells her. The spot is definitely more in shadow than in light.

"I'll make some remarks, they'll read their vows, and then you'll have a minute—two, tops—to sing your song for them, and then there will be hugs and kisses and photos, and then I will firmly but gracefully tell them to move into the hall so the next couple can come in. If you go longer than two minutes, I will have to cut you off—is that understood?"

"Yes."

"Alright." Judge Pao opens a notebook and centers herself on the wedding platform. "I've done this for fifteen years, and I still have my speech out, just in case. Isn't that funny? Don't you think that's interesting?"

"It is," J says. Then he realizes that Judge Pao was talking to Nick, hoping this detail will make it into *The New Yorker*.

No fool, Nick makes a production of scribbling it down.

*Message me when you get here.*

J had taken this to mean, *Don't bother sending me updates every few hours. Don't include me in your life so often. Get used to the distance. We'll be old friends who catch up the rare times we're in the same place.*

Something deeply rooted within him wanted to resist this, to figure out how to bring her back into his world in the way she used to be in it.

But the grounding around the roots was starting to slip.

By uprooting herself, V may have uprooted him, too.

As he packed to leave for New York again, he kept noticing small items of hers throughout the apartment. Books she'd finished at his place and hadn't taken back to her place. A red jacket hanging in the closet. Dried cranberries in the cabinet. A bottle of her preferred vodka in the freezer, only about an eighth full. A charger for her phone.

Nothing that couldn't be left behind, but in communion they still might have some power.

*Maybe not an anchor*, J thought as he locked up the apartment, *but possibly a beacon?*

Then, as he rode to the airport, he tried to transform it from a question to a statement.

Maybe not an anchor, but possibly a beacon.

Awkwardly, the first couple of the day doesn't want a random Swedish musician as part of their ceremony, so J and Nick step back into Judge Pao's small office, keeping quiet as she does her job.

The second couple, however, is willing to have J serenade them. Dylan and Mike, the two interns, have gathered a brief overview of who they are: Allie is a librarian and Claude is a contractor. They met five years ago; Claude's sister worked with Allie and set them up. Both their families are with them today.

J only has a few minutes to digest this information before the families spill into the wedding room. (He created a template beforehand for his wedding songs today, but he'll need some details for each variation.) As the families settle in, J is reminded all over again why he wrote "If You Ever Need a Stranger (to Sing at Your Wedding)"—there is an instantaneous joy buzzing from everyone entering the room; they exude a kind of romantic adrenaline, the euphoria of the long-distance runner crossing the finish line matched with the euphoria of the crowd witnessing the victory.

Judge Pao's smile seems genuine as she calls the couple up and begins the ceremony; J imagines that she, too, must get something out of seeing such happiness, or else her job would be a nightmare of repetition. With just the right balance of humor and authority, she talks about the importance of the day in the eyes of the families and in the eyes of New York State. Then she asks the couple if they've written vows, and when they tell her they have, she takes a step back, as if to render herself invisible as Allie and Claude hold hands, look into each other's eyes, and speak.

Often couples write their vows separately, for a moment of surprise in what's otherwise a fairly formulaic event. But Allie and Claude clearly talked about it ahead of time, because they take the word *vows* literally. Allie vows to be better about hogging the pillows, about reading too late into the night, about keeping her eyes closed for most of the horror movies Claude loves so much. Claude vows to be better about keeping the garbage nights straight, about freaking out when he can't find his keys, and trying to watch movies other than horror movies. They each vow to love the other— "with all my heart," Claude says, and Allie adds, "with all your brain, too," which gets a laugh as Claude amends his vow and repeats it.

Rings are brought to the podium by one of Allie's nieces, and Judge Pao makes it official. J joins in the families' cheers and applause and is riding the moment so much that he's almost surprised when Judge Pao says, "And now, I believe we will have a brief song in honor of the newly wedded couple."

All eyes turn to J as he sheepishly picks up his guitar and improvises a song.

> A librarian and a contractor walk into a bar
> The librarian's name is Allie and the contractor's name is Claude
> They order drinks and nervously sit down next to each other and talk
> The jukebox wakes up and sings for them so soft
> And in the background pirates and rabbis and bears walk in after them
> But Claude and Allie don't notice cause they're lost in conversation
> If you're waiting for a punchline, you'll have to wait until you're old
> As five years later the story's still being told

It's over in less than a minute, but he gets a response like it's the end of a long concert. But then, unlike at the end of a long concert, he is mostly ignored, as Allie and Claude come into the crowd and start the chain of hugs and kisses and congratulations. True to her word, after the proper documents are signed, Judge Pao deftly persuades them to move their celebration out into the hall. The couple and many of their family members thank J as they leave, as if he is a one-man reception line as they pass into the next chapter of their lives.

"That was great," Nick says to him as the information for the next couple is texted in from the reception area. "Now let's do it another dozen times."

Just over a year ago, J had made the ridiculous mistake of allowing his manager to book a small tour in France the same week that

France's team was in the World Cup. When they'd booked the dates, they hadn't realized it was the World Cup, and they certainly hadn't known that France would make it as far as they did. The results were demoralizing—empty crowds from Paris to Marseilles. At one venue in Lyon, J was nearly drowned out from the cheering and groaning and ref-baiting at the bar. And, worse, there weren't many English speakers present, and J's story-songs didn't really carry on tunes alone. The audience reaction ranged from quizzical annoyance to quizzical disdain. Even though he knew the reason for the poor performance, he couldn't stop feeling like a failure. On his short flight back home, he nearly didn't put up a fight when the flight attendant told him his guitar was too big for the overhead compartment. He was ready to leave it on a bench, for a more successful singer to take.

Once he got his luggage and got through customs, he readied himself for the trudge to the taxi stand. He saw the drivers waiting with their plaques, none with his name on it. He saw families reuniting delightedly. And he saw a whole bunch of balloons, as if someone had come from a child's birthday party. It wasn't until he heard his name called that he realized it was V holding the balloons. V, who wasn't supposed to pick him up, had come to drive him home. The previous night, he'd called her and told her what had gone wrong. And now, she was the one thing that had gone right.

They didn't embrace tearfully; that wasn't their style. Instead J said, gesturing to the balloons, "Did you mug a clown on your way to the airport?"

And she replied, "I figured you'd want to pop them on the ride home."

She had brought a hairpin and left it on the passenger seat, and as they drove back to the city, he'd popped the balloons as they both screamed, not so much out of delight but from the sheer desire for catharsis.

It made him feel better.

By the time they got home, the tour was already a story, a bad but funny story.

"Thank you," he said.

"Look, I'm not your car service," V told him. "But I can tell when you need it. And if you need it, I'll be there."

Fast forward a year or so.

(Why is it that we say *fast forward* but never *fast backward* or *fast rewind*? Is it that losing time is a much quicker process than the attempt to get it back?)

J arrived again in New York. Julia was home, but luckily said he could still stay at her place, on the couch. J had looked up the Ace Hotel, and even with a discount, it was still more than he wanted to pay, and possibly more than he could afford. He still smarted that V hadn't offered, almost as if she'd forgotten how expensive touring could be. And this wasn't even touring! This was a free gig for some publicity. And an excuse to come back to New York.

At JFK, the immigration officer actually tallied up the time J had spent in America recently, to make sure he hadn't visited longer than his allotted ninety days. (Apparently, he only had thirty-seven left.) Harried, J rolled his suitcase through the last-chance duty-free and escaped the sliding doors into the outer ring of New York.

He knew V had no idea which flight he was taking. He knew V was busy, and that the AirTrain awaited. And yet . . . as he saw the drivers with their plaques and the families reuniting, he couldn't help but look around, to make sure she hadn't come to surprise him. It was the slimmest of slim chances; he knew this. And still, the disappointment he felt wasn't slim at all.

The second wedding party is dressed entirely in Yankees gear. The bride and groom wear jerseys that have BRIDE and GROOM written on the back where the players' names ordinarily would be, as well as the number 7. The wedded couple isn't wearing caps, but everyone else is.

J desperately tries to remember anything he can about baseball for when it comes time for him to sing.

> You make me feel like I've hit a home run
> With the odds: a billion to one
> The ball's on fire, leaving the stadium
> I'm doing my victory run
> First base, second, third, and fourth
> I'm back where I begun
> I want you on my team from now on
> Put on this ballcap, sign here, and we're done

The next two couples take a pass on having a wedding singer, but J then quickly returns for wedding number three. This time it is just the couple, Mahogany and TJ, and a friend—they didn't tell the interns much besides the fact that TJ has a dog named Lucy, who they wanted to be a witness for the ceremony, but apparently when it comes to legal paperwork, dogs don't count. They ask if J wouldn't mind being a witness instead. J, not really knowing what this meant, said yes.

His first response on seeing them is to think, *Wow, they're children*. They are, in fact, each twenty-one, but that's the tricky thing about age—the older you get, the younger twenty-one looks. They are dressed simply but respectfully for the occasion—her in a white summer dress, him looking a little awkward in a shirt and tie. Their friend is wearing a Beyoncé concert t-shirt. J wonders if this was a deliberate choice, or whether he was asked to be at the wedding while he was doing something else.

Because he is old enough that twenty-one looks really young, J feels the urge to tell them to stop for a second, really think about what they're doing. It is clear from their body language how in love they are, and he wishes that this will be enough.

If Judge Pao, who is even older than J, has any hesitation, she doesn't show it. She beams as if the room is full of family and friends. When she asks Mahogany and TJ if they've written their own vows, they look panicked. The judge quickly tells them not to worry and pulls two laminated cards out for them to read to each other. It is full of the standard pledges, to have and to hold, and both Mahogany and TJ stumble over them in their nervousness. It's only as they are putting the rings on each other's fingers that they start to truly smile, and when Judge Pao tells them they may now kiss as husband and wife, they make it a long one. Their friend videos the whole thing.

Mahogany and TJ step from the platform, ready to leave. Judge Pao reminds them there are some papers to sign, and also that J is going to sing a song for them. They seem to have forgotten the second part—J wonders if the interns really spoke to them or not. Nick gives him a little nod, and he realizes he has to play. He sings:

> Hello my name is Lucy and I'm TJ's dog and best friend
> I'll tell you how Mahogany came into our lives one evening
> I was on TJ's lap as he swiped on Tinder back and forth
> When I saw Mahogany's face I stopped him abruptly with my paw
> I guess I like keeping my pack together, must be a dog thing
> Other girls I'd growl at, but this one I liked by instinct
> I'm a brilliant matchmaker but pickier than most,
> the application list officially closed
> the moment Mahogany got down on her knee and proposed

The couple and their friend don't applaud, but J can tell he chose the right angle. Judge Pao asks J to come sign the marriage certificate as the second witness.

Once he's signed his name, he gets shy thank-yous from both bride and groom, and a hasty display of TJ's phone screen, which shows a very happy-looking dog. Judge Pao doesn't need to tell them it's time to leave—they are out quickly, leaving J up with the judge.

"So young," he says, because he needs to say it to someone.

"Yes, but they know what they're doing. For the most part," the judge says. "You can tell the ones who don't really know what they're doing. But I marry them anyway. Because it's their call, not mine."

The thing about meeting someone when you're both in your thirties is that you know you'll never be truly young together. But still, you can try.

Julia had been home when J finally got to her apartment from JFK, and after he put his things down, she made them some tea, and they sat in the kitchen and caught up. V was the first thing he talked about, and he kept talking for about fifteen minutes. Was he any different from a teenager as he did this?

He waited until it was late at night, which was a mistake because his body thought it was even later at night than the clocks showed. Or maybe it wasn't a mistake at all, because he was so tired that his actions felt like they had all the consequence of a dream. After so much build-up, after so many times deciding not to text to her, it ended up being so easy to just pick up his phone, click on her name, and knock a few letters into the shape of words.

*I've made it to New York*, he wrote. *I wanted to let you know the plane didn't crash.*

Five minutes later, her reply:

*I'm glad. Aren't you tired?*

*Yes*, he typed. *But happy to be here.* "Here" being Julia's apartment. Not the Ace Hotel.

*OK. Thank you for that information.*

*Is this a bad time?*

*Is 12:34 a.m. ever a good time?*

*Were you sleeping?*

*No. But I want to be.*

*I thought you'd want to know I'm here.*

*Now I know.*

*Is something wrong?*

*Why don't people ever ask, "Is something right?"*

*Do you want me to ask that?*

*No. I want to go to sleep.*

J wanted to ask *Are you mad at me?* But he knew that the question itself could be perceived as an act of aggression. Because he was tired, he thought maybe if he dressed it up, made it a little less serious, if would float more easily over the transom.

*Are you irate with me?* he asked.

*Yes.*

*Why?*

*Don't do this. Don't force this conversation.*

*What conversation?*

Thirty seconds went by. A minute.

It was unbearable.

J called V.

She didn't pick up.

*Please pick up*, he texted.

He tried again.

*Seriously. You have me worried now. Please pick up.*

This time, she answered.

"Why are you doing this?" she asked immediately.

"Is it so bad that I want you to know I'm in the same city as you? In the hope that I will get to see you?"

"J, you were just here."

"You say that like it's a bad thing."

He hears something in the background. A voice.

"Is someone there?" he asked.

"George Clooney," V replied. "And Brad Pitt. And Julia Roberts. And even Don Cheadle. Are you jealous?"

"So it's the TV."

"Seriously, it's time for bed. I'm sure you have a wedding thing tomorrow."

"Yes, the one for *The New Yorker*."

"Honestly, I've lost track. Although that presupposes I was ever keeping track, which I don't think I actually was."

"Wow, you're in a mood. Are you sure you're alone there?"

"Do you honestly think I would be on the phone with you if I had someone else here?"

J's mind immediately went to all the nights his texts went unanswered. But he was at least smart enough not to air these thoughts. Instead he said, "I'm sorry I'm keeping you awake. I'll let you go."

That last sentence got a laugh.

"What?" J asked.

"Nothing."

"No. What?"

"It's just . . . all evidence points to you not, in fact, letting me go."

"That's not fair."

"Isn't it?"

J didn't like this. Not at all. He debated: Attack or retreat? Attack or retreat? Attack or—

"Look," V said, sounding completely exasperated. "When I came here, I didn't think you were going to follow me. But that's exactly what you've done. And I don't want that. I've never wanted that."

There was a moment she could have taken it back. Could have said, *I'm sorry, I'm just tired. Let's talk in the morning.* J gave her the opportunity to have that moment. He waited.

But she didn't take it back.

She just hung up.

And J didn't call her back.

*Return to me, return to me, return to me*, J thinks. Then he realizes Nick is talking to him.

"Next up is the Abramovitz wedding. The interns tell me you're going to like this one."

The door opens, and a male couple walks in. One of them, cute and bearded, takes one look at J and actually gasps and steps back, the way singing show contestants on TV do when they realize that the guest coach is someone they adore, like Dolly Parton or Ariana Grande. The bearded guy's spouse seems more amused than annoyed by this.

"C'mon, David," he says. "Just breathe."

David takes some quite visible breaths, then comes over to J and says, "When they said there was a singer who wanted to do a spontaneous wedding song for us, I thought, well, okay. They didn't say your name or anything, but then one of them mentioned that you'd come all the way from Sweden, and I thought, it couldn't possibly be . . . but—I'm freaking out here a little—it actually is you. And that's, like, the most rad wedding surprise a guy could ever ask for."

"It's very nice to meet you," J says, and he means it with every ounce of his soul, even though a bittersweet note is being struck somewhere inside him. How has it gotten to a point where he can bring strangers such ebullient joy, but not the woman he loves?

"I hate to interrupt," Judge Pao says, not unkindly, "but I believe there's a wedding that needs to be performed? And I'm afraid you can't eat that in here."

This last part refers to a giant cake that one of the guests is carrying.

"Oh, we know," the bearded groom says. "It's just . . . we couldn't just leave it out there."

"It took so long to bake it," the clean-shaven groom says, "and he'll never have that recipe agaaaaaaaain."

J laughs, and the clean-shaven groom adds, "He really did bake it. I'm not saying I'm marrying him because of his baking. But . . . it's certainly in the plus column."

The ceremony is as sweet as J imagines the cake to be. When his turn comes, he sings to them:

> At Borough Hall they told them they had a surprise for their big day
> A wedding singer from Sweden had offered to write them a serenade
> When they saw it was who they thought it was they almost dropped
>     the cake
> That David had spent the whole night to bake
> The wedding singer took a good look at them and wondered who
>     they were
> He noticed the way that Christopher comforted his nervous partner
> And how David reciprocated the gesture with a kiss
> And he thought: the reason I sing at weddings . . . is this

Many photos are taken, and Nick assures the grooms repeatedly that he'll forward his recording of the song to them.

"I wish you could join us," the bearded groom says.

"Me too," J replies, and it's not a lie. "But we have to do a few more weddings for the piece."

"A wedding singer's job is never done, I guess! Do you live in New York now?"

J smiles. "I could never live in New York."

It's Nick who asks, "Why not?"

"It's just not a place for me. Too big. Too busy. Too full of itself."

Judge Pao does her velvet-glove routine to keep things moving. After the Abramovitz party takes one last round of selfies and leaves, Nick checks his phone for new texts from the interns and starts laughing.

"What?" J asks.

"You're not going to believe this," Nick says. "The next couple is named *Thor* and *Meta*."

\* \* \*

They don't see J at first when they walk into the room, and J completely understands why. Meta is the first member of a wedding party today to have treated Borough Hall as if it were The Plaza, in terms of attire. At its heart her dress is a simple white, sleeveless, satin sheath. But over it is something that J can only think of as the most elaborate, dazzling fishing net he's ever encountered. It's woven in thicker ropes, but each rope is made of glittery filaments, which give Meta the air of frost in sunlight, even under the municipal lamps.

Thor cannot take his eyes off her. And Meta, at least at first, cannot take her eyes off her dress, trying to prevent it from sweeping too much up off the floor.

"Welcome," Judge Pao says. Then even she can't help but add, "That's quite a dress."

"Thank you," Meta says, lifting her hem to step onto the wedding platform. It is only after she does this that she and Thor see J. He can see it happening—Meta turns, sees him, starts to turn to Nick next, but then stops as if someone inside her has stepped on the brake. She looks back at J and elbows Thor to take a look.

"I can't believe it!" Thor says, breaking out of his Meta reverie with a grin. He leaps down and gives J a huge hug. J hugs back, because to not do so would be even more awkward than doing so.

"When they told us they had a singer, I had no idea . . ." Thor says. "I mean, what are the odds? This is *so cool*."

Meta has not moved from her perch. Meta does not appear to think J's presence is so cool.

"Oh fuck," Thor says, realization dawning. "This wedding is a secret. You can't tell anyone. Not even V. You have to promise."

"Of course, of course," J says.

Thor turns to Nick. "And you can't use our names."

"No names," Nick says. Though he can hardly keep the curiosity off his face. Who are these people?

J walks back with Thor to where Meta and Judge Pao are waiting.

"Congratulations," he says to Meta. He is not going to attempt a hug, or even a handshake.

"Really. You can't tell anyone," she says.

"I promise."

"Okay," she says. "Good."

"I like your dress," J offers.

"It was my grandmother's," Meta replies. J can't tell whether she's serious.

"Time for a wedding!" Judge Pao proclaims.

The ceremony only takes four minutes—Judge Pao's script, the laminated vows. J spends these four minutes not trying to come up with a verse for their song, but instead trying to figure out if Thor and Meta are truly in love, if they really should be taking this step. It's clear that they believe they're in love; even though they haven't known each other long, they've forged a visible togetherness. But is it a durable one? Is there any actual way to know? Even from the inside, it's hard. But from the outside? If someone saw J and V a few months ago, would they have thought they were in love? Forget the private moments. Were there ever public moments where they emanated togetherness, where they would have seemed to the casual observer to be each other's metronome? Or not even the casual observers. What about friends? What did their friends see? Two people in love, or two people trying to be in love, or two people not trying to be in love, or maybe just one person trying to be in love, and the other uncertain of how to deal with that? Thor loves Meta. There's no doubt of that. Well, unless he's just infatuated with her. He's so young—is there a way of discerning a difference? Maybe it's wrong to blame it on youth. What if, all this time, all he really felt was infatuation toward V? What if he was not only infatuated with her, but with their life together? And she must have been too . . . but what if it was something less than infatuation? Something closer to benign enjoyment? Perpetual amusement? Why is Meta so much harder to read than Thor? Is it because she feels less, or just that he shows his feelings more? V never said she was coming to New York to get away from J. She never told him she didn't want him to follow. If she wanted him to let go, why didn't she just tell—

A hand on his shoulder. Nick's. He blinks back to the room that he's in. Sees Thor, Meta, and the judge all watching. Waiting.

J wills on his stage smile, the one that is waiting like a spare tire whenever he doesn't feel like going on. He congratulates the couple. He makes a show of getting his guitar. He quickly thinks of something to sing, then sings it.

> The prefrontal cortex isn't fully developed until the age of twenty-five
> But you can drink at twenty-one, marry at eighteen, and at sixteen you can drive
> Well, what has the prefrontal cortex ever done but overanalyze?
> When the heart knows what it wants it's always right.

"That was so great!" Thor calls out when J is done, running over for another big hug. Then he pulls J onto the platform so J and Nick can be their witnesses. As he signs, J knows two things: That he will, indeed, keep this a secret from V, and that she will inevitably find out anyway. This signature will be one of many clues.

Judge Pao keeps things moving as always, and Nick tells J the next couple asked for the singer not to be present.

"Come walk with us for a second," Meta says, her voice making it clear it's not a request so much as a requirement.

Thor holds Meta's hand as they move into the hallway, her dress even more discordant now than it was in the chapel. She leads them to an empty corner, makes sure that it will remain empty for the near future, then laser-locks her eyes on J's and says, "I want to emphasize, this needs to stay a secret."

"We're planning a real wedding," Thor adds, trying to be as laid-back as Meta is severe. "That's going to be the big deal. You'll be invited, of course. And hopefully will play for us again! Only we'll be the only ones knowing it's the second time!"

"There are serious business implications," Meta continues. "Things are very close to a resolution with the next stages of Secret Project, and we don't want the fact that we're married to be a distraction from that. At all."

"Of course," J says.

"You can't tell V," Thor says.

"Especially V," Meta adds.

"You're in luck," J replies. "I'm not sure V will ever speak to me again!"

Thor laughs at this. Meta can tell he's serious.

Then Thor, seeing that Meta is not laughing, assures J, "Believe me, V loves you. We all know V loves you. So even if you're not speaking now, you will be. You just can't tell her about today."

Meta provides a more measured, "It's true—I doubt you're over yet."

They seem so sure that J and V will talk again that J savors a small bit of hope. What have they seen in J and V together?

"Plus—those songs!" Thor enthuses. "Are you really writing a new song for every wedded couple?"

"Well, the first verse . . ."

"Amazing! There has to be a use for that in Secret Project. We're absolutely going to have weddings on there. How cool would it be to get your own song? We could have you write a bunch of variations, and then AI could take it from there. Let's talk!"

Horrified, yet not knowing what else to say, J says, "Sure. Let's talk."

Meta somehow pulls a phone from the mesh of her dress and checks the time.

"Any big plans for after?" J asks, just making conversation.

Meta smiles and takes Thor's hand. "That's a secret, too."

"Okay, man," Thor says. "Again, it's, like, too amazing that you were the singer in there. Wipe this all from your memory—but I promise we'll never forget it."

Meta smiles sweetly at him. "Never."

And then, as if a spell has been cast, or maybe taken away, they suddenly appear to J as exactly what they are: a newly married couple about to take their first married step out into the world. They practically slide down the banister into the lobby, out of J's sight.

J is called back into the chapel soon enough, for the rest of the day's weddings. There is a couple that brings four of their dogs, for "emotional support," and one friend, to be able to sign a contract. There's a couple with a practically newborn baby named Theo, who spends the whole ceremony looking like he's paused for some reflection, his eyes shut but his ears listening. There's a couple in their forties wearing matching I'M GETTING MARRIED TODAY t-shirts . . . and when the ceremony is done, they remove them to reveal JUST MARRIED t-shirts underneath.

J tries to put all his thoughts about V aside to focus on these couples, but that proves to be impossible. He tries to imagine sweeping her off her feet and getting her to marry him at Borough Hall. Isn't that supposed to be the solution, the conclusion, the top of the mountain they've been climbing together? He can't picture it. Not home in Sweden. Not here. Especially not here. Because to get married in Borough Hall, wouldn't they both have to be living here? And he can't imagine living here. Not even for V.

She's known this all along, hasn't she?

The last couple of the day throws J for a moment—the bride doesn't look like V, but she does look like she could be V's sister.

At least until she speaks, and the most Brooklyn of Brooklyn accents comes out, full of sweaty syllables and puncturing punctuation. She's wearing a dress that is, in its own way, as magnificent as Meta's—this one could very well have been this bride's grandmother's. (As if to support this assertion, the grandmother is present and fussing at the dress.) A photographer click-click-clicks like a paparazzo, and a young kid carries a boom box at least five times older than he is, which blares "Empire State of Mind" so loud the Empire State might get a migraine. Judge Pao signals for the music to end and the service to start. The groom holds out his hand to escort his bride up to the podium as if it's a grand staircase and not a single step. He's wearing a tuxedo that looks like it's never been worn before, and he appears both nervous-happy and happy-nervous. The bride and groom keep holding hands and keep stealing glances at each other instead of looking at Judge Pao as she speaks to them and welcomes them to the next chapter of their life. J thinks, okay, this is a couple that knows each other, that will last a good long time—

Until Judge Pao asks for the rings.

And the groom says, "Oh shit."

And the bride screams, "WHAT THE FUCK, EDDIE? WHAT THE *SERIOUS FUCK*?"

The groom's pranking her, J thinks. But then he's raising his hands, as if he doesn't want his bride to arrest him, and J realizes Eddie actually *has* forgotten the rings and has no idea what to do about it.

Judge Pao tries to intervene and says they don't really need to have rings to make the vows, and that some couples don't, and—

The bride will not hear of it. Her mother and grandmother rush to console her, but she shakes them off, tears in her eyes, saying no, she knew this would happen, that fucking Eddie couldn't even fucking bother to make sure he had the fucking rings on the *biggest fucking day* of her life.

Now more people are on the wedding platform—friends, cousins, who knows? All of them telling the bride it's okay, some of them pulling rings off their own fingers to be used. Eddie tries to defend himself, but a bigger man (his father? the bride's father?) just shakes his head, and Eddie shuts up.

Finally, the bride clears the path between her and the groom, looks him in the eye, and says, "You did this. Not me." And with that, she makes her exit, leaving chaos and Jay-Z featuring Alicia Keys in her wake.

J can tell this is not the first time something like this has happened, or the first time this bride has delivered an exit line. It's just (probably) the first time it's happened in the wedding room in Borough Hall. It makes him think of V—not that she's like that, but this is now, once again, a story he wants to tell her. He wants her caustic, creatively phrased spin on it. Which feels ridiculous at this point.

Because it's the last wedding of the afternoon, and because there isn't any paperwork to sign, Judge Pao actually makes an exit before the groom does, telling J in ten seconds how much she enjoyed his singing and then talking to Nick for about two more minutes with things she might be quoted as saying in his article.

Eventually, a few guys manage to get the groom to hold his head up long enough to be able to leave the room. As he passes by, he says thank you to J, which breaks J's heart. This isn't a bad guy. He just forgot the fucking rings.

Soon it's just Nick and J in the chapel. Someone turns off the overhead lights, so there's only the glow from behind the stained glass.

"So I guess that's it," J says, picking up his guitar.

Nick smiles mischievously.

"Come on," he says. "You've gotta play me their song!"

J is tired. But he also sees the sense in it.

Why should the happy couples be the only ones who get a song? He takes a moment, strums a few chords, and then, as the clerks in the other room close their windows and pack up to leave, he sings:

> There must be a way to solve every lovers' quarrel, I want to think
> As long as the heart was in the right place, if you didn't mean anything
> Forgive Eddie for his sins
> He just forgot the fucking rings
> If there's still love in your heart please take him back in

## THE NINTH WEDDING

The next day, as soon as he wakes up, J texts V:
*I'm leaving tonight. Do you think it's a good idea for us to meet?*
By the time he's out of the shower, there's a reply. It's not a text or a call, but a voice message. He takes a deep breath and hits play.

"Good morning, J. I've thought about it quite a bit, and ultimately I don't see what the point is of us getting together to talk in person. We both know how the conversation will go . . . or if you don't, you should by now. All I've wanted from you is space, and you are unable to give that to me. For all the right intentions, I'm sure. But the intentions don't really matter, not at this point. I need to focus on myself now, and on this new life I'm building. I can't focus on you, not in the way you want me to. I don't want to hurt you. This is not at all about hurting you, even though I am sure it will make you hurt. I don't regret any of our time together, and I hope someday to have more time together. But right now, my time has to be my own. There is no way to co-own it. So I think it's best to say goodbye. And I know this is the wrong way to do it. But don't you think us seeing each other and me saying this to your face would be even worse? Because you would try to stop me, and if you tried to stop me, I would hate you. I don't hate you now. Not at all. I hope this makes sense. I'm just rambling at this point. You know what I mean, don't you? Goodbye, J. At least for now."

V isn't sure how J is going to respond. When her phone buzzes with a new text, she approaches it with trepidation.
*I won't try to talk you out of it*, he's written.
*Good answer*, she replies. Then, with shaking hands, she starts getting dressed.

J rides the subway and feels profoundly resigned. It manifests not as sadness but silence, not anger but emptiness. He is standing on the dance floor after the last song, blinking as the lights are turned on and what once felt magical is now a mundane, borrowed room.

He knows there is nothing he can do. He hasn't done anything catastrophically wrong, but even if he cashes in all his bonus points, they won't get him the prize. He's honestly not even sure what the prize is anymore; the woman he wants to fight for, the woman he wants to be with . . . she only exists in the past. He's figured out that much, at least.

The trick is giving up on V without giving up on love altogether. That is the hard part. The really hard part. Because the lesson can shift so easily from *She isn't worth the pain* to *It isn't worth the pain*.

He has left people for much less than this. He has been left by people for much less than this. He has been cheated on, vivisected, ghosted, and blamed. He has also blamed, also ghosted, been bored or reckless with affections he should have cherished. With V, he had thought it would be different. And, he supposes, it *is* different. It's yet another broken link in the relationship chain, but it broke for a different reason.

The whole time they were together, they should have been working on the times they wouldn't be together, so the distance wouldn't matter. But instead they considered it a positive that when J was gone, neither one felt the need to spend much effort on keeping in touch. Because there was always an end date to the apartness. Now, however, they're really, indefinitely apart, and there's no way to keep hold. She found a new life, and there is no place for him in this new life.

He still doesn't know how this happened. But he is certain now that it has.

The first words she says to him are "I'm sorry." Seeing him so forlorn, so defeated, and knowing that she's the reason the clouds have gathered . . . she doesn't feel regret, but she does feel sorry.

"I'll be fine," he says, brave-facing it. They are at the entrance to Prospect Park in Brooklyn, right by the bandshell. She hadn't wanted them to have another awkward meal. Better to walk around, talk it through.

"I know you'll be fine," she says. She wants to console him, physically console him, then catches herself—if she's going to do this, she has to do it clean. No touching. No nostalgia.

"I'm surprised you like this city so much," he says. Which almost seems ridiculous, because it's a nice day in the park; they are surrounded my people who seem happy with their choice to be here.

She does not point this out.

Instead she admits, "I am, too. But honestly, if work had taken me to London or Paris or Sydney, the same thing would have probably happened."

"You leaving me?"

"Me leaving home."

"Is that what this is about?"

V wants so badly for him to understand this. "It is," she says. "I keep thinking back to Matthias from university. You know, when graduation got close, I understood I had to break up with him. I couldn't see a future for us; he was annoying, self-centered, and needy. I thought it would be an easy break, because of the end of school. But when I told him, 'I think it's time for us to go our separate ways, now that we're graduating,' he told me, 'What are you talking about? That's no reason for us to break up. Neither of us is going anywhere.' It made me so angry then. And what *really* pissed me off is that he ended up being right. Until you, I hadn't even left Sweden. You've taken me places, more than anyone else ever has. But I've felt like a guest, J. You haven't made me feel like a guest, but that's how it's been. Now I don't feel that way. Now I feel I'm actually living somewhere else. And even though it's exhausting, it's also exhilarating. I took control of my life when I was a teenager, but that was a matter of survival. Now I get to do it on my own terms, and even if I fail, I'll still be better for it."

"I wish you'd told me," J says.

"I couldn't tell you because I didn't know." She can't help it; she reaches out and touches his arm, just for a moment. "Sad but true."

J knows this is not about him. She is making it clear it's not about him. But he wants it to be at least a little bit about him.

"I wish I'd asked you to try long distance," he tells her now. "Really try. Not what we ended up doing."

"It wouldn't have worked," V says, in a way that signals to him that she's given this some thought. "That was never what we did. Do you know what I think you want?"

He is almost grateful to her for saying this, because now he actually feels a flash of anger, a coming to life of another different set of emotions. She is cutting him loose; why should he care what she thinks he wants? How is that even part of the equation anymore? Still, he's curious what she'll say, so he says, "What do you think I want?"

He's put needles in his question, and he can tell she's felt them. Still, she answers, "You want someone to come home to. Someone okay with you traveling, but always there when you get back. And the funny part is that I've discovered I might want that, too. Once I get myself steady, I might want someone else steady, who also lets me roam. But here, J. Not there. And you want to be there."

"It's my home," J says.

"I know. Believe me, I know. But the truth is . . . even if we were both in the same place, I'm not sure I want to be the girl that someone else comes home to. I want to do the coming home."

There is still a part of her that thinks she is making a big mistake, that is telling her it's not too late to repair the damage she is doing. Who is she to turn away J's tenderness? Why can't she at least consider giving long distance a try? How will she feel, when he's singing songs that she had no part in—or, even worse, songs that come from the cracks she is leaving in his heart?

But then she thinks about going back and knows she can't.

She convinces herself for the thousandth time to keep going.

The two of them run out of words. What needed to be said has been said, and there were no other words behind it. It used to be that love could carry them through their tightrope silences; it was the safety net beneath them, assuring them that they did not need constant conversation, constant reassurance, to keep steady and true.

Now they're just two people on a rope, walking in different directions.

It hurts every time, J thinks. The end of each relationship is a wound that becomes a scar . . . but they never appear in the same place. There is always room for more wounds, more scars, more hurt.

They walk in the park, and it's nearly unbearable. To fill the void, J starts to tell her about yesterday's weddings (leaving out Thor and

Meta's, of course). He makes her laugh, telling the story of Eddie and the forgotten ring. They walk and talk about other people's weddings for about ten minutes more—the path has taken them on a loop, and they return back to their starting point.

Their tone has shifted into something deceptively pleasant. They don't make a big deal about their goodbye—V wishes him a safe flight, and J wishes her good luck with Secret Project. She doesn't tell him to let her go, not in the way she did in her voicemail. He doesn't point out that it's strange not to know when he'll see her again.

"Okay then," he says at last. They hover for a moment, feel foolish, and both open their arms for a hug. It doesn't last long, but it's also a real embrace, not a politeness.

"Have a safe trip," she says again. Then she turns and leaves. As he watches her go, J can feel his thoughts shift.

She now lives in his life in the past tense.

There is no other place for her.

*Don't turn around,* V tells herself as she walks away, blinking back tears.

Once he returns to the Brooklyn apartment, J calls Julia and tells her that he and V are over. If it's long past time for him to lie to himself, it's also time for him to stop lying to other people. He knows Julia will not tell him that he's wasted the past two years, nor will she tell him that the past two years have been worth it. She will absolutely not tell him he will get some good songs out of it. Instead, she listens and tells him she is sorry for his heart and what it must be going through. She tells him he can stay as long as he needs to, but he tells her he's ready to leave New York City.

On the flight home, there is terrible turbulence, roller-coaster dips. J knows he is in a bad place because as other passengers scream and hold their neighbors' hands and pray, he secretly delights in how awful V will feel if he dies in a fiery wreck, how it will haunt her for the rest of her life.

He makes it back to his apartment, and as he stands there, just inside the door, he feels a new quality to its emptiness, as if it is waiting for its true owner to come home.

The next day he has lunch with Tom. At first, it's easy enough to avoid the topic, as Tom tells him about his mom and George, and how their fourth marriage seems to be the one that's working the best. George's treatments are going well, and Tom's mom has not left his side. They still bicker, but all the blows are softer, almost comfortable. J is happy to hear this.

Then Tom asks, "And how is V? Did you see her in New York?"
And J finds himself saying, once again, "It's over."
So stark. So definitive. So true.
*It's over.*
"What?!" Tom exclaims. "What happened? How is that possible? You two are just . . . wow. I can't believe it."
"I can't believe it, either," he says. "But there it is. Long distance is hard. And long distance when the other person wants a new life is impossible."
"Fucking America," Tom says.
J knows it's not really the country's fault, but the country is easy to blame.
"Yeah, fucking America," he says, raising his glass. Tom clinks it.
"I'm sorry I don't have any words of wisdom," Tom says. "I'm here for you, though. I'm sure it's hard."
J is moved by this, more than he's willing to say to Tom. He understands he'll be seen as the wounded party, and that he has friends who will want to help him with the wounds, some more

gently than others. It's another part of the breakup that he will have to endure.

He tries to resume his normal life. He runs errands, talks to his manager about more touring, meets people for lunch or dinner. He does not go on any apps, or call any exes whose ex status could be easily compromised. He knows that other people rebound with either hope or nihilism . . . but he can't really muster either. He has boarded up that part of his life.

He takes his lead from V about communication. When she doesn't text or call, he decides he won't, either.

A strange thing happens, something that's never happened before on this scale: Weddings begin to fall through.

The first cancellation isn't technically a cancellation—a couple who had emailed about his availability emails back to say that they've decided to keep their wedding small, at a family cabin, and there won't really be need for a singer. J wouldn't give it much thought, but a few hours later, another email comes in. This time it's from Janek, a guy in Poland who first wrote to him even before he was engaged. J was heading to Warsaw for Janek's wedding in October . . . only now it looks like the trip is off, because the wedding is off. *I don't know what to tell you,* Janek writes. *She loves someone else. I guess I'm happy it happened now and not after the wedding. But still, it's a mess. A total mess.*

The next day, the email is from Greta, a stranger in Stockholm who'd contacted J after reading about his wedding gigs in the paper. Her fiancé was a huge fan, and had been too nervous to ask J himself. So she'd emailed, and he'd set up a time to talk to both of them. She'd told him a little already—they'd met at a library, where she was an archivist and he was researching a book about Swedish crime novelists of the 1920s and '30s. On their first date, he'd taken her on a walking tour of grisly murders and unsolved mysteries. The song practically wrote itself.

Now it's their engagement that is chalked onto the pavement. Greta doesn't tell J why—it's not like she owes him an explanation.

*I'm sorry we took up your time*, she writes. *But the wedding is no longer happening. Again, I am so sorry.*

J writes back, tells her it's not a problem for him, and that he's sorry to hear the news.

Then, the next day, he is scrolling mindlessly and sees a headline: "Trouble in Paradise . . . Already?"

Underneath are two photos—one of Celestia and Roger's gala wedding (luckily without a cake shot) and then one with Celestia out walking her dog, looking forlorn. The gossips are saying that contractors are after Roger for unpaid wedding expenses . . . and that Roger has sought comfort not from Celestia but from an unnamed woman with whom he was caught sharing a straw at Starbucks on a day Celestia was posting Hot Sex Tips for Married Women on her TikTok.

It's enough to push J into a serious bout of Kryptonite Syndrome—the implausible yet potentially true belief that your mere presence is souring other people's lives. In this case, J feels like romantic kryptonite. What to do? He's tempted to contact Andreas and Kerstin or Jun and Arthur to see how they're doing, but he's afraid of what he might discover.

Three weeks after his return home, the Talk of the Town piece appears in *The New Yorker*, accompanied by a drawing of J with a guitar, standing on top of a wedding cake.

One of the joys of J's career has been the way great things have happened well outside the bounds of his anticipation—people he's met that he never would have dreamed of meeting, places he's gone that he never would have presumed to get an invitation for. Seeing his name and image in *The New Yorker* font is like that—a completely unexpected goal achieved, not through a master plan but through serendipity.

He posts it on Instagram and the response is fantastic. Other friends see it first in the magazine itself and reach out. Skye DMs with a whole lot of exclamation points. Tara emails with a link and asks him if he saw it. Tom's mom even texts to say she's impressed and told all her friends that someone in *The New Yorker* played at her wedding—especially the friends who hadn't bothered to show.

J scrolls through the list of likes on his Instagram post and sees that V has liked it. But she doesn't text or email or call him to congratulate him. These, it appears, are officially the new rules of engagement. He looks on her Instagram, to see if there's anything he can like in response, but she hasn't posted in two years.

The closest contact he gets is an email from Thor, who is completely delighted with the article, especially because his secret wedding wasn't mentioned. He tells J, *There will be a lot of big news soon!* but doesn't elaborate, except to say that he still hopes J will be available to play his and Meta's official wedding. *It is looking like we'll be coming back home for it,* he writes. *I will let you know dates. Other things have to happen first.*

J looks at his calendar and sees most of his upcoming weekends are free.

He doesn't like it.

Six days later, secret project is no longer a secret. Its purchase is front-page news in Sweden, and it hits a lot of influential sites in both the gaming and finance worlds. The gist in most of the coverage is the same: *Swedish teen wunderkind sells his billion-dollar idea!*

The finer print reveals that Thor hasn't exactly received a billion dollars—just the promise of it, if all goes well. J scours all the coverage for quotes from V, who mostly sticks to the same talking points no matter who she's talking to. "It's the next evolution," she keeps saying. And now it has the funders and tech know-how to become a reality. The new company will be partly based in New York and partly based in Stockholm, thanks to a subsidy from the Swedish government.

J breaks the rules of engagement and texts V. He congratulates her and says he's sure it took a lot of hard, good work on her part to pull it all off. In response, she texts back a simple *Thank you*.

It is unclear to J whether V will be in the New York office or the Stockholm office, and there is no way for him to clarify. Or to know if it even matters.

*It doesn't matter*, he tells himself. *Remember, it's over*.

Two years together can simply unravel. Nothing she's left in his apartment would have any value to her anymore—he mails the few clothes to her office in New York and throws out the toothpaste, the toothbrush, the skin creams. The fact that she could be erased from the apartment so easily makes him wonder what the whole point of it was to begin with. He's left with some memories, some ideas that found themselves into songs. Is that enough to justify all the time spent on love?

A month after the announcement of the Secret Project deal, Thor and Meta announce their engagement. J gets an email from Thor later that day, telling him the date of the ceremony and offering him a ridiculously high sum to play.

Part of J wants to turn down the money, out of some principle he can't accurately pinpoint.

But another part says, *You need the money*. This is the least Thor can do, after wrecking J's relationship.

He writes back to Thor, congratulating him and Meta on their engagement even though he knows they're already married.

He doesn't mention the money, his roundabout way of accepting it.

J is no fool. he knows V will be at the wedding. They will have to see each other.

A month is not nearly enough time to plan a wedding, unless you don't have enough money to afford options or you have so much money that options are limitless.

J wonders if V has somehow been roped into planning the whole thing. Meta didn't strike him as the wedding-plan type, especially when the wedding will be in a Swedish city she's presumably never been to before. Most likely, V is in charge of hiring the right planners and keeping Thor's attention on the company and its tasks.

J can almost imagine how frustrated she must be.

He ventures a text: *As I'm sure you know, I'm playing Thor and Meta's wedding. So if you would like to put in any song requests, I have some influence. Though I suspect you have your own influence over the day?*

To which she replies: *I have been trying to avoid all mention of it.* And then she adds: *That has nothing to do with your songs.*

J smiles, but he also knows he's hit a dead end. Back when they were together, this would have been the start of a long conversation. But while he's slept, his instincts have shifted, at least in relation to her. He knows he is lucky to have gotten a reply, and even luckier to have gotten a clarification. So he draws short of another line of banter, and also draws short of a simple *I hope you're well.* He *does* hope she's well . . . but he recognizes it's no longer important for her to know that.

He tells his friends he's okay, he's moving on, and there are definitely times when he is so lost in his own head—talking with these friends, working on music, watching TV—that he doesn't think of her. But then he will go for a walk and recollection will tug him toward the restaurant where they celebrated birthdays, or the cinema where they argued for a good fifteen minutes about whether Wes Anderson was a genius or simply a creator of beautiful, empty vessels. He has to completely avoid the block where V used to work, because he'll imagine himself a year ago, waiting on the sidewalk to see her after, ready to take her to the bar down the street so she could vent her way through the day's tension to arrive at the evening's calm. The block with her apartment is also a bane; instead of recalling the times they shared there, he instead imagines it a completely frozen space, a personal Pompeii.

From New York, Skye tries to tinker with J's spirits, lift him from afar. *I understand how hard it is*, they write. *It's grief. It's mourning. But it isn't a death. You helped me understand that, even though you didn't know me at all. You are a very good observer of strangers, and I think it would be a mistake to think you're supposed to turn that observation onto yourself. Every now and then, sure. But none of us can observe ourselves all the time. Or the people we love. Our guesses just get more educated, the older we get. And sometimes we still get them wrong . . . but that only makes us better guessers the next time.*

J doesn't want to think about a next time. He still knows there are women he could call up for dates, for sex, for momentary forgetting. But that feels like taking cough syrup to cure a broken leg.

He also knows he could drink. And he does drink, but only with friends, only as a part of conversations that he hopes won't turn into laments. On his own, he resorts to his guitar and his piano, just to see what songs come out. One night he goes down a Paul Simon wormhole, and he can deny what he's doing with "50 Ways to Leave Your Lover" or "Still Crazy After All These Years," but when he's compelled to play "She Moves On" he has to admit to himself what he's doing. Stripped down to a guitar, the song doesn't sound at all like it does on *The Rhythm of the Saints*. It sounds like one of J's songs. He doesn't tear up as he sings it; he isn't particularly moved. But he plays the song five times in a row, as if it holds an essential piece of the puzzle, or at the very least a kinship with what he's feeling now.

Two weeks before Thor and Meta's wedding, she texts him.
*All our business partners are flying in for the wedding. So please, I beg you, no Pamplona. Are we agreed?*
(The Pamplona wedding served far, far too much wine, and J had flubbed a lyric so that "here comes my baby" became "here comes *the* baby." Many gasped, the bride's mother jumped up from her seat, and the bride's father, after the misunderstanding was cleared, still threatened violence.)
He texts back, *You have my word. No Pamplona.*
*It's going to be weird to be home.*
Taken aback, J replies, *I imagine it will be.*
*We should get coffee. Maybe the day before the wedding? It would be too weird to see each other for the first time at the wedding itself.*
So this means she's been thinking about it.
*Of course*, he writes back, trying to keep as neutral as possible. *That makes sense.*
He names a place and time. She accepts and says she'll see him before they know it.

J emails Thor to set up a time to talk to him and Meta about their song.
*You don't need to talk to us*, Thor replies. *You're already our friend!*
J thinks it would be rude to dispute this, and he imagines they're very busy, so he starts writing, based on what he knows.

Perhaps because Thor has called them friends, J feels he should give them a wedding gift beyond his song. He decides to stop by the local indie bookstore. Before he walks in, he checks to make sure that Glenda, one of V's closest friends, isn't behind the register. Coast clear, he heads to the fiction section . . . only to hear Glenda greet him from another aisle, where she's been reshelving.

"Are you here for the new Jonathan Franzen?" she asks—a judgment-laden question if ever there was one.

"No, just looking for wedding gifts."

"Oh, yes . . . *the wedding*."

J and Glenda are not friends, but they are not *not* friends. They've coexisted in V's orbit, but more as planets than moons. From the way she says *the wedding* so knowingly, he understands that she and V are still talking all the time. Glenda has escaped Pompeii.

"It's going to be quite an event," J says, as if he knows more than he really does.

"That's one way of putting it." Glenda stops then and looks J over. In a gentler voice, she asks, "How are you doing?"

"Oh, you know. Keeping busy."

"I kept meaning to reach out, but I wasn't sure if you'd want me to."

"No, no—that makes sense."

"She doesn't want there to be sides. She made it very clear to all of us that you didn't do anything wrong, that it wasn't one of *those* situations. It's just her coming into her own, you know?"

"I am very aware of that—painfully aware of that," J replies, perhaps with a little too much bite. "She is doing what's best for her, which was ultimately not what was best for us. That sums it up, doesn't it?" Then he feels compelled to add, "We're meeting for coffee before the wedding."

"I know. And I hope *you* know that it isn't going to change anything."

J laughs. "Well, it could make it worse. But I appreciate you warning me not to expect her to bring me roses."

Glenda shakes her head. "You're a good guy, J—and I imagine that makes it harder to make sense of what's happened. She's never had thousands of people applauding her at the same time. She's never heard something she wrote playing on the radio, or in a movie. She doesn't have strangers from all over the world writing to her to ask to play at their weddings. I'm not saying she's been jealous—she hasn't been jealous. But she's also been waiting for her turn, her chance to stop jumping from job to job, to create something herself."

"And you're saying she couldn't have done that with me?"

"I'm just saying that's not the way it played out. And when the time came . . . no, never mind."

"Please. Go on. This is helpful," J says, not specifying whether it's helpful for his recovery or simply his masochism.

"I'm just saying . . . based on my own observation, not on what she's said to me, per se . . . even before New York came along, the two of you were stuck. There wasn't any talk of taking it to the next level. You were happy where you were. But relationships like to progress. And when the opportunity arose to take a next-level chance . . . neither of you went for it."

"What does that mean?"

"It means that when V got the call to go to New York, it didn't occur to her to ask you along. And it didn't occur to you to join her on the adventure. I'm not saying it would have worked out even if you'd gone. But it would have been an expression of commitment that neither of you had ever really expressed to each other. Again, I'm not saying you didn't love each other. You absolutely did. But when the moment came for you to love each other more, life took you on different paths. And the path she's landed on . . . it's the right one for her."

It hurts to hear this, particularly because J knows Glenda isn't saying it to be mean. She genuinely thinks it is helpful. And maybe it will be, eventually. But right now, it stings.

"I'm sorry," Glenda says. "Truly, I am."

They make small talk for a little longer—Glenda's four-year-old son is obsessed with a song of J's that is hardly age-appropriate—and J purchases books for Thor and Meta. He maintains his composure until he leaves the shop, and only when he rounds the corner does it hit him again: *It's over, it's over, it's over.* He doesn't understand why this keeps happening, how many times it has to hit him before it finally carves itself into the stonework of his mind. Hope is a tenacious beast, but even beasts have limits.

The wedding planner—who, as it turns out, is *not* V—gets in touch, walks him through the logistics. She also takes great pains to emphasize that he is a guest as well as a performer, and that the bride and groom are looking forward to his presence for the entire event.

Over the next few days, it's not that the words for the wedding song come pouring out, or that they've run dry. J has to work to get to them, and then work to put them all in the right place, to the right tune.

Be suspicious of any writer who says it's usually otherwise.

He has no idea when V is flying in. So the day before they're supposed to meet, he wonders if she's close, tries to sense her presence. Could he sense it before, or is this a fiction he's telling himself after the fact? When she walked into a room, definitely. But a city? Was his affection's radar ever that encompassing?

She's cut her hair again.

Not radically. But it's also not entirely familiar, so immediately his presumption of familiarity takes a hit.

"I like your hair," he says as they sit down for coffee. He doesn't particularly like it, but he wants her to know he's noticed.

"Thanks," she says, unfolding her napkin and putting it on her lap. "I'm still not sure about it."

"It's good to see you," J says, even if the word good doesn't fit right. If he were being honest, he'd say *It's inevitable to see you*, or *It's almost like seeing a stranger now, to see you*.

"I'm glad we're doing this," V replies. "Seeing each other before the big day. The wedding is going to have enough drama already."

"Really? Is something wrong?"

"No, no—it's just that the families haven't met before. Everyone besides Thor and Meta think it's happening too quickly. But since the families don't have any financial leverage here—Thor's paying for it all himself—there's not much they can do."

J understands he could say, *Plus, they're already married*. He's tempted—just to have that frisson of accomplishment, proving to V that he knows something she doesn't.

"You must be so busy, with everything happening," J says instead, and V tells him all about Secret Project, and the challenges ahead. It's all so boring, now that he doesn't have any stake in it. He wonders if she's rich. That's nearly impossible to ask. So instead, when she's done, he asks, "Are you going to stay in New York?"

"For now."

"Meaning . . . months? Years?"

"I don't know. That's all I can give you."

"Surely, you don't have to give me anything." J sees this as a light, morbid joke. That's all.

But V sighs and says, "Please. Let's not fight."

"This isn't fighting," J points out.

"It's not getting along, either. And I want us to get along."

"I think I've done a very good job of respecting your wants, V," J says. "But when you ended things between us, your wants stopped being a priority of mine. You do understand that's how it works, don't you?"

V sits back, backs down. "Okay. That's fair."

J is tempted to point out that she is no longer the sole arbiter of fairness, either, but decides to keep that to himself. Instead, in a friendly tone, he asks, "Are you seeing someone in New York? Surely it can't be all work."

"I'm not seeing anyone. But I might, J."

She says it gently, even considerately. She doesn't ask him if he's seeing anyone else. She knows that's not the issue.

"Okay," J says. Then he repeats it. "Okay."

This is the moment of true understanding, the one that is almost transcendent in its absoluteness. She has been telling him this for weeks, months. Now he feels it. It isn't that she doesn't want to be in a relationship. It's that she doesn't want to be in a relationship *with him*.

Even though he's known it's over, has been dealing with it being over, it's still startling to J how much this wrecks him.

"What happened to us?" he asks.

"No single thing," V answers, unsurprised by the question. "No single moment, no single turn. It wasn't like I was miserable. I was never miserable, J. It was more about meaning, about definition, about living with as little dissonance as possible. I was . . . how do I put this? I know: I was a lyric set to the wrong music. The words were clear to me. But the music of everything around me wasn't supporting those words. At times, it was working against those words. So I had to change the music. And part of that was separating from you, looking for a better match, or maybe no match at all. You weren't wrong for me, J—but you weren't right for me, either. Not in the kind of relationship we had, that vague space where we don't want to use the words *boyfriend* and *girlfriend*, but we don't want to use anything more serious, either. So where does that leave us?"

She is not asking J this question. So he lets her keep speaking, to answer it.

She says, "Perhaps selfishly, I still want us to talk. Because I love our talking, especially when it's not about us. Which I understand is quite a thing to say right now, but I'm going for it. I don't want to ghost you. I don't want you to ghost me. We are too smart to let ourselves be haunted. But the only way to avoid it is to get through this hard moment of redefinition. You will naturally think it's harder for you, and I won't dispute that. But please know it's also hard for me."

"I don't doubt that," J says, with no trace of bitterness. But he also . . . doesn't care. He doesn't care how hard it is for her. He doesn't care how she feels about their future. He doesn't care about her desire to not be haunted. If anything, he feels like a ghost right now, at this table but no longer at this table. He is standing aside, watching this person who looks like him politely go along with what she's saying. Because he really doesn't want to fight. He doesn't want to argue. He doesn't want anything out of this conversation anymore.

"Thank you," she says. "I hoped you wouldn't."

For the next half hour they have what could only be called a normal conversation. It feels like those first hours after a noisy but harmless storm passes through, and the fact that it's not rainy takes on a different meaning than it had before. J is happy to let his ghost sit there and chat amiably. V tells J not only about Secret Project, but also some of the people she's met in New York, how it's felt like the first time since university that she's had to go out of her way to make new friends. (J nods, sympathetic.) Because she doesn't want her social life to be entirely about work, she's joined a running club, and now has three friends with whom she runs on Wednesdays and Sundays and drinks with on Fridays. Fiona, Theresa, and Janet. (J forgets their names as soon as she says them. He does not need to know the new cast of characters in her new life.)

She asks about his songwriting, and he gives her what paltry update there is. He tells her about what happened with Skye and Detroit, and George (whose prognosis remains good) and Lisbet, and also about a strange nervousness he feels about playing Thor and Meta's wedding.

"But you've played so many weddings before," V says. "Why would this one make you nervous?"

"Honestly, it was probably you," J tells her, unable to stay a ghost for too long, and feeling the need to put some of his blood back into the conversation. "Not just the fact that you'd be there, but also the fact that Thor is your boss, and basically the only reason I'm there ties back to you."

"I think you'll be fine. Thor is a genuine fan. And Meta . . . well, I can never get a read on her. But I'm sure that if she didn't want you playing, you wouldn't be playing at her wedding."

J sighs.

"What?" V asks.

"Maybe I'm just tired of weddings." It's not that he hasn't had the thought many times before, but it's rare for him to say it out loud.

"Why?"

"I think when I have things going on in my life, I enjoy it. But when I don't, I feel like I'm a spectator in the world, and the weddings make that more obvious. I don't mind being an observer, but I find it hard not being able to share my observations."

"You can still share them with me," V offers.

J can tell: She really means it.

Still, he says, "You've got to be kidding."

"You haven't lost me," V says.

"How can you say that? I have."

"No. You haven't. We have a choice here, to either devolve or evolve. I want us to evolve. And the only way to do that is to keep talking, to talk this through. So when I say you haven't lost me, you have to take me at my word."

"No," J says. As simple as that, it's exactly what he means.

"What do you mean, no?"

"I mean, it's over. Although I recognize that you would like to still have all the good parts of our connection while severing the other parts, that isn't how this is going to work. I lost you, and you've lost me. I loved you, and ultimately that didn't matter—that's the worst feeling of losing there is. Even if I end up believing that we weren't meant to be together, and even if we manage to evolve into some other kind of relationship, if we talk ourselves through . . . there is still the overwhelming feeling of failure. Not just in terms of you, but in terms of making any relationship work."

V nods. "I know what you mean. But I think it's also a trap we fall into—staying in something that isn't right because we don't want to have failed, because we don't want to lose. When I got to New York, I told myself, *This is your chance to try to be alone.* Which at first sounds horrifying, because the whole world seems to be telling us that we should never be alone, that the only way to find happiness is to find someone else to be there with you. I have spent my whole life trying not to be alone. And for all I know, I won't end up alone. But I'd at least like to give myself the option. To not feel I've failed because I am stepping away from what we have in order to navigate more on my own. What's funny is that of the two of us, I feel you're much better at being alone. But you also have much more pride than I do, so it makes sense that you'd hate to lose more than I do."

"I at least seem to have the pride-fall pattern down well," J says. "If only I was smart enough to see it coming—but I guess pride doesn't let you see it coming, does it?"

"You're going to be fine," V says. "We're each going to be fine. Don't you feel that, at least a little bit, right now?"

And he has to be honest with her. He cannot make himself a ghost.

So he tells her, again, "No."

There are hundreds of thousands, maybe millions, of songs about falling in love, being in love. There are more about having your heart broken. But how many songs are there about loving someone and having the nature of that love change? How many songs are there about going from lover to friend, from sex to affection? How many songs are there about being happy alone?

Walking home, J wonders these things.

He knows, theoretically, that V is right: He hasn't really lost her, if he chooses not to lose her. But at the same time, he doesn't feel a reason to make that choice. Maybe he doesn't have the right songs to guide him. Or maybe there's a reason there are ultimately more songs about heartbreak than about anything else.

V texts an hour later suggesting that, since they both have to be there early, they go to the wedding together. J says he'll just meet her there. He is surprised when he gets a call from V at nine.

"Get your tux on and come early," she tells him. "Thor and Meta seem to have hit a snag. And Thor's asked for both of us to come to their hotel to help."

J meets V in the lobby. He is in his tux and is carrying his guitar. She is in what could only be a bridesmaid dress, tight and teal.

"I chose it," V says, tracing J's glance. "Believe me, the other options were worse."

"I thought Meta would dress her bridesmaids in black."

"Yeah, well—that's not how it played out."

"So why are we here?"

"I think Meta's having some pre-wedding jitters."

"Okay . . . but why are *we* here?"

"I guess we're about to find out."

She leads J to the elevators, and he isn't at all surprised when she puts in a key and hits the button for the penthouse suite. How else are newly minted tech billionaires meant to live?

The elevator opens into a foyer, and even though V has the key, she rings a doorbell to announce their arrival.

It is Thor who answers. Like J, he is in a tuxedo. Unlike J, he looks like he's never been in a tuxedo before. Everything seems just a little misaligned, and his posture suggests the whole outfit might fall to pieces if he makes the wrong sudden move.

"I'm so glad you're here," Thor says to V and J. "I honestly don't know what to do. Come in."

Instead of a groom, he looks like a high schooler cast as a butler in a school play—J half expects him to ask to take their coats. Thor has always seemed young to J, but never nervously so. Now the nervousness seems to have risen to the surface.

"Where's Meta?" V asks.

"In the bedroom."

"And what's going on?"

"She doesn't want to go through with the wedding. Having her family here and my family—it's too much."

"Thor," V says. "We've talked about this. Maybe it *is* too much."

J is surprised by her tone. It is not the sound of a coworker. It is the sound of an older sister.

"I know, I know," Thor says. "Meta and I talked this over, many times."

"How can you have talked it over many times? You've only known each other for months! And now you want to get married!"

J's ears perk up further. She really doesn't know they're already married.

Thor looks at J, and all is understood: The secret is still a secret. J is here right now because he is the one who, through sheer accident, knows the truth.

"You love each other," J says. "Isn't that right?"

"Yes," Thor says emphatically. "That's not the issue here at all. The issue is the wedding, and how scary it is."

"Let's go see Meta," V says. "It's pointless to have this conversation without her."

Thor leads them to the bedroom. There, Meta is lying on the bed in leisurewear, staring at the ceiling. Next to the bed is a mannequin in a wedding dress, hovering like an angel or a ghost.

"Hello, Meta," J says.

"Hello," she replies, not moving. She sounds worn out and looks like a teenager with a migraine. J feels they should be talking about whether or not she feels up to going to class, not whether to call off her wedding.

Thor sits down at the foot of the bed and tenderly puts his hand on Meta's ankle. "We appreciate you two coming over," he says to J and V. "We didn't know who else we could talk to."

For months now, J has seen Thor as a minor character in V's story, the young boss who whisked her away and then took the town while she burned the midnight oil. Now he rewinds the story and plays it with Thor as the main character—a nineteen-year-old whiz kid who had been immersed in his Secret Project since high school, who had probably never left Sweden until the money guys came calling. So he moved to Manhattan with a crew of adults; of them, V was probably the most human, since she worked in publicity, not programming. His family stayed behind. His friends, if he'd managed to have any in high school, stayed behind. Then he met a girl, and suddenly she became New York City to him. He didn't make other friends, except possibly a few of hers. He lost himself in love before he ever found himself in any other way. Now, when life wobbles, V is the closest person he has who isn't Meta.

And Meta—she may have stayed nearer to home than Thor, but the fact is that even if she has relatives and friends in other rooms of the hotel, none of them have been summoned to this suite. Which speaks volumes to J as well.

Meta closes her eyes, then says, "I've gotten so caught up in planning that I haven't let myself stop and wonder if I should be doing this at all. I think it's been weeks since I slept well, and I kept telling myself it was because I was anxious about meeting his mother, and anxious about my parents coming all the way to Sweden, and anxious about getting everything right even though I was making calls from six hours in the past, thousands of miles away. But now I'm wondering if it wasn't just that. I'm wondering if we're about to combine elements that were never meant to combine. We wanted coalescence, but what if we get combustion instead?"

V looks over to J with raised eyebrows: *Do you want to take this?*

He signals back, *Not at all. All yours.*

"It's natural to feel that way," V begins. "I don't know many brides who haven't. So let's put it into that perspective. But I also feel that it's not too late to change your mind. If you go in there and say, 'Hey, we've decided not to get married,' everyone will understand. Marriage is a big step, and you don't have to take it now. The two of you are so young, and your love is so young. You don't need to make it grow up fast."

"I'm not sure getting married is the issue," J says delicately.

"Of course it is," V replies, somewhat dismissively. "You're not saying they have to get married, are you?"

"No, not at all. It's just . . ."

"It's just *what*?"

J looks to Thor beseechingly and says, "You have to tell her."

V shifts her glance from J to Thor. "Tell me what?"

Thor turns to Meta, who opens her eyes, looks at him, and nods. She sits up and he reaches for her hand. Only when the hands are clasped does he look at V and say, "That we're already married."

"WHAT?"

"We went to Borough Hall and got married a few weeks ago."

"I happened to be there when they did," J adds.

Now she swings back to him. "You mean, you knew this whole time—"

"We swore him to secrecy," Meta says.

"Still. Wow."

J waits for more, but V remains stunned. He turns to Meta and Thor and says, "So . . . are you regretting now that you're married?"

"No," Thor says.

"Maybe a little. But not a lot," Meta says at the same time.

Thor stares at his wife for a second. "Honey?"

She touches his cheek with her free hand, soothing. "I mean, no. I'm glad we're married. It's just that . . . before it was just the two of us, and now it's going to be everybody. That's the problem."

Thor nods in agreement. Then he turns to V and J, who are now side by side facing the bed, and asks, "What do we do?"

J and V look at each other then—and this time, there aren't signals as much as sympathies. J understands: Both of them want to have an answer to give the young couple, and neither of them has any idea what that answer is. Even though they have been on the earth almost twice (!) as long as Thor and Meta, even though they've been in far more relationships and attended far, far more weddings, they cannot solve anybody else's crisis any better (or worse) than they can solve their own.

J realizes: Thor and Meta might not even know he and V have broken up. What if the reason he's here is because they think he and V are still together?

Still, there has to be *something* from all the weddings he's attended that he can share with them. There has to be some helpful truth he's gleaned from all the stories he's witnessed unfolding.

What he finds himself saying is, "You have to understand that none of it matters. Nothing about a wedding matters. It is created to be an exception—the one time your life together is purely for show. It should never interfere with how you feel for each other, or what you mean to each other. You share your vows in front of other people so they will understand what has happened between the two of you . . . but that part has already happened. It's like when a scientist makes a great discovery and then a year later announces that discovery in a scientific journal so everyone can know about it. Your love is the discovery. The wedding is the scientific journal."

Thor and Meta don't look particularly comforted by this.

"I have an idea," V says. "Both of you, stand up."

Thor lets go of Meta's hand and stands. Once he does, Meta swings her legs around and pulls herself up.

"Face each other," V commands.

They do. It's an incongruous sight, with Meta in her leisurewear and Thor in his tux.

"Now, I want you to exchange your vows."

Thor turns his head to V. "They're in the other room. Oh, no—wait. I have them on my phone!"

He goes for his phone, but J tells him, "No. Stop. Not on your phone."

"And not with any notes," V adds. "Speak from your heart. Both of you."

Thor nods, and without needing to be told, he and Meta clasp hands again.

"You first," Meta says, smiling.

He smiles back. "I knew you were going to say that."

He falls silent for a second, sorts things out in his mind. Then he starts.

"I am lost. Before I was considered successful, I only sometimes knew what I was doing, and now that I am considered successful I *really* have no idea what I'm doing. I know you get that. When it comes to business, I'm not just over my head—there are times I feel like I am at the bottom of the ocean, staring up, trying to remind myself what the sky looks like. The pressure is *enormous*. There is no way to hear anything besides my own thoughts. It's scary. And what you've done . . . it's like you've built me a trap door at the bottom of the ocean. When I go through it, I'm on land again. I can breathe. There's a breeze, and trees, and clouds. And most of all, there's you. I know the opposite of *lost* is *found*, but with you, it's *finding*. That's what I feel like we're doing. We are constantly finding. Right? That is the thing we most have in common. Our desire to find. And it just so happens that finding someone else who has a desire to find is the thing that can make a person like me feel least lost. With you, I know what I am doing."

As Thor says this, his eyes run to tears, even as his mouth smiles at the tears, as if to say, *Isn't it funny that tears are happening?* One of the most intense human urges is the one to wipe away tears, but Thor clearly doesn't want to let go of Meta's hands. So he lets them trace their way down his face. To J, a crying Thor should be the antithesis of the happy-go-lucky guy he's seen so many times before. But J doesn't feel it's contradictory at all. If anything, Thor has just reversed things a little. Right now, he looks lucky-go-happy. The tears ride along with that.

"Most of my life, I've met my friends playing games online," Thor goes on. "Even when it was just building things on *Minecraft*, that was a hallowed space for me. So naturally I wanted to stay in those spaces with my work and give people more of a way to connect. I still think there is value in that. But at the moments when I doubt myself the most, I worry that I am slowly becoming a computer. Every time I go online, I lose a small part of my humanity. I feel if I hadn't met you, I might have wired myself too much into the machine. I would have lost sight of the real pleasures of roaming a city late at night, or having someone run her finger down my chest. Because I didn't know pleasures like that before. I stayed indoors. You make me want to be outdoors, among others. You make me want to step away from all my screens, all my simulations. I am so grateful for you. There's no way you could possibly know."

"I know I should end this with a vow. I vow to do my part to see that we will always take care of each other. I vow to live with you in the real world, and to support you in all the ways money can't buy. I vow to always take you seriously, but to not take life too seriously. I vow to deal with my failures honestly and with my successes just as honestly. I vow that this is going to be a wild ride . . . but worth the trip. I vow to love you now, and I vow to understand I will come to love you even more. This is just the beginning."

Meta frees her hands . . . but only so she can wrap her arms around Thor, standing on her tippy-toes to give him a long kiss, then holding him as he closes his eyes and hugs her close. J feels the affection swell within him for both of them—and for love in general. He looks to V, who seems to be patiently waiting for the embrace to end so the vows can continue. He smiles at her, trying to get her to smile back, but she's too lost in thought.

When Meta and Thor finally let go of one another, Meta looks at V and says, "I suppose it's my turn now."

"Yes," V replies with a smile. "Please, go ahead."

"I think before I start, I need to explain my name to you all. Thor knows all this, but if what I'm going to say is going to make sense, the two of you should understand it as well.

"The story goes like this: When she was pregnant with me, my mother listened obsessively to classical music. That was her biggest craving. Especially toward the end, when she was put on bed rest—instead of watching TV she would put on her headphones and listen to certain recordings on loop. At some point, she decided on my name. Not from the name of a piece, or a composer, or any of the players. No, it was the conductor's name that glowed bright to her—Zubin Mehta. If I'd been a boy, I would have been named Zubin. Since I was a girl, I was named Mehta.

"In school, kids thought Mehta was weird, but Meta was cool. So decided to embrace it, especially once I got to high school and realized how meta it was to be called Meta. I legally changed my name.

I made a big deal of it, because my girl self made a big deal out of everything. And then I met Thor, and within five minutes of meeting him, I was telling him this story. In fairy tales and fantasy novels, you're warned to never tell a stranger your true name. But I did. And because of that, it didn't feel like we were strangers anymore."

With that she turns from J and V and shares her full attention with Thor again. She smiles at him in a way that shows she's feeling lucky-go-happy as well.

"I didn't write anything out. I knew you would, but I just wanted to see what hit me. And this is it, right now: The fact that you, more than anyone else in the world, know my true name and know my true self. My parents know my true name, of course, but somewhere in my childhood they lost the ingredient of kindness, and now I'm more wary of them than ready to share my truths with them. Which leads to this whole wedding dilemma. But putting that aside . . . I often feel you are the only person in the world who really knows me. And the reason you know me is because from the start you've cared in a way that nobody else has. I know I don't make it easy. But you understand why. Which is why you deserve to know my name and to wear so many of my thoughts. It's not you I'm afraid of; it's everyone else. I promise. And I vow that every tangent, every spiral, every trajectory I take will always end up home with you. Are we clear, soldier?"

It must be a joke between them because Thor guffaws, then says, "We are clear, sir!"

J wonders: If he had met V at nineteen, could they have been this close, this certain? If they had met before their adult lives began, would there have been less conflict, less pressure to make it all balance? Because wouldn't they have smiled and laughed like this? Wouldn't they have been able to tunnel-vision themselves into thinking an eternal commitment was a good idea?

He looks at V, but her focus is on Thor and Meta. She hasn't finished her ceremony yet.

"The vows have been exchanged. Do you want to exchange rings as well?"

Thor's smile fades. "My brother has them."

V holds up a hand. "No worries. It's a possessive tradition anyway. Plenty of time for that later. I think what our bedroom wedding needs is a song. Do you happen to know anyone who could perform a song right now?"

"Here?" J says.

"Yes," V replies firmly. "And then, when you're done, I'm going to ask you two how you feel and what you want. See what the song says to you."

J leads them to the piano in the suite. Thor and Meta sit down next to each other on the couch, hand in hand, an expectant audience.

> In you I see myself
> In you I see someone I loved
> Your stupid youthful ignorance
> I'll tell you where it can be shoved
> I want to warn you
> I want to teach you
> I want to tell you to cover your ears
> and ignore every word I have to say
>
> Because I think that you will make it
> but I know the rules for traveling in time
> If I tell you how things went for me
> will that change your path further down the line?
> Cause I'm a sad old time traveler
> trying to find the point where things went wrong
> but you don't get a second chance, once it's done it's done
>
> You learn so much that you can't unlearn
> You burn so soft but you can't unburn

> And for every time you're hurt the ice sheet grows
> Silently it snows
> Ask Antarctica, it knows
>
> So open your ears now
> not to me but to each other
> You are young now, you are here now
> Even Antarctica is filled with flowers
> Do you hear the song
> playing softly
> from somewhere
> deep within?
> That's the song that my song wants you to sing

He isn't paying any attention to Thor or Meta. He's looking at V, and V can't look J in the eye. She's said goodbye and he's said goodbye, but this is it, the real goodbye, the jagged corners of the break. What more can he wish Thor and Meta than that they avoid such a fate?

"Thank you, old man," Thor says when J is finished, completely oblivious to what has just occurred. "Though really, you're not *that* old."

Meta, however, looks at V sympathetically, and then at J with a little less sympathy. "I promise to ignore every word you say," she tells him. Then she reaches over for Thor's hand and holds it tight.

V recovers and turns her attention back to the young couple. "So," she says, "now we reach the moment of decision. Thor and Meta, do you feel you are married already?"

"Yes," they both say.

"Do you want to be together for as long as it takes?"

"Yes," Meta says, at the same time Thor says, "Absolutely."

"Do you feel any need or desire to repeat this in front of all your guests?"

"No," they both say.

"Then I now pronounce you Thor and Meta, as you were meant to be. If you'd like to kiss, go ahead."

They do. At length.

"Now," V says when they're through, "here's how I suggest you proceed: Cancel the ceremony, tell everyone you eloped, and keep the party. You don't need any witnesses—that's what we're here for. What you need are people to celebrate you. And celebrate they shall. I picked out the DJ, after all."

"And you don't want me to perform, do you?" J asks.

"I don't think so," V says. "I think that song doesn't go any farther than this."

Calls are made to certain family members. Texts are sent to everyone else. Meta's mother is aghast, and the wedding planner has a panic attack, but everyone else is fine. Some, J suspects, are even relieved to not have to sit through yet another wedding ceremony, including the rental priest, who will still be paid for the day.

For about an hour, J gets to see what V must be like at work. She takes the things that could veer into chaos and sets their course for completion. When Meta gets overwhelmed by the messages from her mother, V takes her phone and manages the crisis. When Thor starts to get fidgety after the hairstylist and makeup artist arrive for Meta, V orders Thor and J to the minibar, then the balcony, so they can have a quiet toast and stay out of the way.

Once the new timing of the day has been confirmed, makeup and hair are near finished, and two other bridesmaids—a cousin and a high school friend—have arrived, V turns to J and says, "My work here is done." Thor hugs each of them for a very long time before they leave, and Meta just shakes her head, as if to say *There are no words right now*. V tells her not to worry—it's all a party from here.

It is only when they are away from everyone else, waiting for the elevator, that J has a chance to tell V, "Good job."

He expects her to reply with something along the lines of "I know." But instead her shoulders sag a little, and her expression is tinged with sadness, not achievement.

"Is it?" she asks.

"What do you mean? You saved the day."

"But do you really think they should be married? They're so young, J. And I *encouraged* them."

"They're in love. Truly in love. Isn't that what matters most? And they were already married. You didn't lead them to the altar."

"Yes, I'm aware of that—thanks for the tip-off, by the way."

"They swore me to—"

"It's okay. Really. I guess right now I wonder why we do this to ourselves."

"You mean, weddings?"

"Sure. Let's say I mean weddings."

J reaches up and touches her arm. "Come on. You don't mean that. You were all adrenaline in there, and now it's fading out. Even if you have doubts that Thor and Meta will make it. And even if *we* didn't make it . . . that has nothing to do with them."

"Yes, I know that," V says. "It just exhausts me sometimes."

"That's definitely a key part of it."

"Don't stop playing weddings, J. What you do . . . it's a form of kindness. And love needs to be given as much kindness as possible."

"I just keep thinking I'll find something here."

"All the weddings in the world can't teach you about love. Only love can teach you about love."

The elevator finally arrives. They step inside and V hits the button for the lobby.

"I'll keep that in mind," J says.

The elevator doors open. J steps out, but V doesn't leave.

"I'm actually going to go back up to my room to change out of this dress," she explains. "I'll see you at the party. Save a dance for me."

"I guess I'll have coffee," J says. "Even though I'm tempted to change into your dress."

"It's not your color."

With that, she releases the door-open button, and the doors close on her looking out at him.

J feels an impossible combination of sensations, wound and scar at once. His relationship with V is over, but it also feels *completed*.

He stares up to the penthouse, wishing Thor and Meta luck, and strength, and humor, and flexibility, and music, and honesty, and time.

He knows they will need all of it, every day.

# THE TENTH WEDDING

Eleven months later

It is the night before the wedding, and the brides and the wedding singer have broken into the hall where the ceremony and party will be held. The brides do not particularly look like brides—there is nothing white or lacy about their outfits, and there's nothing nervous in their expressions. The wedding singer looks like a wedding singer, but only because he is carrying a guitar.

*Broken into* is probably not the right phrase—one of the brides arranged for this rendezvous with the help of the site manager, a rehearsal with no one else around. The site itself is the Appel Room at Jazz at Lincoln Center, a remarkable space hanging over Columbus Circle, one wall a complete glass lookout over the street and Central Park.

Even at midnight, there is a steady stream of headlights and taillights, punctuated by the green-yellow-red signals of traffic lights.

The singer heads to the stage. The brides choose to sit in the third row, on the aisle.

"Are you ready?" J asks.

And Nadine, one of the brides, replies, "As we'll ever be."

About two months ago, J was interviewing Nadine and Frances on Zoom for the song for their wedding. Nadine's story was an inspiring one; she'd been married to a man who was relentlessly berating and possessive, making her feel both out of luck and out of options. But then she met Frances and realized she didn't need to be in a loveless marriage. Nadine left her husband, and her lawyer got her an excellent settlement. She enjoyed being on her own, but realized she enjoyed life even more when she and Frances were together. One thing led to another. And now, here they were, two women in their fifties, one getting married for the first time, one for the second.

"Your relationship to love changes, depending on who you're with," Nadine told J. "You give up on it because you feel it's given up on you. But it hasn't. You just weren't with the person who could help you reach it in its fullest."

"Do you feel like a different person, now that you're with Frances?" J asked.

Nadine shook her head. "I feel like I was always me. But I changed my shape for him in a negative way. And I've felt more my real shape with Frances. Same thing with my relationship to love. Love is change. I tried to bend it to make it work. But it won't allow itself to be bent for too long, not if you're honest with yourself."

"So she found the strength to fix it," Frances said.

"Something like that," Nadine replied, not wanting to take the credit.

After hearing their story, J asked if they had anything else they wanted to add.

"Actually, we do," Nadine said. "We appreciate you asking about our stories. But we were wondering . . . instead of writing about us, could you maybe write a song that sums up what you've learned from singing at all these weddings over the years? We know that's not what you usually do, but when we talked about it, we feel like we want to be the ones sharing our story at our wedding. What we'd love if for you to touch on something greater, something bigger than us. That's what we'd really love."

No one had ever asked him this before.

"I'm not sure I know any more about love than anyone else," J confessed.

Nadine waved this off. "I don't believe that for a second."

"Okay, I'll try," J promised. He really liked these two strangers, and also liked having a new assignment for once.

The riskiest part was trying to articulate what he'd learned about love.

He'd been down in the dumps about a relationship that had looked promising but had never really shifted out of neutral—this wasn't the woman after V, but the woman *after* the woman after V.

Neither of these women had left a scar, only a slight irritation that went away quickly enough. With V, the scar was there, and he felt it from time to time, but it also didn't take up as much of his skin as he'd thought it would.

They hadn't stayed in touch. Or, more precisely, they'd only stayed in touch the same way that everyone else stayed in touch, through social media posts and occasional comments. He hadn't blocked her, nor had she blocked him. That would have been too much of a statement for either of them. So instead there are these passive infiltrations of information—a picture of her in her new (large) apartment; a picture of her in a helicopter with Thor and Meta; a picture of her more and more with a man who, with one click, J sees is an economics professor at NYU. It's like reading the summary of the new season of a TV show he used to watch. And V has no doubt seen J's photos from the road, plugs for gigs all over Europe. He didn't post about this trip to New York because it's not a public performance. And even though he is aware that at any moment he could turn a corner and find V, perhaps accompanied by her NYU professor "friend," J also doesn't feel any obligation to tell her he's in town or ask her for coffee.

She remains past tense. Possibly past-past tense, if such a tense existed.

But it still took a while for him to come back around to love.

Preparing for Nadine and Frances's wedding, he thought about the last wedding he'd played at—Janek from Warsaw had gotten back together with his girlfriend, so J had made a delayed trip to Poland to add his musical blessing to the ceremony. And that was what it had felt like—a blessing, both to the wedded couple and to J himself. Because that's what music could be, wasn't it? At weddings and funerals. At the most intense moments and also the most mundane. Music could make things better. Maybe not for any longer than the song lasted, but while the song was there, it always did some of the lifting of the moment. The singer provided that lifting. The singing made everything momentarily lighter.

J thought about all the times he'd given up. And then he thought about all the times he returned. There was a reason music was always there for him. And part of that reason was the ability and the opportunity to share it.

That was something he'd learned.

*Last*, as an adjective, means the end.

*Last*, as a verb, means to endure.

Most of the songs he writes, most of the songs he wants to share, navigate this contradiction. Because this navigation—that is the gift he can offer to the couples he sings for. That is what he's learned, and what he's still learning.

J took his assignment for Nadine and Frances seriously. He even thought of it in different terms: If he were to only write one more love song, what would he want it to say? Would it be a falling-in-love song or a you-broke-my-heart song? Which would represent love most accurately? He wanted to ask his friends what they thought—he was sure Skye would have some ideas—but that wasn't what Nadine and Frances had asked for; they wanted it to come from him, and from what he'd seen.

He thought of V. Of course he thought of V. But he wasn't writing for her, or anyone who had come before her, or anyone who would come after her. He thought of all the couples he'd written songs for, trying to find the universal theme beneath their individual stories.

For weeks it eluded him. Then one night, he listened to the recording he'd made of his conversation with Nadine and Frances, and there it was, a single sentence buried in the middle:

*Love is change.*

What if he *had* turned to V the minute she told him about going to New York and said, "Hey, let's do this thing together"? What if he'd been able to set up a new version of himself as she set up a new version of herself? Would those versions have found a way to be together, in the same way that, say, George and Lisbet managed to reunite even when the stakes were higher than they'd ever been before? Or what about Arthur and Jun surrendering parts of each of their "I" in order to become a "We"? Even Thor and Meta, who haven't even reached the age of knowing what it's like to be a grown-up in the grown-up world . . . how many changes do they have ahead of them, both individually and as a couple?

The uncertainty doesn't just come from wondering how well you know the person you love. It comes from wondering how well you know who they will become, who you will become, and what that will mean for each other. And then going for it anyway, based on the hunch that it's going to work it out, that whatever changes you make will end up being compatible. There are so many times you'll want to give up. And so many of those so many times, it's right to give up.

But when love works?

That's the giving up on giving up. That's the song coming through the noise.

What more can he wish Nadine and Frances than the capacity to adapt, and adapt, and adapt? What more can he wish them but the shape-shifting persistence of love?

Now here he is, about to play the song to an audience of two. Nobody else has heard it first.

Yes, he can see V in its DNA . . . but mostly he sees his own experience woven in the helix of words and music. It will become a song he'll sing at weddings all the time, with the two original brides' permission. Many listeners won't understand at first why he's singing it, but by the time he gets to the end, most of the people in the room who've experienced love will understand what he's getting at.

He looks at Nadine and Frances holding hands in the third row and flashes through all they must have gone through to get to this point. He doesn't really know them, but this wedding has given him a reason to get to know them a little, to be gifted with a sample of their music, and to give back music of his own.

The microphone isn't on. The speakers are asleep. It's just a man on a stage, using his voice to reach the couple in the audience.

He shares with them what he's learned.

> Every lovesong is a curse
> At first so sweet at its arrival
> But when I've written down its words
> It stares back at me like a stuffed animal
> The very thing it was to capture
> vanished in the moment after
> It just slipped right out of my little hands

New York City's never done
If it was it wouldn't be New York City
And you can jump into the Hudson
but the second after it's a different entity
Loving you is loving a motion
A warm current in the ocean
That's how I wanted my songs to be

So this is the last lovesong that I'll sing
A promise to leave the heart open
To never fall in love with what's been
And if I ever should write a lovesong again
I would set a key and a tempo
Then let you lead on the piano
and we'd just make it up as we go
That's the only good lovesong I know

Every lover is a ship
Over time rebuilt and changed
Every board replaced bit by bit
Until all that's left is the lover's name
Sometimes I let go of the rudder
I close my eyes and shudder
And I whisper softly that I love her

Oh this is the last lovesong that I'll sing
A promise to leave the heart open
To never fall in love with what's been
To greet the unknown with a grin

This is the last lovesong that I'll sing
An ode to whatever fate may bring

**Kisses scattered to the wind**
**A lovesong to all that's changing**

When he is through, they applaud. He takes a bow, then walks off the stage to meet them in the aisle. They give him a long hug, then when it's done, Nadine says, "That isn't the last love song you'll ever write, is it?"

"No," he replies. "But you know what I mean."

The brides smile, and at the same time, both of them say, "I do."

## AUTHORS' NOTES AND ACKNOWLEDGMENTS

The two of us first connected when David sent an email of admiration to Jens after listening to a lot of Jens's music while writing a novel in the 2000s. Our paths kept crossing at intervals, until a few years ago, when Jens messaged David and said, "I have an idea . . . and it might work as a book." It is extremely appropriate that music and words brought us together and led us here.

The idea for the book was based on Jens's inadvertent career as a wedding singer, spurred by the song "If You Ever Need a Stranger (to Sing at Your Wedding)." That said, the weddings and the wedded couples in this book are entirely fictional, even if a few of the wedding details (like passing out inside a cake) are true. Likewise, V, Thor, and Meta are entirely fictional, and not based on anyone specific in either Jens's or David's life.

The book was written over the course of three years. For half the weddings, David wrote the chapter and then Jens conjured a song to fit the couple in the chapter. For the other half, Jens gave David a song, and David had to come up with a wedding to lead to that song. The overall arc of the story, some of the details about weddings, and a few observations about love were discussed, but by and large, when a chapter appeared in Jens's inbox, it was a surprise to him, and when a song appeared in David's inbox, it was a surprise to *him*. Jens's initial plan was that the songs from the book would be compiled as an album, but after a while he realized that the album wouldn't make much sense on its own, so he decided instead to write an album that followed the book's narrative from J's and V's perspectives, sometimes adding new scenes taking place between the book's chapters. David revised the chapters to match the new songs, although there may be a few details that don't align in the end.

There are many people we have to thank for their help in the creation of the book.

Thank you to everyone at Abrams Press, starting with our stellar editor, Zack Knoll, and continuing to our wonderful publicity director, Taryn Roeder, and marketing director, Kim Lauber. Thanks as well to Ruby Pucillo, Kristen Luby, Jamison Stoltz, Michael Sand, Holly Dolce, Lisa Silverman, Eli Mock, Diane Shaw, Deb Wood, Sarah Masterson Hally, and Christine Edwards and the entire sales team. Thank you also to everyone at Recorded Books for the audio edition.

Thanks to everyone at Secretly Canadian, Jens's record label, including Ben Swanson, Maxie Gedge, Rachel Glago, Jessica Park, Robby Morris, and Gloria Van Ditmar.

Huge gratitude to Bill Clegg and everyone at the Clegg Agency.

David would like to thank: his parents, for always letting him play music; the rest of his family, all of whom seem to like getting mixes; Nick Eliopulos, who loves the Lekman oeuvre as much as he does; Gabriel Duckels, who heard a lot about this book as it was created; Mike Ross, who takes his music very seriously, which deserves serious respect; Billy Merrell, for being Billy Merrell; Adam Goldman and David Abramovitz, for their enthusiasm for this project; and to all the friends he shared living space with while working on the book, primarily in Cape Cod, which is, strangely enough, not a bad place to be when you're writing a book set in Sweden.

Jens would like to thank: his parents, his sister, and her family; his friends Reese Higgins and Annika Norlin for listening to the songs and giving invaluable feedback; Alex Hardi and Erik Sjölin, for good advice over countless glasses of wine on Capri; Daniel Fagerström and everyone else who was involved in the recording of the album and the audiobook songs; and, most of all, thank you to all the couples I've played for over the years.

And finally, a shoutout to Julia Rydholm. Had Julia not worked in David's office at the same time as touring in Jens's band, it is highly unlikely we would have remained in touch to the degree we did. So, really, it could be argued this book wouldn't exist without her.

## ABOUT THE AUTHORS

DAVID LEVITHAN is the author of numerous acclaimed novels, including *The Lover's Dictionary*, *Every Day*, *Boy Meets Boy*, and *Two Boys Kissing*. His other collaborations include *Nick & Norah's Infinite Playlist* with Rachel Cohn and *Will Grayson, Will Grayson* with John Green. He can often be found with headphones on, a devoted music listener . . . but it's safe to say that nobody will ever ask him to sing at a wedding.

JENS LEKMAN is a singer and songwriter from Sweden with several beloved albums such as *Life Will See You Now*, *Night Falls Over Kortedala*, and *Oh You're So Silent Jens*. He was once voted the fifteenth-sexiest man in Sweden by *ELLE*. Then he dropped down to number thirty-three, and since then he hasn't been included in their list. He works part-time as a wedding singer.

If you loved *Songs for Other People's Weddings* and want to hear the music come to life, scan this QR code to listen to the album!